ABOUT LAST NIGHT—

"I accept," Ellie announced, the words bursting from her, startling Mason. Her eyes widened even more, as if her declaration had surprised her, too.

"I'm sorry?"

"I . . ." She fidgeted with the edge of the catalogue she'd been reading. "I considered your—proposal last night. And I accept," she said firmly.

Mason's reaction was instantaneous: desire ripped through him. Images of laying her across her desk and making love to her right there flashed through his mind in vivid detail.

But in the next second, guilt gripped his chest with such force he could barely breathe. He couldn't simply have sex with her and walk away. Could he?

"That is," Ellie said quietly, "if the offer still stands."

BOOK YOUR PLACE ON OUR WEBSITE AND MAKE THE READING CONNECTION!

We've created a customized website just for our very special readers, where you can get the inside scoop on everything that's going on with Zebra, Pinnacle and Kensington books.

When you come online, you'll have the exciting opportunity to:

- View covers of upcoming books
- Read sample chapters
- Learn about our future publishing schedule (listed by publication month *and author*)
- Find out when your favorite authors will be visiting a city near you
- Search for and order backlist books from our online catalog
- Check out author bios and background information
- Send e-mail to your favorite authors
- Meet the Kensington staff online
- Join us in weekly chats with authors, readers and other guests
- Get writing guidelines
- AND MUCH MORE!

**Visit our website at
http://www.kensingtonbooks.com**

Wanting What You Get

Kathy Love

ZEBRA BOOKS
Kensington Publishing Corp.
www.kensingtonbooks.com

For my Mom and Dad:
Thank you for believing in me—
even when you weren't quite sure
what I was doing.
I love you!

ACKNOWLEDGMENTS

I want to thank my wonderful critique group, The Tarts.

Thank you, Kathy, Chris, Janet and Kate for identifying with these characters that I love so much.

Julie, thank you for all the phone conversations. You know that you are invaluable to me, my dear, dear friend.

Thank you to my fantastic family.
I love you all.

Thank you, Treena, Lisa, Kristen, Jen and Tim.

And as always, thank you, Todd and Emily.
I love you with all my heart.

Prologue

"Ellie-phant, you lost?"

Ellie Stepp studied the tip of her worn sneaker and pretended not to hear Mark Legere's loud question or the snickers that followed.

"She's not lost," a voice Ellie recognized as Josie Nye's answered for her. "Coach Ramsey is making her do extra gym classes because she's so . . ."

"Fat," Eric Dunton provided.

There was more mocking laughter.

Ellie continued to scuff a toe on the highly glossed gymnasium floor. She could get through this. She could.

It had been her worst nightmare when Coach Ramsey had told her she'd have to make up her missed gym classes or fail. Classes she had missed because she conveniently kept forgetting her gym clothes.

Now she wished she had just brought the dreaded t-shirt and shorts in the first place. Gym was terrible, but it was far worse when she had to make it up with the senior class. Seniors, the high school's elite.

She could survive this. Fifty minutes, that's all.

She shot a quick glance at the large, round clock on the far wall. No, only forty-six. Anyone could survive that.

She tugged at the t-shirt that was a bit too snug. It

was borrowed from her older sister, Abby. Abby was at least a size smaller, if not more.

"Yo, guys."

Upon hearing those two simple words said in a deep, rich voice, she felt like the tight tee was strangling her, and Ellie knew there was no way on earth she was going to survive the next forty-something minutes.

"Mason, dude, you rocked last night."

Ellie lifted her head slightly to see Eric Dunton thump a tall blond on the back. Mason Sweet, the senior class's *most* elite.

Mason shrugged. His broad shoulders moved gracefully under his white t-shirt.

Ellie fought to inhale.

A group of seniors circled around Mason like they were his disciples. In many ways, they were. After all, he was the quarterback of the Millbrook Millers. He was the most popular boy in school. One of the smartest, although her sister Abby was officially the smartest. But Mason was the wealthiest. And he was definitely the best looking.

Ellie believed he might well be the best-looking boy in the world. Definitely better looking than any of the young actors in the teen movies that all the girls were crazy about.

His thick hair was a rich, warm color—honey streaked with pale gold. And his eyes were gray and shone like polished silver when he smiled. And that smile . . .

"Okay, kids, let's get this game of hoops going," Coach Ramsey called, clapping his hands together loudly, snapping Ellie out of her reverie. Nervousness churned in her belly.

The kids lined up against the wall. Ellie remained rooted to her spot, slightly away from the others.

"Mark, you're captain. And . . . Mason, you're captain," the coach decided.

Ellie doubted that Coach Ramsey really had to think about the choices. Mark and Mason were the best athletes in the school. Of course, in her opinion, Mason was the very best.

She watched Mason step to the white line marking the perimeter of the gymnasium floor. He was born to be a team leader. Born to be the best. Born to shine.

"Ellie!" Coach Ramsey waved an arm. "Get over here with the others. You're not going to get picked standing way over there. Come on."

Ellie shuffled over to the other kids.

"You might as well stay over there," Eric Dunton whispered as she passed. "You're not going to get picked anyway."

Again, Ellie acted like she didn't hear the gibe and sank against the concrete wall beside a girl who looked relatively friendly. The girl shifted away from her.

"Okay, Mark, you get first pick," the coach said, and the horrible and demeaning process began.

As each person was chosen by one of the teams, Ellie felt like pieces of her clothes were being stripped away, leaving her more exposed. More noticeable.

Finally, there were only three people left fidgeting under the scrutiny of the selected kids.

It was Mason's turn to pick. He looked at the scrawny boy in glasses that stood to her right. Then his gray gaze stopped on her and lingered.

"Man, don't pick the ugly Stepp sister," Eric groaned.

Mason glanced at his friend and then back to her. Their eyes locked for a moment, and Ellie fought the urge to tighten her arms around herself and look at the floor.

Something akin to pity darkened his eyes; then he chose the scrawny boy.

Mark automatically picked the deceptively friendly-looking girl beside her.

And that left Ellie against the wall alone—naked for everyone's perusal.

"All right, Ellie, you're on Mason's team," Coach Ramsey said.

Several kids on her appointed team groaned.

"Come, guys," Coach Ramsey warned, although Ellie suspected he commiserated with the team.

Reluctantly, Ellie left the wall and stepped out to the middle of the gym floor to join her team.

"Man, why couldn't the tall, ugly Stepp sister be the one that had to make up a gym class? At least she might be able to play basketball," Eric muttered. "Even the geeky one isn't as tubby as this one."

Ellie hated to wish this on anyone, especially her sisters, but she wished either Marty or Abby were here, too. They were stronger, braver.

Mason cast another look at Ellie. This time there seemed to be another emotion mixed with the pity in his eyes, but she couldn't label it.

"Ah, stop your whining," Mark Legere said, wearing a smug grin. "At least Mason didn't choose her. He just got stuck with her."

Ellie wrapped her arms tightly around herself and pretended she didn't hear.

Chapter 1

"Ellie, stop tugging at your dress. You look great."

Ellie smiled at her younger sister. She knew Marty's compliment was given just to be kind, but the gesture was appreciated. She ceased fiddling with the bodice of the fitted gown and clutched her bouquet of red roses and cream-colored lilies instead.

"You look great, too," Ellie told her, but her claim wasn't an empty reassurance. Marty did look wonderful in her gown. The dark red satin emphasized her lithe curves and flattered her coloring perfectly.

Whereas Ellie looked like a sausage stuffed into a crimson casing. Or, more appropriately, like one of Maine's famous red hot dogs. But to be fair to herself, Marty could wear a potato sack and look fantastic. Marty was a model; it was her job to look gorgeous. Being a librarian didn't require looking good—thank goodness.

But today wasn't about herself, or Marty, or their dresses. It was Abby's day.

Ellie glanced across the Millbrook Inn's foyer to find her older sister. Abby looked beautiful, too. Her wedding gown was ivory satin, bias cut and off the shoulders. The style was exactly the same as Ellie's and Marty's, except Abby's skirt was fluted with a slight train. And she didn't look like a sausage—or a hot dog, for that matter.

Abby's cheeks were flushed and her eyes sparkled as she beamed at her new husband, Chase. He grinned back, and they just looked so . . . in love.

Ellie had never actually pictured Abby falling head over heels. She had hoped, but to be honest, she thought Abby might be a lost cause. Abby had always been the practical sister. The scientist who needed tangible proof about everything. That had included true love. Then she met Chase Jordan again after years of living away from their hometown of Millbrook, Maine, and suddenly love seemed to be very tangible. As tangible and unavoidable as a well-aimed brick to the side of the head.

The couple kissed, and Ellie smiled with a certain measure of satisfaction. She had once told Abby that true love existed, and Abby had scoffed at her. It was nice to be right, especially about this topic.

"Ladies," a voice like merlot, rich and smoky, said from behind her.

Ellie's fingers itched to pull at her gown again, but instead she turned to look at the owner of the wonderful voice.

"Mason," Marty greeted him like they were old friends, which they never had been. Marty had been three years behind him in school, and then she had moved to New York right after her graduation. They'd probably never spoken before tonight.

While Ellie had seen him around town at least a couple times a week for years, but she wouldn't consider him an old friend, either. Just an acquaintance. An acquaintance that she was staring at as if he were a total stranger.

But it was hard not to stare. He was breathtaking in his charcoal gray tuxedo with a lighter gray waistcoat and cravat. His hair was shorter than she had seen it in years, and he had it combed back from his forehead, making him look very debonair.

"Drinks," he offered, with an endearing smile that made him appear more boyish, but no less debonair.

Ellie's fingers strayed to her dress, but she caught herself before she started tugging.

"Oh, you are a lifesaver," Marty said with great enthusiasm, accepting a flute of champagne.

Mason took an appreciative sip of his drink, some amber liquor in a highball glass. "Yes, I do believe I got this just in time."

They both let out grateful sighs.

Marty and Mason would make a perfect couple, Ellie realized, looking at the two of them side by side. They were both tall, lean, and beautiful.

But Ellie was the maid of honor, and Mason was the best man. So that effectively made them a couple for the evening. Much to Mason's dismay, Ellie was sure.

Though they had only a couple more duties to complete. Walking into the reception, dinner, the bridal party dance, and that was it. Then Ellie could breathe again. Well, as much as a snug satin dress would allow.

"Are you sure I can't get you a drink?" Mason asked, turning his quicksilver eyes on her.

Ellie blinked. "No, I'm fine."

Mason shrugged. "Let me know if you change your mind."

He likely thought she was a goody-two-shoes, which she supposed she was, but that wasn't why she didn't drink much. She was just on an eternal diet, and she didn't want to give up precious calories on alcohol. Her theory was, why have a strawberry daiquiri when she could have strawberry shortcake?

"Guys," Tommy Leavitt, Chase's other groomsman, called to them. "I think they are getting ready to introduce us."

Marty joined Tommy, taking his arm. They crossed to join Abby and Chase, and that left Ellie alone with Mason.

She looked up at him. He held up a finger to signify that he was almost ready, downed his drink, and then placed the empty glass on an end table beside a large fern. He offered her his arm. "Ready?"

She nodded and slipped her arm through his. She could feel his warmth and strength through the layers of worsted wool and cotton. And for a brief moment, she wished she had taken his offer for a drink. Maybe it would calm her nerves.

At the large double doors that led into the ballroom, Erin Theriault, the wedding director for the Inn, lined them up.

"Okay, Ellie, you're with Tommy." She placed a hand on Ellie's shoulder and started to maneuver her toward Tommy, but Mason held fast to her arm.

"Erin, Ellie and I are supposed to walk in together," Mason said.

Ellie found herself tugged against Mason's side, surrounded by his arm and his spicy scent. It took her a moment to gather her wits and notice Erin was frowning at them, puzzled.

"That's right, you two are the best man and maid of honor," the wedding director finally said. "For some reason I saw you with Marty, Mason."

Disappointment plunked heavily in the center of Ellie's chest. She'd, of course, had the same thought earlier, but it stung to know someone else saw her sister and Mason as the better match, too. No one would mistake the short, chubby librarian and the tall, dashing mayor as a couple. Not even in the concocted couples of a wedding party.

She straightened away from him, but he left his arm looped around her shoulder.

When Erin left to arrange the train of Abby's dress, Mason leaned close to Ellie's ear and whispered, "Now, see, I definitely see myself with you."

Air rushed out of her lungs, and Ellie didn't know how to respond, or if she even could.

She glanced up at him. A mischievous twinkle danced in his eyes.

He was flirting with her. Mason had never flirted with her, ever. But that was all it was, flirtation, a bit of fun. It wasn't real. She still felt light-headed and warm. Her cheek tingled where his hot breath had grazed her skin.

He straightened, a frown marring his brow. "You don't look thrilled with the prospect of being my date for the evening."

Ellie swallowed, then managed to say with a relatively steady voice, "This is hardly a date. We're just the best man and the maid of honor."

"So, you can't imagine anything more?"

Ellie's eyes widened, but, thankfully, before she had to formulate a response, the double doors opened, and they were introduced to the waiting guests.

"You look flushed. Are you okay?"

Ellie started, nearly dropping the fork she was using to push around bits of her pecan haddock. She glanced at Abby and forced a smile. "Of course. Just a bit warm. Satin doesn't breathe."

Abby studied her for a moment; then her frown disappeared as she accepted Ellie's explanation. "The dress looks gorgeous on you, though."

Ellie continued to smile, but her face felt taut and fixed. She knew she should say something more. Make small talk, but she couldn't think of anything. Not with Mason sitting on the other side of her. So she resumed piling her fish into a small mound.

Mason hadn't made any other odd comments since they'd sat for dinner. He had escorted her to the table. He'd made the best man's toast. Most of which

she couldn't recall because her mind had been awhirl
with confusion and shock.

Then he had sat down beside her and acted like
he'd said nothing unusual. He didn't flirt. He made
observations about their dinners. He chatted with
other guests. Ordinary stuff. In fact, everything was so
normal that Ellie started to think she had imagined
Mason's earlier remarks.

She had to have. Mason had never given her a second glance. Sure, he was always friendly and polite, but
men like Mason Sweet did not flirt with women like
Ellie Stepp. It just didn't happen.

She cast a furtive glance at him. He sat back in his
chair, long legs crossed at the ankle, talking with Carly
Porter. He and Carly had dated briefly in high school,
and it was evident that she was still interested in
Mason after all these years. She leaned over him, her
cleavage nearly eye level with his face. And in Ellie's
opinion, Mason didn't seem exactly disinterested in
her, either. He seemed quite pleased to be talking
with her. And what wasn't pleasing? As well as having
first-rate cleavage, Carly was slender with long, shiny
brown hair and green eyes. But she was also engaged
to Phillip Daigle, an accountant in Bar Harbor. Still,
Ellie got the impression that Carly wouldn't turn
down any invitation Mason offered.

She turned her attention back to her dinner. It was
cold, and the cream-covered asparagus had con-
gealed. She started to push that into the shredded
pile of fish. Then she set her silverware down and
reached for the glass of white wine that had accompanied the meal. Given that dinner was pretty much
a wash, why not splurge?

She took a sip. It wasn't half bad, so she took another.

"I hope the company isn't driving you to drink,"
Mason said, his voice close to her ear.

Startled, she nearly choked but managed to swallow the wine and set the glass aside. She turned to find Mason leaning very close and Carly gone.

"No," she breathed. "I . . . I decided I wasn't very hungry." Her explanation didn't make sense, really, but it was the best she could do.

"I noticed." He glanced at her plate. "You seemed to have a real vendetta against that fish."

She glanced at her plate and winced. Playing with her food, that was definitely poor etiquette. "I'm just not hungry, I guess." Again the comment seemed sort of lame. Carly would probably have had a witty comeback.

Mason didn't seem to notice. In fact, for a moment, she thought he wasn't even listening. He surveyed the room. A restrained look of distaste twisted his lips. "Well, weddings will do that to a person. Take your appetite right away."

Ellie glanced at the room trying to see what he saw, see what was so unpleasant. Guests sat at round tables; candlelight flickered and crystal glimmered; the soft music of a classical guitarist played under the din of talking and laughter; flowers adorned everything, making the room look magical, beautiful.

"The wedding didn't ruin my appetite," Ellie said, feeling the need to defend Abby and Chase's hard work. "I think everything is beautiful."

Mason glanced back to her; he seemed almost surprised by her voice. Then his lips curved into a half smile. "Chase and Abby have done a great job with the wedding. I know they will find every happiness."

She nodded and started to look away.

"And you're right."

She paused, waiting for him to continue.

The distaste in his gray eyes disappeared completely, and they became intent. Again he leaned close to her. "Everything does look absolutely beautiful."

Heat burned her cheeks. She shifted in her chair.

He couldn't possibly have meant that last comment in reference to her. No, not possible. She was imagining things again.

When he abruptly excused himself to go to the bar, Ellie decided she was definitely finding innuendos that didn't exist. Maybe it was the wine, although she'd started imagining things before her few meager sips. Maybe it was the tightness of her dress. Or maybe it was the romance of Abby and Chase's wedding. Whatever it was, she was absolutely inventing any signs of flirtation from Mason Sweet.

Mason leaned on the bar and watched the reception.

He lifted his refreshed drink from the bar and took a deep swallow. The whiskey burned his throat. It was a familiar, almost comforting sensation, not foreign and strange like the thoughts and feelings he'd been having all evening.

He had expected to feel uncomfortable about being in another wedding. He'd managed to avoid them since his own nuptials, and he would have been just as happy to steer clear of them forever. But Chase was his best friend, and despite Mason's own opinion of the state of matrimony, he did believe Chase and Abby were a great couple, and they would have a wonderful life together.

Yeah, he'd been prepared for his usual cynicism, the lingering resentment toward his ex-wife for her duplicity, and even the general self-loathing that always accompanied any thoughts of his past. All those feelings were old news, but what he was feeling tonight . . . Well, this was new news. New and strange and inexplicable.

His gaze roamed over the crowd until he found Ellie standing with her sisters at the edge of the dance floor. She was short, so when people walked up to chat with Abby, he'd lose sight of her. But then the person would move, and he could see her sunny, corkscrew curls, her wide cornflower blue eyes and bowed lips again. She smiled at her sister, Marty, and dimples appeared on either side of her pink lips. She looked like a radiant little cherub fallen to earth.

There! That. That was one of the strange and inexplicable thoughts. Mason shook his head slightly as if he could shake the random, odd thought out of his mind.

He had never noticed Ellie Stepp before, let alone pictured her as a little angel. No, that wasn't true. He had noticed her—as the nice, shy little bookworm. He had noticed she had a pretty smile. Hell, he'd even noticed she had the bluest eyes he'd ever seen. But he'd never felt attracted to her.

Although he could pinpoint the exact moment when Ellie Stepp moved from cute acquaintance into the object of his desire—when he saw her walking down the aisle of the church toward him. There had to be something very sacrilegious about the wave of lust that had washed over him. But he hadn't been thinking of burning in hell at that particular moment. Nope, he'd been thinking that he'd rather be burning up the sheets with Ellie Stepp.

She came down the aisle, her steps measured, the narrowness of her skirt inhibiting any large movements. The restricted movement, however, did reveal the sway of her walk, and the close-fitting crimson satin displayed the roundness of her hips, the fullness of her breasts. Ellie had a striking, voluptuous figure hidden under all her baggy sweaters and long skirts.

Just as she'd reached the front of the church, she'd glanced at him. Just a quick look, but Mason had felt it like a lightning bolt. For that brief second, he could have sworn they'd been on the same wavelength: both attracted, both yearning.

But he'd obviously been wrong. Every time he'd

attempted to flirt with her, she had looked uncomfortable. No, more than uncomfortable. She looked like she wanted to run away. That wasn't the reaction of a lady who was madly attracted. Wildly repulsed, maybe.

He took another swallow of his drink. So, he would ignore this sudden and puzzling attraction and spend the rest of the evening acting like a perfect gentleman. And hopefully, when Ellie was shrouded in her flowing clothes, his libido would start acting normal.

"You aren't checkin' out my wife, are you?"

Mason turned to find Chase standing beside him. "Don't tell me you're going to be one of those domineering, jealous types."

Chase grinned. "So, how you holding up?"

"Fine." *Other than I suddenly want to jump your sister-in-law's bones.*

"I do appreciate you doing this for me. Let's face it; if it hadn't been for your little pep talk, I might not be here today."

Mason shook his head. "Nah, you'd have come to your senses. It might have taken a hell of a lot longer, but you would have eventually."

Chase chuckled and clapped Mason on the back. He started to order a drink, but a whistle stopped him and drew both men's attention in that direction. Both men were shocked to see Nathaniel Peck strutting toward them in full police uniform. Nathaniel was Millbrook's chief of police and, as far as Mason knew, had *not* been invited to the wedding. But it was very Nathaniel to just show up. He was a little aggressive and even more abrasive. And for whatever reason, he did consider Chase and Mason his friends.

"Chase, you have this place decked out," Nathaniel said, looking around.

Chase offered Nathaniel an easy smile, handling

the other man's crashing his wedding with good grace. "I hope no one called the police on us."

"Nah." Nathaniel chuckled and leaned against the bar, looking as though he was settling in for the evening. "Yep, this place looks great. Really nice. And look at all the gorgeous ladies here tonight." He was quiet for a moment; then he added, "Check out that Stepp sister."

Mason followed his stare toward the three Stepp sisters.

"Mmm, she looks like a delicious, shiny, red apple in that dress," Nathaniel said with great appreciation. Then he let out another low whistle. Shaking his head, he added, "And I'm just the fella to peel her right out of it."

Mason set down his drink on the bar with more force than necessary and faced Nathaniel. "I don't want to hear you talk about Ellie like that."

Nathaniel cocked an eyebrow, then grinned. "Now, who said I was talking about Ellie Stepp? As a matter of fact, I was talking about the model sister there. What's her name? Martha?"

"She prefers Marty," Chase informed Nathaniel, but not before he gave Mason a curious look. When Mason ignored him, he clapped a hand on both men's backs. "Now, if you will excuse me, I believe I'll get back to my wife."

Mason turned toward the bar and considered ordering another drink. He tried to ignore the remaining tension that constricted his chest. A tightness that had appeared as soon as he'd thought Nathaniel was admiring Ellie in that fitted red gown.

"So, you're taking this whole best man/maid of honor thing quite seriously, aren't ya?" Nathaniel nudged him with a shoulder.

Mason suppressed the urge to shove him back. "What do you mean?"

"You got all bristly when you thought I was check-ing out your date for the evening. I'd say that's right gentlemanly of you."

Mason grunted.

Both men leaned against the bar, backs to the rest of the room. Nathaniel ordered a drink.

Mason wished Nathaniel would leave and then he could order a drink, too. "Aren't you on duty?"

Nathaniel took a sip of his drink and shook his head. "Just got off. Can I buy you a drink?"

Mason was surprised by the man's offer.

"I mean, you aren't driving tonight, are you?" There was an undertone to the police chief's question.

Mason gritted his teeth but then managed to say calmly, "No, I'm not." He turned to the bartender. "I'll take a whiskey, straight up. On the police chief, here."

They both remained silent, sipping their drinks and lost in thought, until a light tap on Mason's arm gained his attention. He turned and Nathaniel fol-lowed. Ellie and Marty stood behind them. Since Marty was closest to him, he assumed she was the one who had touched him. Ellie was keeping her distance, her hands knotted together.

"Well, hello there," Nathaniel said, before Mason got a chance to speak.

Marty glanced at the tall police chief, the gesture polite but indifferent, the reaction of a woman who was used to men trying to chat with her. "Mason," she said, "it's time for the wedding party dance."

Once more Nathaniel found his voice first. "Did it hurt?"

Marty shot Nathaniel a confused look. "Excuse me?"

"Did it hurt?" he repeated.

"Did what hurt?"

"Did it hurt when you fell to earth?" Nathaniel

stepped closer to her and trailed a fingertip down her bare arm. "Because you must be an angel."

Marty jerked away and shot Nate a look that would have killed a smaller man, or maybe a smarter one.

Mason looked at Ellie. She watched the other two, a slight frown turning down her lips. He couldn't help wondering if he'd sounded as stupid to her earlier this evening.

Lord, he hoped not.

"I've seen some of your modeling work," Nathaniel said, the sentence filled with innuendo.

Marty glared at him. "Do I know you?"

Nathaniel straightened, traded his drink to his left hand and offered her his right. "Nathaniel Peck, chief of police. And I'd certainly like to get to know you much better."

Marty's eyes widened just slightly, and Mason could have sworn he saw hatred flash through them, but then she turned her attention back to Mason, ignoring Nathaniel's extended hand, her face blank. "I think we're needed on the dance floor."

Mason nodded and followed Ellie and Marty as they headed to the center of the room where Chase, Abby, and Tommy waited.

Just as they reached the polished parquet, the first strains of Elvis's "I Can't Help Falling in Love With You" began.

He suddenly felt ill. He lurched to a stop and tried to take a deep breath. *It's just a song. A wedding standard.*

A hand touched his arm.

"Mason, are you all right?" Ellie frowned at him, her blue eyes dark with worry.

He cleared his throat and forced a smile. "Yes, I just happen to like other Elvis songs better. Say 'Kentucky Rain' or maybe 'In the Ghetto,'" he said.

Ellie watched him for a moment; then a small smile

curved her mouth, merely hinting at the dimples on either side of her lips. "But not particularly appropriate for a wedding."

Her smile seemed to help. He focused on it. He caught her hand in his, concentrating on how small her fingers were—how warm.

He led her onto the floor to join the already dancing bridal party.

He pulled her against him, tighter than he should. She held herself rigid, and her movements were stiff, but he couldn't relax his hold. He needed to feel Ellie's softness, her warmth.

The liquor he'd consumed this evening had started to take its effect. He was a bit light-headed, and he didn't want to think about the memories this song brought back. He wanted another of Ellie's sweet smiles.

"It's not the jumpsuits or anything."

Her curls tickled his chin as she looked up at him. "Excuse me?" she asked, confused.

"I like *Kentucky Rain* or *In the Ghetto,* but not because they were released during Elvis's jumpsuit phase."

She blinked; then another smile lurked on her lips. "Are you sure?"

"Absolutely." He was silent for a moment. "It might be the cool kung fu moves, but definitely not the jumpsuits."

This time a full-fledged smile deepened her dimples and caused her eyes to sparkle. And she seemed to relax a little. "I like early Elvis."

He nodded. "Now, I can see that about you." He grinned down at her. She was shorter than he had realized. And softer. He liked the curve of her hip under his hand and the feeling of her small hand in his. She had such tiny hands.

His ex-wife, Marla, had been almost at eye level with him. Her lithe body firm from all the Stairmaster and treadmill she'd been obsessed with doing an hour every day. And her fingers had been long and elegant like a pianist's.

"This was our wedding song." Mason wasn't sure whether it was the booze or just the need to tell someone that made him speak.

He could feel Ellie's reaction. She paused just a fraction of a second; then the little hand on his shoulder caressed him, just barely, nothing more than a twitch of her fingers, really.

"Marla wasn't an Elvis fan, jumpsuits or otherwise, but I convinced her."

Ellie continued to watch him, her eyes full of compassion.

"She didn't want a d.j. Thought it was tacky. She wanted an orchestra or a string quartet or something, classical music and waltzes."

Again those tiny fingers twitched.

"I never was sophisticated enough for her."

Ellie was silent for a moment, and then she said adamantly, "She wasn't good enough for you. If you were mine, I'd never ask you to be anything different than what you are. Never."

Mason stopped turning her around the dance floor and stared down at her, startled by her resolute manner, but more so by the words themselves.

If you were mine . . .

Ellie looked away from his probing gaze, her cheeks darkening to a red only a few shades lighter than her dress.

Another wave of dizziness washed over him. "So tell me, Ellie, do you want to be mine?"

Chapter 2

"*If You Were Mine.*"

Ellie's head snapped up when she heard the words that had been haunting her for the past two days.

Prescott Jones, her assistant and right-hand man at the library, stood on the other side of her cluttered desk holding up a book. The cover showed a bare-chested man and buxom woman locked in an amorous embrace.

"It's in," he said, oblivious to the fact that he had given her such a start. "We got four copies. And I bet they'll all be checked out before the day is through. I think Harriet Dodge called at least eight times last week to see if we'd gotten it yet."

Ellie took a deep breath, realizing he was talking about Amanda Austin's newest steamy romance novel, not her stupid, *stupid* comment to Mason Sweet at the wedding.

"Good," she managed in a calm voice. "Get it catalogued and on the shelf. And maybe you should give Harriet a quick call and let her know we have it in."

Prescott nodded and started out the door of her tiny office; then he paused in the doorway. A frown drew his auburn eyebrows into a nearly straight line over his pale blue eyes. "Are you all right?"

Ellie forced a smile. "Of course."

He studied her for a moment. "You just don't seem yourself."

"I'm just a little tired after all the weekend's festivities."

"How was the wedding?"

"Lovely."

Prescott waited for a moment as if he expected her to elaborate, and when she didn't, he simply nodded. "Well, I'll get the new stock into the database."

Ellie watched him leave and then turned back to her computer. She stared at the spreadsheet open on the computer screen. Now where was she? Outlining the library's events for the month of October. She positioned her fingers on the keyboard and stared at the screen. The grid and the few entries she'd already made blurred as her mind returned to the wedding.

Mason's words repeated in her mind, crystal clear. *Do you want to be mine?* said in his distinct drawl. The feeling of his arms around her, strong and warm. His spicy scent like cloves and bergamot. His gray eyes like storm clouds and thunder. It was all so sharp in her mind. Yet, she still felt like she must have read it in one of the romance novels she loved. Men did not ask her questions like that, especially not men like Mason Sweet. Even now her heart raced at the memory, but realistically she knew he couldn't have meant anything by it.

After the dance finished, there had been no more interactions between them. Although, for the remainder of the reception, Ellie could feel Mason's eyes on her. She would glance toward him, and he'd be watching her, an unreadable expression on his face. But even with all the exchanged looks, they had avoided each other.

Ellie had decided that her dumb comment had just made him wonder about her, wonder why she would even say such a thing. That had to be why he was watching her but not approaching. He probably thought she was a stalker, some creepy, obsessed woman who had created all sorts of elaborate scenarios about him.

If you were mine, I wouldn't want you to be any different than you are. How creepy was that? It sounded like she'd actually thought about his marriage and how she'd have acted if it had been her married to him.

Of course, she had. She'd thought about being with Mason since sixth grade. He'd been in the seventh.

Ellie had been waiting in front of the Millbrook Middle School for the buses to arrive. An eighth grader, Bruce Gross, had stolen her hat, a hideous stocking cap that had been her father's when he was a little kid. Ellie loved the cap, a piece of a father she could barely remember.

She hadn't pleaded for it back or chased after Bruce. It would have been pointless. So she clutched her books to her chest as he taunted her, pretending the jeers didn't hurt.

Then out of nowhere, Mason had come up to Bruce. He was already a head taller than the bully, but much thinner.

"Give it back," he'd said.

"Mind your own business, Mason," Bruce had sneered, saying Mason's name like an insult.

"Give it back," Mason had repeated.

"Screw off."

Then Mason had drawn back and popped Bruce right in the nose. Bruce had doubled over, dropping her hat. Mason scooped it up and handed it back to her.

"Here," he'd said with a look of smug satisfaction, then shook his hand because the punch had hurt his knuckles.

He'd gone back to his bus and ridden away like a knight into the sunset.

Later, Ellie had discovered that Bruce had been harassing Mason's girlfriend and a couple of her friends. Ellie supposed that seeing Bruce tease another girl had been the last straw for Mason. He'd actually defended her in an effort to save his girlfriend from further bullying, but it didn't matter to Ellie. In her eyes, that moment had made him a hero. And she'd had a silly, unrequited crush on him ever since.

But it was really time to grow up and let the crush go. At the very least, it was time to stop rehashing the events of the wedding. Just like the hat, there had to be extenuating circumstances behind his behavior— like he'd been uncomfortable being involved in a wedding after his own marriage had failed. Or he'd drunk too much. Or both.

She straightened in her chair, the old leather creaking under her weight, and focused on the computer screen.

She had far too much work to do to idle away time daydreaming about Mason. She'd wasted too much of her life already dreaming about Mason Sweet.

"Hello? Ellie? Are you in there?"

Ellie looked up from her tea, muddled. How long had she been staring into the creamy brown liquid?

Marty sat beside her at the kitchen table, her knees practically level with her face, her toes curled over the edge of her chair. She watched Ellie like a concerned gargoyle.

"I've been blathering on for ages. Have you heard anything I've said?" she asked.

Ellie shook her head. "No, sorry. What were you saying?"

"I was telling you about that idiot, Nathaniel Peck. How did he become the chief of police, anyway? He's always been a menace to society; he shouldn't be the one trying to get the menaces off the street."

Ellie understood Marty's reaction; while Nathaniel had never bothered her, he wasn't the nicest person. And he had been very mean to Marty in the past. High school had been painful for all the Stepp sisters. But she didn't think Marty would want to discuss her history with Nathaniel, so she simply said, "He can be very overbearing."

"And a pig, no slur intended. At the wedding, he asked me if my photos were airbrushed, or were my breasts just naturally smooth and unblemished."

Ellie nearly choked on her tea. "He did not!"

Marty held up her hand in some attempted imitation of the Girl Scout salute. "I swear."

"Smooth and unblemished?" Ellie grimaced.

"I know!" Marty exclaimed. "Like in real life, I have blotchy, discolored boobs or something! I've only posed topless twice in my whole career, and every pig in the world saw those two pictures. I knew I shouldn't have done that Calvin Klein ad campaign."

"That was pretty piggish," Ellie agreed. She got up, stepping over a sleeping Chester, Chase and Abby's dog that she was watching while they were on their honeymoon, and stuck her teacup in the microwave. She *had* been staring at it for a long time. The tea was beyond tepid.

She needed to stop this. Her earlier pep talk had done little good. She'd managed to get all her scheduling done, but she didn't remember actually doing any of it. Hopefully she hadn't scheduled the Millbrook Quilters and Alcoholics Anonymous meetings on the same night. That was the only drawback of having one of the nicest meeting rooms in Millbrook. It was always booked, no room for mistakes.

She'd have to double check tomorrow. The Quilters met every third Tuesday. AA met every Wednesday. It wouldn't do to have a bunch of confused ladies with pinking shears and batting showing up there.

If she couldn't stop obsessing about Mason, this was exactly the type of thing that was going to happen.

"Are you planning to get your tea?" Marty's voice snapped Ellie out of her musing. "The microwave has been dinging away at you."

Ellie shot her sister a self-conscious look. "Sorry, my mind is not working today."

"What's eating at you, anyway? You've been acting strange ever since the wedding. Are you upset because Abby fell into the abyss of wedded bliss?"

Ellie laughed. "No, I'm thrilled for her. Even though your description of marriage makes it sound very appealing, indeed."

"Blah," Marty said dramatically. "I'm never getting married. I can't imagine being stuck with the same man, day in, day out, for my whole life. Men are far too annoying."

Ellie frowned. "You're too young to be so bitter. And what about Arturo? You were madly in love with him. I thought for sure you two would marry."

Marty made a disgusted noise. "I'm pleading temporary insanity. See, if I was so wrong about Arturo, then I could potentially end up with someone like Nathaniel Peck." She shuddered.

"What about the man you're dating now?" Ellie asked.

Marty unfolded her long legs from the chair and crossed to the sink. She turned on the faucet and re-filled her water bottle. "Rod," she finally answered, but the name was said with no emotion, like she was reading it from a list. A list of people she didn't know.

Ellie waited for her to say more, but she didn't. She stared out the window over the sink.

"You know, I was thinking," Marty said, her voice suddenly animated again, "we should go out and rake up all the leaves in the backyard and jump in them like we did when we were little."

Ellie let the topic slide. Her little sister hadn't wanted to discuss her current boyfriend since she'd arrived home. And Ellie saw far too little of her to ruin their time together by pushing the issue. But she suspected it was an issue. Marty looked tired, and several times Ellie had noticed that she looked unhappy.

Marty turned from the window and leaned against the sink, her dark eyes probing. "So what happened at the wedding that has you brooding?"

Apparently Marty didn't have the same misgivings about prying into Ellie's life.

"I haven't been brooding."

Marty gave her a dubious look. "You've been all quiet and sullen. I call that brooding."

"I haven't been sullen," Ellie insisted. "I've been introspective."

"Tomato, tomahto."

Ellie shook her head. "You're still such the irksome little sister."

"And you are still such the secretive sister."

Ellie's eyes widened with shock. "I'm not secretive."

"You never told me or Abby anything when we were growing up. You were the one who always listened to our problems. But you never told us any of yours."

Ellie thought about that for a moment. "I guess I didn't have any problems worth discussing."

Marty made a noise that stated she didn't believe that for a moment, but instead of arguing, she opened the freezer and began to plunk ice cubes into her water bottle.

Ellie sat back at the kitchen table and fiddled with the handle of her teacup. Part of her wanted to tell Marty about the incident with Mason, and about the dumb thing she'd said to him. She wanted her sister to reassure her that Mason had likely forgotten the whole event already.

Ellie took a sip of her tea. Marty was right; she had been quiet. She hadn't been brooding, though. Fixating, maybe, but brooding, no. Maybe it would help to tell someone about her concerns.

"It's . . ." She was unsure where to start. It was too preposterous to be said aloud. At least not with any measure of sincerity. "I think Mason Sweet was flirting with me."

Marty stared at her.

Ellie shifted on her seat. She knew it was too incredible to be believed.

But when Marty burst out laughing, well, that seemed a bit unnecessary.

Marty rushed to the table and fell onto one of the chairs, still laughing.

Chester jumped up, tail wagging, ready to get involved in all the excitement.

Marty reached across the table and caught one of Ellie's hands, squeezing it.

"Ellie, you are the queen of understatement."

Ellie frowned, unsure what she meant.

Marty's laughter calmed after several deep breaths. She grinned a huge, toothy grin that had graced many a magazine cover. "You *think* he was flirting with you? Well, I *know* he was flirting with you. Girlfriend, he was practically drooling over you all night."

"No, that's not true," Ellie said skeptically.

"Every time I saw him, his eyes were fastened on you."

"Really?" Ellie had begun to believe the only reason he'd kept looking at her was that she'd kept looking at him.

Marty nodded. "He watched you the whole night."

Ellie didn't know how to respond, or even if she

should believe her sister. Although Marty had no reason to make things up.

"I honestly thought there must be something going on between you two, but since you'd never mentioned him, I didn't think I should ask. Is there anything going on?"

Ellie's eyes widened, and she felt heat burn over her cheeks. "No!"

Marty's smile broadened, if that were possible. "Well, I got the distinct impression that Mason would like there to be something going on."

Okay, this wasn't what Ellie had expected. She'd figured Marty would listen to her story and then tell her exactly what she'd already told herself a thousand times. *Mason was distraught over the wedding and not acting like himself. He likely didn't even remember anything either of you said.* Those were the reasonable responses. Not . . .

"I'm tellin' ya, he looked like he could have eaten you up with a spoon."

"No," Ellie insisted; she knew she sounded a bit panicked, but this was not good. She didn't want to hear things that were going to make her think about the man even more. The point of talking to Marty was to rid her mind of Mason, so she could think like a rational human being again.

Ridding her mind of Mason. That was a laughable concept, given that Mason was never too terribly far from her thoughts anyway. She fantasized about him, pictured him as the hero of the novels she read. But she didn't fixate on him like she had since the wedding. She might be sadly obsessed with the man, but she could usually relegate her fantasies to the appropriate time and place. Marty's disclosure was not going to help her situation in the least.

"You must have misread him," she suggested with a measure of insistence.

Shaking her head, Marty said, "I don't think so."

Ellie fought the urge to groan. Even if he had been interested in her, which she still couldn't believe, what was she going to do with the knowledge? She couldn't imagine herself approaching him about it.

"Maybe I did assume more than what was really there," Marty said, although the words were phrased slowly as if she was struggling to understand what Ellie wanted to hear. "It could have been the romance of the evening. Or the dress. You did look great in that dress."

A pent-up breath escaped Ellie. Now, this was what she'd expected to hear. She reached out and scratched Chester's ear, letting the dog's warmth and soft fur calm her.

"I'm sure it was the wedding," Marty said again, seeming to sense that was what Ellie wanted to hear.

Ellie continued to pat Chester, and the room was quiet for a few moments. Until Marty asked, "You are crazy about him, aren't you?"

Smiling, Ellie said, "Chester is a sweet dog."

"No," Marty said, softly, "not Chester—Mason."

Chapter 3

The shrill ring of the telephone sounded before Ellie had to respond, and she had the relieved feeling of being saved by the bell.

She jumped up and grabbed the receiver of the old avocado green telephone that hung on the wall near the door leading to the living room.

"Hello," she said cheerfully, thrilled to talk to whoever was on the other end. The caller was her savior.

"Ellie?" It was Prescott, and he didn't sound nearly as happy. He sounded anxious.

"Prescott, is everything okay?" Out of the corner of her eye, she caught Marty making a mooning expression that she neither understood nor had the time to ponder.

"Not really. As you know, tonight was the monthly meeting of the board of trustees."

Did she know the monthly meeting was tonight? Yes, it was the second Monday, although she hadn't remembered until this instant.

"Okay," she said, not really sure why Prescott felt the need to remind her of that fact. Unless, of course, he was on to her inability to schedule the event calendar with any competency. She knew it was only a matter of time.

"Harriet Dodge came to me after the meeting with some interesting news."

Well, apparently he wasn't calling to tell her she'd messed up the meeting. But then, she had made up this month's calendar before she'd lost her capacity to think about anything other than Mason Sweet.

"She wanted me to know that Everett Winslow attended the meeting tonight, and he's pushing for the trustees to consider taking money from the library budget and putting it toward the school."

"What?" This announcement caught her attention. The library was barely surviving on the budget they had now. They couldn't afford to lose more. But Everett Winslow was the chairman of the school committee, and he had a lot of pull in Millbrook.

"Everett is hoping to get a new football field for the high school," Prescott told her.

Everett Winslow had also been the football coach in Millbrook for years.

"Ellie? Are you there?"

"Yes, sorry. I'm just trying to digest this."

"It's terrible. He's talking about taking over $20,000."

"$20,000! We can't lose that!"

"No, we can't. We have to stop this. If Everett Winslow has his way, the Millbrook Public Library will end up closing," Prescott said, agitated.

Ellie realized she'd never heard him raise his voice. If anything, he tended to whisper—a direct result of working in a library, she guessed. "I'll think about it. That won't happen. The trustees have to know what will happen if we lose that kind of money."

"They know," he said. "They also know that Everett Winslow isn't a man to be messed with."

A sick feeling roiled in Ellie's stomach. Prescott was definitely right. Everett Winslow was a force of nature.

"Okay," Ellie said, taking a deep breath to calm the queasiness. "Thanks for letting me know. I'll think of something."

"*We'll* think of something," Prescott stated.

"Right. See you tomorrow."

"See you tomorrow." The line clicked dead.

While Ellie had been on the phone, Marty had come to stand near her, leaning a hip on the frame of the living room door. "What's happened?"

Ellie held the receiver for a moment before hanging it up and turning to her sister. She explained the situation in a brief, condensed version. She was too upset to elaborate. She sat down numbly and leaned forward to rest her cheek against Chester's fluffy back. Her eyes burned.

Marty followed her, placing a reassuring hand on her shoulder. "But there does have to be a way to stop Everett Winslow."

Ellie raised her head and sighed. "I don't know. He's a member of the Millbrook good ole boys. He has a big support system that will vote whatever way he asks them to."

"Even if their vote threatens the library?"

Ellie shrugged. "I don't know."

"Well, we have to think of something," Marty said, her temper flaring, which it did easily.

This time the situation did warrant a little anger. A lot of anger. Ellie began to pace the kitchen.

"Wait, didn't Mason beat Everett Winslow in the last mayoral election?" Marty said.

Ellie nodded, surprised her globetrotting sister would be up on Millbrook politics.

"Then you need to get Mason on your side. He's obviously got more pull with the people of Millbrook than Everett Winslow."

Ellie thought about that. It did seem likely that Mason would have more influence.

"I guess it wouldn't hurt to approach him."

"Well, go do it," Marty insisted.

Ellie gave Marty an incredulous look. "It's—" She

glanced at the clock. "It's after nine. I can't show up at his house this late at night."

Marty looked equally incredulous. "This is a major problem, a dire one. I think he'll understand your lapse in etiquette."

Ellie considered Marty's point. She was right. This was a huge, potentially disastrous situation, and she did have to deal with it now. She couldn't wait and risk the chance that Everett might get to Mason first. Ellie didn't think Mason would vote for anything that could hurt the library, but it wasn't worth the gamble. If Mason did back Everett Winslow, it would be the last nail in the coffin for Millbrook Public Library.

"You're right."

Marty went to the coat tree in the corner of the kitchen and retrieved Ellie's cardigan. She held it as Ellie slipped her arms into the sleeves. Then Marty grabbed Ellie's purse and handed it to her.

"Good luck," Marty said.

"Aren't you coming with me?"

Marty hesitated. "I have to walk Chester."

Upon hearing the word *walk*, Chester was on his feet and waiting anxiously at the door.

Marty gave Ellie a shrug and a 'What can I do?' look.

The entire drive to Mason's, Ellie debated her decision. That is when she wasn't questioning her sister's motives in making her go right that moment—and alone. She did think it was better to approach Mason without her sister. It seemed a bit unprofessional to bring a sibling along. But she would much rather have spoken to him with Prescott or even Nancy, the crotchety bookmobile librarian, at her side. Not that she was concerned that she couldn't make a valid argument in the library's favor. She would just feel less nervous with a support system.

Maybe Mason wouldn't be home. Or he could be in bed. She looked at the digital clock illuminated on her dashboard. She doubted that Mason was the type to be in bed at 9:30 P.M.

When she rounded the corner that led to his house, she reconsidered. The huge house was dark, except for one light burning upstairs. Maybe he was in bed.

She pulled into his driveway and immediately turned off the engine and headlights. His car was in the driveway, so he was home. But she couldn't very well barge up, pound on his door, and demand his support while he stood there in his jammies. Well, she *could*, if her heart could handle seeing Mason Sweet in his pajamas.

She should have just called. Why hadn't she thought to call? But it was too late now. She was here.

She hesitated, then decided to just go up and knock lightly. If he answered, then he wasn't in bed. And if he didn't, she'd go to his office tomorrow morning. Like she should have done in the first place.

She got out of the car, shutting the door softly, and picked her way up his walkway. The hulking shadow of his house loomed in front of her. She could hear the crash of the surf on the cliffs near the house, and damp, chilly sea air ruffled her curls. She suddenly felt like the heroine in one of her grandmother's old gothic novels. A shiver snaked down her spine, and she scolded herself for being so childish.

When she reached the door, she stopped to debate her idea again. This was important. She could do this. She could.

She raised her hand and was about to knock when a voice came out of the pitch-black night and stopped both her hand and her heart.

* * *

"Ellie Stepp. Now this is a surprise." Mason sat in the darkness, lounging in a wicker chair, his feet propped up on the porch railing.

When the nondescript sedan had pulled into his driveway, he'd been unsure who it was. But as soon as Ellie had stepped out of her car, he'd recognized her silhouette immediately. Ellie had never been to his house before, and he wondered if it was his own thoughts that had brought her here now. He'd thought about her a lot since the wedding.

As she'd approached the house, he'd assumed she would notice him sitting on the porch. But she had been too preoccupied to detect him. In fact, she'd been absorbed in a conversation with herself, whispering in a quiet voice that he couldn't quite hear.

Now she stood before him, a hand pressed to her chest.

"Mason?"

He didn't recall her ever saying his name before. Odd, given the fact he'd known her for years. It sounded nice; she had a soft, lilting voice. Sweet and gentle.

"Yes. Sorry to scare you."

"My gosh," she said, "you really did." Her lilting voice sounded breathy, and sudden, vivid images of other things that he could do to make her breathless flashed into his mind.

"I was just outside having a nightcap and enjoying the autumn air."

He could make out the nod of her head, but he wanted to see her face. He rose, leaving the fifth of scotch on the porch floor beside his chair. "Let's go inside. It's rather hard to see out here."

"Yes."

He moved past her to open the door, giving her a wide berth. He wanted to touch her, but she was nervous, and he was afraid she might dart if he did.

Or maybe he was afraid she'd vanish—*poof!*—like an apparition. A figment of his imagination. Maybe even a drunken hallucination. Whatever the case, he wasn't going to risk her disappearing yet.

Flipping on a light, he led her into a large foyer. To one side of the spacious entrance, a staircase curved up to the second floor. Straight ahead, a door led to the dining room, and to the other side of the foyer, a set of double doors opened into a living room. He walked into the shadowy room and turned on a lamp.

When he looked back to Ellie, she stood in the doorway, unease written on her features until her eyes began to scan the lavish room before her.

"This room is beautiful," she said in awe. She reached forward and touched her fingers to the burgundy velvet of the chair nearest to her.

The strangely erotic movement of her hand stroking the fabric hypnotized Mason. He managed to tear his gaze away and look at the room.

He rarely spent any time in here, despite the fact that the room really was beautiful with vaulted ceilings and stunning molding. The antique furniture fit the style of the house to a tee and showcased the most striking feature of the room, a white marble fireplace, perfectly.

This had been his ex-wife's favorite room. That was probably why he never came in here.

He sank onto the sofa, crossing his feet on the highly polished coffee table. "This was all Marla's doing. She was an antique nut."

Ellie's fingers stopped caressing the velvet, and she looked uncomfortable again.

"Please have a seat," he offered, patting the cushion next to him. Instead of joining him, she sat in the chair she'd been touching, pulling her long black sweater around herself as if she was cold.

"So what brings you to see me at this time of night?"

Mason could think of a reason that would be particularly appealing, but he doubted that sweet Ellie Stepp was here to offer him a night of unbridled passion, much to his disappointment.

"I'm sorry to bother you so late," she immediately apologized. "But—well, I need to ask you a favor, and it couldn't wait until morning."

Mason straightened. A favor that couldn't wait 'til morning. That sounded like sex to him.

"I've just discovered that Everett Winslow is rallying the community to take funds from the library budget and put them toward the school budget—for a new football field."

Football, budgets, Everett Winslow. These topics didn't sound like pillow talk. Mason blinked. It took his mind a few moments to switch gears and grasp what Ellie was really telling him.

"Everett Winslow wants a new football field," he finally said.

Ellie nodded, not seeming to notice that he was acting like a muddled dimwit. "Yes, apparently he's even approached the library's board of trustees about it."

Mason dropped his feet to the floor and leaned forward, his elbows braced on his knees. "I'd think the trustees would see no advantage to Winslow's request."

"I would, too," Ellie agreed. "But I don't think we can count on it."

Mason knew that her doubt was valid. Everett Winslow was a member of one of Millbrook's oldest families. He had friends and he had money. That gave him a lot of power, power he loved to wield.

"But why would he be going after the library?" Ellie asked.

Mason thought about it for a moment. "I would guess this isn't aimed at the library in particular. He's just trying to find a place where he can take money without angering too many townsfolk."

Ellie stared down at her clasped hands. An upset expression turned down her pretty mouth.

Mason immediately felt angry. Angry that a place Ellie loved and took such pride in might not mean the same thing to the rest of the town.

"Winslow must want the new football field because of his son," Mason said, trying to get her thoughts off his reasoning, and the wounded look out of her blue eyes. "Dale Winslow is doing very well this season, and there has been some buzz that he might even get some college recruiters looking at him next year."

Ellie frowned. "A new football field would help him get recruited?"

Mason shrugged. "It couldn't hurt."

The injured look faded from her eyes and was replaced by confusion. "Dale comes to the library all the time. He's a very smart boy. He doesn't need a sports scholarship to get into a good school. Why, he'll probably get an academic scholarship. And even if he doesn't, his father can afford to pay for any university he might want to attend."

Mason was amazed that Ellie was naïve enough to believe this really came down to money. It was about that scholarship. A scholarship was prestige. A concrete sign that Winslow's kid is the best. And a sports scholarship, in many ways, was even more prestigious. After all, even fewer kids could kick or run or throw. That made Winslow's kid very special, indeed. Special and cursed.

Mason knew. He'd spent his youth in the same situation as Dale. Struggling to succeed so he could win his father's love and respect. Love that should have been his unconditionally, not given based on his triumphs. But all too often that was how love worked.

Mason had no use for love, in any form. He didn't want it or need it.

He did, however, want and need another drink.

"Do you want a drink?"

Ellie seemed bewildered by the sudden change in topic, but she gave him a polite little smile. "Water would be fine."

"Water," he repeated with disappointment. Man, it was hard to find a good drinking buddy. Too bad Chase was on his honey . . . Chase was probably having sex.

Mason gritted his teeth. Talk about a one-track mind. He rose and had to grasp the arm of the sofa to steady himself. The room had suddenly started to list to the left.

After a few moments, the room righted itself, and he headed to his study where he kept a well-stocked bar. He poured himself a whiskey, straight up, and downed it. He stared into the empty glass.

Everett Winslow really was a piece of work. It galled him that the man was always trying to show his power in this town. Winslow could pay out of his pocket to have a new football field built, but it was more significant if he could get the town to vote his way.

Mason suspected Winslow knew he would never support him on this proposal. And every avid Millbrook sports fan who had supported Mason in the last mayoral election would then be in Winslow's camp. And Mason knew that Winslow intended to win the next election. Maybe if Winslow had attended the last town council meeting, he'd have realized he didn't need to go to all this effort. Mason was already los . . .

He didn't want to think about all of this.

Mason refilled his glass and finished the fiery liquor in one smooth swallow.

He didn't want to think about the next election. He didn't want to feel sympathetic for Dale Winslow and the difficult future that lay ahead of the poor kid. He didn't want to think about his ex-wife and her perfect furniture. He didn't want to think about any aspect of his failed marriage. He didn't want to think about any of his failures.

He especially didn't want to think about the library and Ellie Stepp. No, that wasn't true. He *did* want to think about Ellie. He'd thought about her a lot since the wedding.

He had nearly convinced himself that his sudden attraction to her was completely a fluke. The effect of his apprehension at being in a wedding and the fit of that amazing red dress she had worn. Without that exact combination, Ellie Stepp would simply go back to being his best friend's sister-in-law and the town's head librarian.

But as soon as he had flipped on the light in the living room and had seen her adorable face, tousled curls, and sky blue eyes, well, he knew his theory was shot.

Tonight she wore a billowy, flowered skirt; a plain, button-down shirt with only the top button undone; and that long black cardigan that she thought hid all her lovely curves from him.

Nope, stress and a tight red dress had nothing to do with his attraction. He still found her sexy as hell.

Refilling his drink once more, he headed for the kitchen to get her glass of water. The hallway seemed to have fallen prey to the same tilting that the living room had earlier, so he used the wall to balance himself. But once in the kitchen, the floor leveled out again, and he got her ice water with no further incident.

When he returned to the living room, Ellie stood at the window, gazing out into the night. She turned when she heard him.

"The view during the day must be amazing," she said.

Mason studied the way her skirt draped alluringly over her rounded hips. The black cardigan had fallen open to reveal the full curve of her breasts.

The whiskey he'd drunk was warm in his belly. He knew Ellie would be warmer.

"The view tonight is pretty amazing, too," he said.

Ellie blushed.

He stepped forward and offered her the water. "Here you go."

She hesitated, then reached forward to accept the glass. Her fingers brushed his just briefly, but Mason could feel it throughout his body, like someone had touched a lit match to the alcohol coursing through his veins.

She took a sip of the water and then looked around like she didn't know what to do next. Finally, her eyes returned to his.

"So, will you help the library?"

For some reason, the question sent the pleasant burn inside him into a hot rage. Here he stood, wanting Ellie down to his marrow, and all she wanted was the influence that his position in the community could get her.

Well, this time he wanted something in return for his help. Maybe he needed a favor, too.

"If I give you my support, what will you give me?"

Ellie frowned, confusion evident in her pure blue eyes. "I—I don't know. What do you want?"

Mason pretended to ponder the question. "Let's see . . . well, library membership is free, right?"

Ellie nodded.

"Hmm," he continued to ponder. He took a step forward and leaned against the wall.

She watched him, her expression so open, so trusting. It made him want her more.

"I have it," he finally said, a slow smile curling his lips. He reached forward, took her glass, and then set both his and hers on the coffee table. He straightened. "And I really think this proposal will suit us both fine."

She waited for him to continue, and again he was struck by the guilelessness of her angelic face. A twinge of guilt tugged at his conscience, but liquor and lust squelched it.

"I'll back you on the library," he said purposefully, "if you sleep with me."

Chapter 4

Ellie's eyes widened, and although her mouth was wide open, she couldn't seem to draw in a breath.

Mason Sweet had just said he would help her, if she—if she slept with him. Her first reaction was to wonder why on earth he'd want her to sleep in his bed. Then her stunned mind realized that what he was proposing had absolutely nothing to do with sleep.

He couldn't mean it like it sounded. Why would a man like Mason Sweet need to make a bargain like that?

"Are you drunk?" she asked, honestly bewildered by his suggestion.

Mason straightened to his full height, his wolfish smile slipping just slightly. "Hardly; why do you ask?"

"Because I can't imagine why you would want to make such a proposal."

"Can't you?" he asked, his grin returning, and Ellie found her pulse racing.

He moved closer, leaning on the window frame, boxing her between the sofa, the window, and him. "Didn't you see me watching you after our dance?"

Ellie didn't respond except to step back. The windowpane was cold against her back and incongruent with the heat that radiated from her cheeks and Mason.

"I wanted you then." His voice was low, and she could feel it stroke over her skin.

He inched closer; his legs brushed the edge of her skirt.

"I want you now."

Ellie's mouth fell open, but before she could manage any other reaction, Mason pulled her against him and caught her mouth with his.

His lips moved over hers, demanding things she didn't know how to give. She felt like she was being sucked into a whirling, dark vortex where sensations and emotions were coming too fast, too violently.

She pushed at his chest, and a slight squeak escaped her. He must have understood her panic, because suddenly his mouth gentled and began to caress and coax her. And as quickly as she had felt like she was sinking, Ellie then felt like she was floating, adrift on long, smooth waves of desire. Desire lapped over her, through her.

She was lost in a sea of longing. In a sea of Mason's heat, his taste, his scent. The hands that had been pushing at him now clutched the front of his shirt.

A small moan vibrated in the back of her throat and received an answering groan from Mason.

His hand slid up her side and cupped the underside of her breast. His touch was strange, but nice. Then his thumb brushed over her sensitive, distended nipple, and she was catapulted right back into a drowning swirl of passion.

She pulled back, startled, and this time he released her.

The stillness of the room was filled with the harsh bursts of her breathing.

For a brief moment, Mason appeared as shaken as she was, but within the blink of an eye, the cool, composed Mason returned.

"As you can see, I think my proposition will be quite

satisfactory for both of us," he said, a small, satisfied smile on his beautiful mouth.

Ellie stared up at him, amazed that he could be so calm when her heart still pounded painfully in her chest.

"What do you think?" he asked as he brushed a curl from her heated cheek.

She pushed past him, needing to put space between them and bumping her knee on the sofa in the process. She crossed to the doorway before she looked back at him.

He leaned against the wall, his arms folded over his chest, watching her.

"I—I have to go," she managed.

He nodded like he didn't care whether she stayed or not.

Ellie hesitated for just a moment. "Bye," she said, and started toward the front door. As she fumbled with the doorknob, Mason's voice caused her to pause.

"I look forward to helping you," he drawled, the words low and wicked, "with great anticipation."

Ellie didn't look back, instead concentrating on the knob until she managed to get it open, and she fled.

Ellie was over halfway home before her breathing was back to normal and her brain could think with any sort of clarity. She had needed to put distance between herself and Mason. She needed to be alone to try and make sense of the events of the night.

Slowing her car, she pulled off the road onto the shoulder and pushed the gearshift into park.

Mason was willing help her and the library, but only if she—helped him. She supposed she ought to be offended, but she wasn't. Mason Sweet, the mayor, the best-looking man in town, one of the most popular, a guy who could have any woman he wanted, wanted to have an affair with her.

Okay, it was only a one-night stand, really. But there was still something oddly flattering and definitely exciting about his strange proposal. Gorgeous men did not barter sex with shy, chubby librarians.

She touched her fingers to her lips. They still felt hot from Mason's kiss. *Mason's kiss.* She had fantasized about kissing him so many times. She had imagined sweet, gentle kisses. Long, passionate ones. Even quick, possessive ones. But never had she envisioned anything as terrifying and absolutely thrilling as the real thing. Even when she felt completely overwhelmed by him, it still felt . . . fantastic!

Her mouth curved into a huge grin, and a surprised laugh escaped her. She was going to accept his proposal.

She was going to be like one of the wild and headstrong heroines in the romance novels she loved. She was going to go for the gusto. She'd sat on the sidelines her whole life. Now, she intended to live a little.

Her life was orderly and tidy. And she had to admit it was often a little dull and lonely. It was time to lose control. To be wild. And this was the person she'd wanted her whole life. Sure, she was scared, but if she let this opportunity pass, well, it wouldn't ever come her way again.

She'd do it!

She grinned down the dark road until her conscience, her insecurity stepped in; then her determined smile slipped.

She *was* jumping headlong into a situation that she had no idea how to handle. After all, a single kiss from the man had her completely, well, flustered. How on earth would she ever get herself together enough to have . . . to be with him?

Okay, if you can't even say the word, how will you ever actually achieve the deed?

She rested her head on the steering wheel. Warmth from the car heater and the melodious tune from the radio cocooned her. She closed her eyes and tried to dampen her self-doubt. Slowly, the words of the song playing penetrated her racing mind. The female voice was singing about being with the man of her dreams, even if it was only for one night.

Ellie straightened. She could do this. She *could*. She wasn't going to let this chance pass her by. She was going to be with her dream man and help the library. If she didn't, she would always regret it.

Marty looked at the clock on the VCR again for the fifth time in as many minutes. It was only ten past eleven, hardly late, especially by her standards. Ellie was fine.

She tried to concentrate on the cooking show that she had been only half-watching.

She shouldn't have let Ellie go alone. Ellie had needed the support. She was the shy, timid sister who had always counted on her sisters for encouragement.

Marty petted Chester's head. He stretched out with a long, satisfied sigh, taking up over half of the couch. Marty stuck her cold feet under his chest. She tried to focus on the television chef. He was whisking something in a small bowl. What was it that he was making again?

Why had she goaded Ellie to go see Mason tonight, anyway? For some reason, she'd thought trying match-making was a good idea. It was a terrible idea.

Mason Sweet seemed like a nice enough guy, but there was something cold about him. A harshness to his eyes and a cynicism to the set of his mouth. He wasn't right for softhearted, sensitive Ellie.

Maybe she should go find Ellie. Although, she had no idea where Mason lived. This really had been an awful idea.

Chester lifted his head, and his tail moved slightly. Marty stopped pretending to listen to the TV and tried to hear what had caught Chester's attention.

The front door opened, and Chester hopped off the couch to go greet the caller.

Marty started to rise but decided against it. She didn't want Ellie to see that she'd been worrying.

"Hey, Ellie, is that you?"

"Yes."

Ellie walked into the living room, Chester at her side, and both woman and dog looked absurdly happy.

"So did you see Mason?"

Ellie nodded.

"And things went well?"

Ellie smiled again. There was an odd, dreamy quality to her expression. "Yes."

Marty gritted her teeth. She wanted to shout, 'Well, what the hell happened?' But instead she asked, "So he'll help?"

That strange, mysterious smile deepened. "Yes, we came to a very agreeable arrangement."

Marty frowned. This situation didn't seem to require an arrangement to her. It seemed more of a *yes, I'll help you* or a *no, I won't help you* sort of thing to her.

"I'm going to bed," Ellie said, heading down the hall to the stairs. "'Night."

"'Night," Marty called after her, sure her voice was riddled with confusion. Ellie was definitely acting peculiar. And Marty was fairly certain her hair was tousled and her lips looked puffy and red.

Chapter 5

How could the simple sound of a coffeemaker brewing be so deafeningly loud and so painful? Mason propped his elbows on the kitchen table and glared at the offensive machine. He didn't even want coffee.

Struggling to his feet, he trudged to the refrigerator and opened the door to peer inside. There were a few beers; an open can of ravioli; a couple slices of hard, dried-out pizza; some gourmet mustard; a jar of capers; and a full bottle of Bloody Mary mix.

A cup of the loud, obnoxious coffee? Or a cold glass of the dog that bit him? He grabbed the bottle of mixer and headed to the cupboard to get a glass. With glass in hand, he went to the freezer for some ice. As he captured a couple of cubes, a wave of familiarity slammed over him.

He'd gotten a glass of ice for someone last night.

Ellie Stepp. She'd been here. He'd gotten her a glass of ice water. He'd kissed her.

Dropping the ice cubes back into the freezer and absently placing the empty glass on the counter, he staggered over to the table and fell into one of the kitchen chairs.

He'd kissed Ellie Stepp. Judging from his headache, he had drunk a lot last night, but he would have thought, no matter how much liquor he drank, he'd remember that.

He concentrated, trying to ignore the pounding in his skull. Why had Ellie been here?

The library? Yes, that was it. There was a problem with the library. And . . . Everett Winslow was trying to take money from the library. For a football field. And Ellie wanted Mason's help rallying votes for the library versus the field.

He nodded with a touch of relief, feeling better that things seemed to be coming back to him. But the reassurance was short-lived.

So what did kissing Ellie have to do with any of this?

A sickening feeling, which had nothing to do with his hangover, washed over him. He'd told Ellie he would help her if she had sex with him.

He dropped his head to the table and groaned. *Shit.*

After a few seconds, he raised his head and squinted at the clock. It was eight o'clock. The library opened at, what? Nine, maybe ten. He'd go to his office to check in and make sure nothing urgent needed his attention; then he'd head over to the library and offer Ellie his deepest apology for being drunk . . . drunk and horny.

He wiped a hand over his face and groaned again. This was not good. He had probably scared the shy woman half to death. He knew he could be a jackass, but this was bad, even for him.

Heading to the shower, he went over his apology in his head.

"Ellie, I just want to apologize," he said aloud as he stepped into the scorching shower spray, wincing only slightly before he continued, "for being . . . for being . . . the world's biggest ass."

This was so bad. How could he expect to be forgiven for suggesting something so inappropriate? It was inexcusable. It was made even worse by the fact that she was his best friend's new sister-in-law. Chase would not be too pleased if he heard about this.

See, this was exactly the kind of trouble a guy found

himself in when he didn't get laid on a regular basis. Inevitably, his cock did the thinking for him.

And he and his cock had been doing a lot of thinking about Ellie Stepp. Since the wedding, she'd been a very popular topic of reflection.

Her soft lips pressed tremulously against his flashed through his mind. Funny, he could barely recall making his offensive proposal, but the texture and heat of Ellie's mouth were as clear as the steamy water running over him.

She had been so sweet, so unsure in his arms. And despite her fear, she had responded. She'd tasted like fresh air and sunshine. She'd been so soft and yielding in his arms.

He closed his eyes and let the water sluice over him, hoping it would wash away everything—his headache, his embarrassment, his memories, and most of all, this raging need to touch Ellie Stepp again.

After a few moments, he opened his eyes. It wasn't working. He looked down at himself. One part of his anatomy in particular wasn't listening at all.

He would definitely have to find a woman to satisfy his libido. But Ellie wasn't that woman. Ellie was the kind of lady who needed a long-term relationship. Mason didn't intend to offer that kind of commitment to anyone.

So, he would apologize to her and the whole incident would be forgotten.

His cock pulsed against his stomach; it obviously didn't believe him, either.

Fortunately, maybe unfortunately, everything seemed to be in order at his office. The biggest issue of the day seemed to be whether Elton Grindle had had a fishing permit when he'd caught the largest fish at the annual bass-fishing contest.

Mason suspected he hadn't. He couldn't remember Elton ever having a fishing license, but by Mason's way of thinking, Elton had still caught the largest fish, license or no. Plus Elton was eighty-three years old. Let the old fella win.

So the biggest problem at the mayor's office didn't hold a candle to the problem in the mayor's private life. And although it would have been much nicer to stay in his office debating fishing permits and avoiding Ellie altogether, he couldn't.

"Ginny," Mason said as he left his office and passed his secretary's desk, "I've got to run an errand, but you can reach me on my cell."

Ginny, an average-looking woman with short hair and a pointy chin, nodded. "Okay, boss."

She always referred to him that way, and Mason had the distinct feeling it was her own private joke. He had no doubt that she considered herself the real boss.

He walked down the granite front steps of the Millbrook Town Hall and made a right. The library was located just two buildings down and across the street. As he approached the old building, he really looked at it, maybe for the first time in years.

The estate had once been a sea captain's, not unlike his own house. Whitewashed with black shutters, it had a mansard-style roof, tall multi-paned windows, and a front porch.

Renovations had been done through the years with sections added to accommodate more books, but the additions stayed true to the style of the original building.

Most of the flowers had gone by now, but in the summer the grounds were alive with bright colors and scents. And they had children's story time on the shaded lawn when the weather was nice.

The library was beautiful, a perfect place to hold the stories of history and fantasy worlds and adventure and love. A perfect place to be watched over by a shy, sweet beauty like Ellie Stepp.

Sex, my friend, that's what you needed. When you start seeing a woman you've known for years, a woman you've never even noticed until recently—as some sort of enchanted fey guardian of the books or whatever . . . well, it is the dire need for sex talking.

Or perhaps just insanity.

Either way, he needed to get this situation under control. And he would.

The library was quiet when Mason entered. Prescott Jones, an agreeable, unassuming guy who had moved here from Bangor a few years ago, sat at the check-out desk.

The desk was actually a U-shaped counter made of dark, polished oak, holding a computer, papers, and piles of books that waited to be returned to their proper places on the shelves.

"Mayor," he greeted with an affable smile that revealed a row of glaringly white teeth.

Mason blinked. He thought his hangover was better, but obviously his senses were still a bit hypersensitive.

"What can I do to help you this morning?" he asked.

Yeah, the wholesome, chipper thing was a bit too much this morning, but he managed to ask, "Is Ellie in yet?"

Mason could have sworn that Prescott's smile slipped just a bit.

"Yes, she's in her office. I'll get her." Prescott started to come out from behind the desk, but Mason raised a hand to stop him.

"I'll go. It's back this way, right?" Before Prescott could answer, Mason strode in the direction he'd pointed.

Sure enough, past the shelves labeled BA-BI, a door was half open and through the crack he could see part of Ellie's face and her tousled, blond curls.

He lifted a hand to knock, but when his weight shifted, the old wooden floor creaked.

Without looking up, Ellie said, "Do you remember if we ordered one or two copies of the new Jane Blackwood novel?"

Mason hesitated, then pushed open the door. "I don't recall."

Ellie's head snapped up. "Oh," she uttered; her lips formed a cute little 'o,' and her cheeks grew pink. "I thought you were Prescott."

Mason smiled. "I figured. Sorry to disappoint."

"No," Ellie shook her head, "you didn't." She looked uncomfortable.

He stepped further into her tiny office and closed the door behind him.

When he turned back, Ellie looked even more ill at ease. He could hardly blame her. After all, the letch who'd bargained sex for his political backing was between her and her only escape route.

He tried shifting away from the door, but then he nearly loomed over where she sat.

She stared up at him with large, wary eyes.

He cleared his throat and tried to think of how to start. "About last night—"

"I accept," Ellie announced, the words bursting from her, startling him. Her eyes widened even more, as if her declaration had surprised her, too.

"I'm sorry?"

"I . . ." She fidgeted with the edge of the catalogue she'd been reading. "I considered your—proposal last night. And I accept," she said firmly.

Mason's reaction was instantaneous: desire ripped through him. Images of laying her across her desk and making love to her right there flashed through his mind in vivid detail.

But in the next second, guilt gripped his chest with

such force he could barely breathe. He couldn't simply have sex with her and walk away. Could he?

"That is," she said quietly, "if the offer still stands." Her face colored a deeper pink that matched the rosy color of her sweater. Her cornflower blue eyes were so filled with guardedness that he felt like an even bigger cad than he already had.

"About that proposal," he started, knowing he had to withdraw it even though he longed to continue the arrangement and take her to his bed.

Ellie looked down at the catalogue, running a small finger along the edge of the pages.

He lost his train of thought for a moment, entranced by the unintentionally seductive gesture.

"It was," he said more determinedly, "a mistake."

Ellie's head shot up, apprehension furrowing her brow.

"But I'll be glad to back you against Winslow without any—compensation."

Her blue eyes had darkened to the color of stormy seas, and they seemed to well up. With relief, no doubt.

She looked down at her desk. "Thank you," she murmured so quietly he had to lean forward to hear her.

"Don't thank me," he said grimly. "I want to help."

She nodded, still not making eye contact with him.

He studied her bowed head for a moment. Deciding the best thing to do was leave the poor woman alone, he said, "I'll be in touch once I've found out where Winslow stands with the community."

She nodded again, and the movement caused a tear to roll down her cheek and splatter on the catalogue. The wetness seeped into the paper, leaving a dark splotch.

Mason immediately castigated himself as the world's biggest jerk. "Ellie, I am sorry about last night." The words sounded so inadequate, but he couldn't think of anything better.

She shook her head but refused to look at him. "It's okay. No apology necessary."

A derisive laugh escaped him. "I owe you far more than an apology."

Ellie finally lifted her head, and her tear-filled eyes ate at his conscience.

"You shouldn't have to apologize for realizing you made a mistake."

Mason frowned. To him, that seemed to be the exact time a person should apologize.

"How you feel is how you feel. Or in this case, how you don't feel." She gave him a tremulous smile.

His frown deepened. What? She was speaking far too cryptically for his hungover brain. "I'm not sure I follow you," he finally admitted.

"I'm . . . I'm just saying," she struggled for the right words. "I'm not surprised you decided that it was a bad bargain."

"It was a terrible bargain," he agreed.

Ellie winced. Another tear tumbled down her cheek. "Right." She wiped her eyes, the gesture resolute. She took in a deep breath. "Thank you again for your help."

Mason was confused by her sudden dismissal. He had thought she would be thankful he wasn't following through with the arrangement. Instead, she seemed hurt.

Suddenly, the truth hit him. Ellie *wanted* a one-night stand with him. She had accepted his vulgar offer not for the library, but for herself.

Well, damn, this was an outcome he hadn't considered. An odd sense of smugness and an overwhelming rush of desire came over him.

Of course, Ellie's wish to be with him didn't change the fact that she was a completely unsuitable woman to have a fling with. But he wasn't going to let her believe that he didn't want her.

Because he did. Damn, he did.

"You think I decided to end this deal because I don't want you? Because I don't want to sleep with you? Well, that's crap."

Ellie looked embarrassed. "Please, Mason, don't do this. You don't have to."

"I'm not telling you this to make you feel better. And I'm certainly not telling you this to make myself feel better. Because frankly, it's going to be hell, knowing that I could have you. But I won't. I'm telling you this because it's the truth. Hell, last night's kiss should have showed you how much I want you."

"I . . ." Ellie blushed a deep scarlet. "I want you, too." The words were no more than a whisper, said so honestly and with such conviction that Mason felt overcome by them. By her.

"But I can't do this." It nearly killed him to say it.

The wariness returned to Ellie's eyes.

Mason moved around the desk so he could touch her, even though he knew he should stay away. Far, far away. His hands caught her upper arms. "Ellie, you aren't the kind of woman who has an affair and I can't offer you anything more."

Ellie gazed up at him and, again, he was struck by the openness and sincerity in her eyes. "I want whatever you can offer."

He stared at her for a moment, and then despite his better judgment, or maybe judgment played no role at all, he pulled her up from her chair and kissed her.

Chapter 6

This time, when Mason's lips captured hers, Ellie was ready. She wanted this so, so much.

She returned the ravenous pressure of his mouth, mimicking his motions with timorous determination, hoping her own hunger made up for her lack of finesse. Her hands traced his muscles covered by the fine material of his suit, trying to memorize every contour of his arms and shoulders.

When her hands sank into the thick, silky hair at the nape of his neck, a deep rumbling moan escaped him, and he leaned her back so she was half across her desk. His hands roamed over her back and sides, slipping under her sweater, and found the hem of her cotton blouse, making contact with her bare flesh.

She clutched him, once again feeling overwhelmed by the longing that raged through her. It was all-consuming and unreasonably strong. Far too strong for her to handle.

She vaguely realized she might very well have her one-night stand right here on her desk. Did that count as a one-night stand if it didn't happen at night?

It didn't really matter. Nothing mattered except Mason.

Abruptly, he dragged her back up to her feet and broke the kiss, taking a step away from her.

She wove, confused by the sudden stop. Her heart-beat seemed incredibly loud in her ears until she realized the insistent pounding was at her office door.

"Ellie," Prescott's muffled voice called from the other side. It was apparent from his worried tone that he'd been knocking for a while.

She hadn't heard a thing. She glanced at Mason.

He ran a hand through his hair and scowled at the door.

"Ellie!" Prescott called again.

She cleared her throat and answered in a shaky voice, "Come in."

Prescott stuck his head in, casting a questioning look from Ellie to Mason and back to Ellie. "Is everything okay?"

She self-consciously tugged her sweater around herself and forced a smile. "Yes, we were just—just discussing how we are going to solve the problem with—with Everett Winslow."

Prescott's pale eyes scrutinized her, and she had the distinct feeling he didn't believe her. Then he frowned at Mason. "So you are going to help us?"

Mason glowered back. "Yes, I plan to help *Ellie*."

She could feel Mason at her back as he took a step closer to her.

Ellie glanced over her shoulder at Mason and then looked back to Prescott. The two men glared at each other like two angry dogs fighting over the same bone. She could swear they appeared almost jealous.

Well, that proved it. There was something in either the air or the water. Or maybe the Earth had fallen off its axis because everything was definitely askew.

Golden boy Mason Sweet wanted an affair with her. Mild-mannered Prescott Jones looked ready to fight Mason to the death. And she had been more than willing to lose her virginity right there on her desk—in the middle of the day—at the public library.

* * *

Mason stepped past Ellie. "I'll call you tonight," he said with a possessiveness he didn't even recognize or understand. All he knew was that he did not like the protective look in Prescott Jones's eyes.

It was clear that the assistant librarian thought Mason was a threat to Ellie. Which in truth, Mason was, but what bothered him most was that Prescott seemed to have the hots for Ellie. Mason couldn't imagine why he cared. So what if Ellie's nice, unassuming coworker had a thing for her? That wasn't any of his business.

If Mason was planning to pursue her, then that would be a different story.

Although the look Prescott narrowed at him as Mason left the office made him want to inform ole Prescott that Ellie was taken. Hands off. Instead, Mason gave the other man an answering scowl and left the library.

The sun was high in the sky, and the air had warmed considerably. Or maybe it was just residual heat from his encounter with Ellie. He shouldn't have kissed her, but the invitation she presented was too much. Her wide eyes, her impossibly pink lips. She was irresistible.

But he was going to resist. He wasn't a heroic guy, but he was going to try to be. In fact, tonight he was going to look for a lady to help him assuage his pesky desire. Ellie Stepp wasn't the only cute woman with eyes like crystal clear skies and lips like sugary cotton candy.

"Mayor Sweet."

Mason snapped out of his reverie, recognizing the voice immediately. He looked up to see Everett Winslow descending the town hall steps. "Everett," he greeted coolly.

Winslow jogged down the last few steps. "You're just the man I hoped to see."

Everett Winslow was about fifteen years older than Mason. But only a few wrinkles around his eyes and some gray hair at his temples showed the age difference. He had a trim, athletic build, and he always sported a wide, practiced grin as he did now.

Everett offered him a hand, which Mason accepted in a brief, firm shake.

"What can I do for you today, Everett?" Mason asked as if he didn't know the answer.

Winslow's smile deepened, and a sly gleam sparked in his eyes. "Ginny just told me you were over at the library."

Mason's own congenial smile almost slipped. *How did Ginny do that?* She knew everything that happened in this town. It could be quite helpful, but when her wicked powers were used on him, it was more than a little bit unsettling.

"Yes, Ellie Stepp had some interesting news for me," Mason said, keeping his voice neutral. "She said that you've approached the library's board of trustees about possibly voting some of the library's budget over to the school board."

Winslow nodded. "Yes, I did. And that is why I'm here today, too. To see if I could rally any interest from the town council."

Mason pretended to consider Winslow's proposal. "Well, I do think a new football field would be a grand addition to the town." *Yeah, right.* "But I'm afraid I can't give you my support. Not at the cost of the library."

Winslow nodded with an understanding set to his mouth, although there was no disappointment in his eyes. Mason had given him exactly the answer he had wanted.

"Well, Mayor, thank you for your time," he said with false sincerity.

"Any time, Everett," Mason replied with his own faked candor.

Mason watched Winslow stroll down the sidewalk. There was a bounce to his step not fitting for a man who had just lost the backing of the mayor.

Mason's suspicion was correct. Winslow did want them on opposite sides of this issue. And Mason had no doubt this debate would divide the town. Once again, the two men were going to see exactly which of them held the power in Millbrook.

Mason hoped it would be him. But after the past few weeks, he couldn't be absolutely sure.

Unfortunately, there was nothing he could do but let the games begin.

"I'm not sure Mason is going to be much help," Prescott said.

Ellie frowned up at him from where she sat on the floor reorganizing the children's books. Kids were rough on the Dewey Decimal System. "Why do you say that?"

Prescott crouched beside her, tackling the shelf next to the one she was working on. "I don't know. I've just heard some things, that's all."

"What have you heard?"

Prescott shrugged, looking at the books rather than at her. "I've heard a few people who've attended town council meetings recently say that Mason wasn't . . . he hasn't been himself lately."

Ellie immediately bristled. "Well, that's neither here nor there. I know Mason will do everything he can to help us."

Prescott was quiet for a moment, and then he asked softly, "How well do you know him, Ellie?"

That gave Ellie pause. There didn't seem to be a time in her life when Mason hadn't, in some vague way, been a part of it. But she didn't know him, not really. She'd kissed him. She planned to sleep with him, but neither of those things meant she really knew him. Strange, given how personal both acts were.

"I know him well enough," she said, although there wasn't the vehemence behind the words that she'd hoped for.

Again Prescott was silent, sorting and shifting.

"I was wondering," he said after several moments, "would you be interested in going out to dinner tonight?"

He had asked her to dinner many times before, but after his reaction to Mason today, she wondered if Prescott thought there was more to their friendly dinners than she realized.

She glanced at him. He continued to organize the shelves, nearly finished with the Ls. There was no indication on his boyish features that her answer really mattered to him.

She was reading more into his reaction in her office than was actually there. She'd never even considered before that Prescott might think about her as anything other than a friend and, hopefully, a decent boss.

"I think I'll have to pass tonight."

Prescott nodded with his usual easy acceptance.

"Marty's still in town," she added.

"Right," he said with a smile. Ellie had never noticed that Prescott had a very handsome smile.

The customer bell on the check-out desk rang, and he got up to wait on whoever had rung.

Ellie watched him leave. Maybe things would be simpler if she was attracted to Prescott.

Ellie glanced at her wristwatch. It was almost ten o'-clock. She hated to be so pathetic that she was waiting for Mason's call with bated breath, but she was.

She began to read her book, rereading the same paragraph she had read three times already. Obviously, any sort of comprehension was beyond her at the moment.

Dropping the book onto the couch, she rose and decided to go look for something to eat. She'd just gone grocery shopping and the refrigerator overflowed with food, but nothing looked appealing. She crossed to the window to look out into the dark autumn sky. Then she looked at her watch again. Officially ten o'clock.

Marty looked up from the kitchen table, where she sat going through a stack of guidebooks about Sweden. Her next modeling job was at a resort in Stockholm.

"What are you doing? You're making me jittery."

Ellie shot her sister an apologetic look. "I'm just antsy tonight."

"Why?" Marty absently flipped another page of *Stockholm for Swingers*. The artwork on the book looked like it was from the seventies, although the binding looked as perfect as if it had never been opened before.

"Where on earth did you find that book? And why?" Ellie asked, trying to change the topic.

Marty moved her hand so Ellie could see one of the Millbrook Public Library stickers across the base of the binding.

"No," Ellie said, surprised, and moved to pick it up. She flipped through the pages. There were lovely shots of men with big bushy sideburns and women with kinky perms grinning in Jacuzzis or in restaurants. There was even a lovely shot of a group of swingers on a nude beach.

"I had no idea we had such a fine book in our library," Ellie said, lifting an eyebrow. "Have you found any places that you plan to visit?"

Marty laughed. "Nah, I just took out every tourist

book you had about Sweden. I'm not really interested in swinging. Although I'm sure Rod would love it." The last part was muttered so quietly that Ellie wasn't sure if she had been meant to hear it or not.

The phone rang, and Ellie actually jumped.

"I'll get it," she said quickly and ran to grab the receiver.

"Hello." She sounded breathless and a tad desperate.

"Hey," a low voice drawled on the other end of the line. "Is Marty there?"

Ellie felt the heavy, sinking sensation of disappointment in her belly. "Sure, she's right here." She held the receiver out to Marty.

Her sister didn't look nearly as excited about the phone call as Ellie had been.

Ellie went back to the living room to try to read her book and to offer Marty a bit of privacy. Her plan didn't really work as Marty's voice rose angrily, and Ellie could hear every word.

"Rod, that will still leave me plenty of time."

Pause.

"Rod, it's only a few days longer than I'd originally planned. I want to see my sister again before I leave, and she'll be home in four days. I'll see her for an evening and a day and take a late flight from Bangor to New York."

Another pause.

"Yes, I take my career seriously." A small pause. "Rod, you wouldn't. No, this is my shoot."

Quite a long pause, then finally Marty said with dejection. "All right, I'll be home tomorrow night. Are you happy?"

Then her voice quieted, and Ellie couldn't hear anything more.

Ellie was really worried about her sister. It had been apparent since Marty had gotten home that something was wrong. She wasn't eating, and she didn't seem to sleep. Ellie heard her up roaming around the house all hours of the night. Ellie knew that this Rod-person was part of Marty's distress, but since Marty refused to talk about him, Ellie had no idea how involved they were. But after what she had heard of this conversation, it was clear that he was very involved in her modeling career.

"Well," Marty said, "I'm sure you heard that I have to head out tomorrow." She sounded dejected.

Ellie nodded. "Do you think you can get on a flight?"

Marty shrugged. "Yeah, I'm really disappointed that I won't get a chance to see Abby again. But you know my crazy, jet-set career. It keeps me dashing."

Ellie could see that Marty was quickly regaining her bravado. She thought Marty hid behind false bravado a lot, and she admired her baby sister for having so much fortitude.

"Well, this is our last night," Marty said, all of her upset gone from her voice, although a little tension lingered in her stance and around her mouth. "We need to do something."

"What did you have in mind?"

Marty thought for a moment; then her eyes lit up. "Let's go to Bar Harbor to that bar on Cottage Street. The one with the microbrewery attached."

Ellie looked down at her baggy cotton pajama bottoms and her loose t-shirt. "You want to go out?"

Marty nodded adamantly.

Ellie looked unsure. "It's a work night."

"Oh, don't be an old poop. I don't know when I'll be home again."

Ellie's next thought was that Mason was going to call and she'd miss it. But she glanced back at her sister, waiting for an answer and giving her encouraging looks. She didn't see Marty often and she did want to spent time with her. Plus, Marty needed a little cheering up. It would be selfish to say no.

"I'll get dressed."

Marty let out a happy whoop. "We are going to have a great time."

Chapter 7

The Bear's Den was a cozy place that catered primarily to locals. The main room was open with a bar to one side of the room. Square tables and ladderback chairs were arranged in front of a small stage. Past the bar was a little area in an alcove that contained a few tall, round tables and bar chairs.

"Let's sit in the main room. You can't see the band from the corner over there," Marty said, leading her to the table closest to the stage.

The "band" was made up of two men with acoustic guitars and microphones. They played a song Ellie didn't recognize, but both men had nice voices and the music was soothing and folksy.

"What can I get you ladies?" a waiter about ten years younger than them, with a knit cap and a goatee, asked them once they were seated.

"I'll try your ale," Marty said.

"I'll have an iced tea," Ellie said.

Marty frowned. "Come on, Ellie-Ann, have a drink."

"You have the drinks," Ellie said with an indulgent smile. "I'll drive."

Marty shrugged, seeming to find that trade-off agreeable. She began to sway to the music.

Ellie scanned the room. It was relatively quiet. A couple guys sat at the bar, hunched over their beers. A young couple sat a few tables back, eating dinner.

From the way they were dressed, in expensive hiking boots and fleece pullovers, Ellie guessed they were tourists in for the nice autumn camping that Acadia National Park offered.

Another couple sat in the alcove, but Ellie could only see the woman from her angle. The woman was a tad overdressed for the place, in a pair of tight, black slacks and a silk blouse. Her thick, dark hair was cut into one of those perfectly arranged, carefree styles that Ellie envied.

She touched her own hair. Her riot of curls was carefree, too, but not due to an intended style. Her curls just had a mind of their own.

Oh, well, there was no point worrying about it. After all, her hair was the least of her problems. There was her weight, which she had struggled with her whole life to no avail. And her face, which was absurdly round with pudgy little cheeks. And there was her height. How had she ended up being just over five feet tall when both her sisters were over five foot nine? Marty was six feet tall, for goodness sake.

Ah, it wasn't worth obsessing about. She was what she was. And there were moments when she wouldn't want to be anyone else for the world.

Her mind drifted back to her encounter with Mason today. His kiss had been wonderful. She hadn't been as nervous as the first time. She still found him frightening and exhilarating at the same time, but it was like a roller coaster at an amusement park. Even though she was scared, she never wanted the ride to end.

She sighed.

"Okay, what has you looking so dreamy?" Marty asked. "Or should I say who?"

Ellie immediately suppressed the silly smile she was wearing and tried to look nonchalant. "I was just thinking about . . . work," she said lamely.

"Work?" Marty sounded unconvinced.

Ellie nodded.

Marty suddenly looked horrified. "Please don't tell me you've finally given in to Prescott Jones."

"Huh?"

"Prescott Jones. Please don't tell me you've never noticed the way he moons over you. Every time I come to see you at the library, he follows you around like an adoring puppy dog."

Ellie gave her a disbelieving look. "No, he doesn't."

Marty rolled her eyes. "Oh, please!"

The waiter returned with their drinks.

"Are you sure?" Ellie asked after the waiter left. "I mean, it could just seem like he's following me. The library *is* small."

Marty rolled her eyes again. "I can tell the difference between following and accidentally running into. He follows."

Ellie considered Marty's words and the fact that she had wondered the same thing about Prescott herself today. Before she had really thought out her words, she confessed, "That's funny, because Prescott interrupted Mason and me in my office today, and he didn't seem very happy." As soon as she finished, she knew she'd said too much.

"What did Prescott interrupt you and Mason *doing* in your office today?" Marty asked, leaning her elbows on the table.

Ellie bit back a groan. She could feel her cheeks burning, and she knew Marty was too keen to miss her reaction. "Mason came to tell me he would back the library against Everett Winslow."

"I thought he told you that last night."

Marty really was too sharp.

"Yes, well, he just wanted to discuss a few things."

"Did this discussion involve using lips and tongues for more than forming words?"

"Marty!" Her eyes widened in shock.

Marty chuckled. "You don't have to kiss and tell if you don't want to, but I couldn't help noticing that you looked pretty well kissed when you came home from Mason's last night."

Ellie could feel her cheeks grow hotter. She took a sip of her iced tea, hoping the cold liquid would cool her warm skin.

Marty took a sip of her ale. "Okay," she said when Ellie didn't speak. "I'll drop it."

Ellie took another sip of her tea, and she realized she did want to tell Marty. She needed to share this. "We did kiss."

Marty slammed a hand on the tabletop. "I knew it!"

Ellie's cheeks still burned with embarrassment, but she felt relief, too. Somehow telling Marty made it seem more real.

"Sooo," Marty said, encouraging her to disclose more.

"It was very nice."

"Nice?"

"It was wonderful," Ellie admitted.

Marty smiled gladly. "Are you planning to go on a date or anything?"

Ellie's own smile slipped a notch. "I think we will get together sometime." Once, anyway.

Marty nodded and reached across the table to squeeze her hand. "I'm glad. It's about time you found some happiness."

Ellie frowned, perplexed. "Why do you say that?"

"Well . . ." It was her sister's turn to look a little uncomfortable. "You've spent a lot of time alone since Grammy died. And when she was alive, you spent all your time helping her. It's time to live for you."

Even though Marty could never know it, her words made Ellie feel even more confident about her crazy decision to sleep with Mason. It was something for her. To hold to herself when the days grew lonely again.

Both sisters fell into silence, listening to the soothing music and sipping their drinks.

"I've got to use the ladies' room. If the waiter comes back, can you order me another ale?"

Ellie nodded. She watched Marty cross the room. The two men at the bar followed her journey, too. One of the guys nudged the other with his elbow, and Ellie could hear their bawdy laughter over the musicians. Marty disappeared into the bathroom, oblivious to the stir she'd caused.

Ellie shook her head and turned back to the band. She didn't want to be like Marty, to garner that much attention. But she did wonder what it would be like to have men notice her. Well, notice her and think she was attractive.

Of course, Marty claimed that Prescott had noticed her. Ellie couldn't quite believe that. It seemed rather implausible that she'd worked with Prescott for years and had never been aware of his interest.

Ellie might not have been blessed with Marty's beauty, but Marty had certainly been blessed with Ellie's imagination.

To be honest, Ellie didn't really care if *men* found her attractive. She'd be thrilled if only one man found her pretty. One man in particular. And it appeared, amazingly, that one man did.

Ellie smiled to herself and softly hummed along with the song the band was playing. She wondered if Mason had called. She'd finally purchased an answering machine, so hopefully, if he had, he had left a message.

She looked around, remembering Marty wanted another ale. She couldn't help noticing that the woman in the alcove was being embraced by her companion, and from the angle of her head, she appeared to be getting kissed quite soundly.

She looked away, feeling a little too much like a voyeur, and searched for the waiter. He was nowhere in sight, but the bartender, a short, stout woman with a masculine-looking haircut, was just leaning against the bar, watching the musicians.

Ellie retrieved her purse from the back of her chair and approached the bar.

"May I have a Black Bear Ale?" Ellie asked the bartender.

The woman nodded but didn't say a word or even crack a smile. She left to pour the ale.

One of the men who had been watching Marty leaned closer to Ellie.

"Ole Addy ain't too friendly, but she's fast with the drinks." The man smiled to reveal a missing tooth, which was too bad, since the man appeared to be in his thirties and had nice, twinkling eyes.

Ellie managed a shy smile back.

An ale was thumped down in front of her, and Addy waited for her money, still not saying a word or smiling.

Ellie rummaged through her wallet until she found a ten. Addy took it, crossed over to an ancient cash register, and returned promptly with Ellie's change.

"See," the man said, leaning toward Ellie again. "Fast."

Ellie smiled nervously again.

The man on the other side of the sparkly-eyed man sat forward. "Seems you don't talk much either, but you've got a real pretty smile."

Ellie felt herself blush, and she had no idea how to react to the two men's attention.

She didn't have to consider her embarrassment long because Marty appeared at her side, a troubled look on her face.

"Ellie, I'm not feeling too well. I think we should go."

Ellie nodded, concerned by her sister's sudden agitation. "Okay, I got you another ale, though."

Marty reached in front of Ellie and slid the full ale to the twinkly-eyed guy. "Here you go. On us."

The man didn't hesitate to accept the drink. "Hey, thanks."

"Let's go," Marty said, her voice insistent.

Ellie frowned. "Are you feeling that sick?"

Marty nodded vigorously. "Yes. Yes. Very sick." She caught Ellie's arm and jerked her toward the door.

Bewildered, Ellie followed her sister, although she glanced around. She had the sensation she might have forgotten something. She had taken only a few steps when a glimpse of tawny hair and a familiar laugh caught her attention.

She peered over to the alcove, now in full view. Ellie could clearly see the lovely brunette, and now she could also see the companion that held her rapt attention.

Ellie's stomach plummeted as she immediately recognized a pair of sleepy, gray eyes and the lopsided, charming smile. Both were burnt indelibly into her brain.

Mason sat close to the brunette, his hand on her thigh, his fingers brushing a strand of her long, shiny hair from her cheek. Just at that moment, Mason's gaze moved from his female friend and locked with Ellie's.

Ellie stumbled, falling against her sister. Marty tried to steady her, but it was too late. Ellie hit the floor with a resounding thud.

The musicians stopped their playing and silence filled the bar.

Ellie lay there for a moment, praying for the floor to open and swallow her. But it didn't. Instead, a couple of pairs of hands tugged at her.

Reluctantly, she righted herself into a sitting position and allowed the hands to pull her to her feet. The hands belonged to Marty and the man with the missing tooth and nice eyes. His friend stood there, too, a concerned expression on his face.

Ellie didn't look over at the table in the alcove. Instead, she offered the two men a feeble smile and murmured her thanks.

"Ah, don't worry about it," the man said, his own smile wide and gapped. "I've fallen so many times leaving this place, it's little wonder there ain't big ole holes in the floor on either side of my bar stool over there."

Ellie managed another smile, appreciating his sympathetic words. She suspected that her fall might have been less distressing if it had been caused by overindulgence rather than pure clumsiness. And she would definitely feel better if Mason hadn't been there to witness her klutziness.

Marty recognized Ellie's mortification, said a quick thank you to the men, and then led her out of the bar.

Mason watched Ellie leave, her sister's arm protectively around her. He was filled with an overwhelming sense of loss as the door swung closed behind them.

When Ellie fell, his first instinct had been to rush over and make sure she was okay. But he hadn't. He'd stayed where he was. Because, despite his consuming desire for Ellie, he knew he was doing the right thing by remaining with Natalie.

He looked at the woman sitting across from him. The woman he'd called after work to meet for a drink—and perhaps a bit more. A woman who understood the score.

Mason knew that even though Ellie said she was

fine with a similar arrangement, she wasn't really prepared for it. As far as he knew, and he did have Ginny's fiendish gossiping abilities on his side, Ellie Stepp had never so much as dated anyone.

Mason glanced over at the two men who had been talking with Ellie. He'd seen them here before, at the same spot at the bar. Mason had also seen the interest in their eyes as they helped Ellie. One of the men had even said something to the effect that "the little one was as sweet as a red, ripe cherry." Then they'd chuckled, and Mason had suppressed the sudden urge to go over and bash their heads together.

The men's reaction to Ellie did, however, bring up an interesting question. Men definitely noticed her. Hell, Mason was practically drooling over the woman. So why didn't she date?

"Mason?"

Natalie's voice startled him.

"I'm sorry, did you say something?"

Natalie smiled. She had a large, wide smile with lots of even, white teeth. There was something a little predatory about it. "I just asked if you knew that woman who fell."

"Nope," he said easily, although he couldn't quite figure out why he lied.

"Poor girl. She seemed a bit bumbling."

Natalie's words weren't exactly insulting, but for some reason, they offended Mason. "She slipped. It happens."

"She probably had a bit too much to drink."

Again, Natalie's words were conversational rather than judgmental, but he felt the need to defend Ellie. "She doesn't drink."

Natalie raised an eyebrow. "I thought you didn't know her?"

Mason took a drink of his whiskey and water. After he swallowed, he managed a composed smile. "I don't; she just doesn't look like the type that would get tipsy on a weeknight."

Natalie looked unconvinced but shrugged as if the topic had become boring to her. "Listen," she said in a soft voice, like she was suggesting something quite wicked, "why don't you come over to my house, and I'll make you one of those Irish coffees you like so much. Neither of us cares about getting tipsy on a weeknight."

Mason's smile widened. He knew what followed Natalie's very intoxicating coffees. And it was exactly what Mason needed to rid him of his improper longing for the proper Miss Ellie Stepp.

Chapter 8

Natalie's house was new. She and her ex-husband had built the two-story cape five years earlier. Despite its classic New England exterior, the inside was very modern. And in Mason's opinion, quite cold and uncomfortable. But it suited Natalie.

Not that Natalie was cold. She wasn't, and he knew because she was nestled in his lap, quite hot.

Her lips roamed down his neck, and her fingers worked on the buttons of his shirt.

He closed his eyes and leaned his head against the back of the leather sofa, trying to focus on her hands. They were now inside his shirt, caressing his chest.

She flicked her tongue over his bottom lip and then captured his mouth in a sure, decisive move.

Mason had always enjoyed Natalie's expertise, her confidence with him. But tonight, her skilled moves felt too deliberate. It wasn't about passion; it was about gratification.

Suddenly Ellie's kiss earlier today replayed in his head. Her tentativeness. Her artless and vulnerable response. The way her hands knotted into his hair and she held on like she might drown in desire.

Mason groaned into Natalie's opened mouth and shifted around on the sofa until she was pinned under him. He deepened the kiss, plundering her mouth.

He had a gorgeous woman who wanted to satisfy him right here in his arms. *Stop being a fool and enjoy it.*

Natalie moaned and clasped him.

He ran his hands over Natalie's body, stroking her through her clothes. She was lithe and lean. A body created by hours of working out and a low carb/high protein diet. A body most men would pant over.

He stroked a hand up her back under her silky blouse. The individual bones of her spine protruded under her smooth skin. She wriggled under his touch, and her hipbones jabbed into his stomach. He moved his hands over her belly, which was flat and hard, to her breasts.

Under her lacy demi-bra, her small breasts jutted into his palms like firm little plums, pert and compact, not soft and supple.

He nearly groaned with frustration. Natalie was a beautiful woman, a sexy woman, but she wasn't the one he wanted. He wanted softness and warmth. He wanted sweet shyness and guileless enthusiasm. He wanted Ellie—and he wasn't a fool for passing up Natalie; he was a fool to think he could sate his need with someone else.

He untangled himself from Natalie's limbs and sat up.

"What is it?" She frowned up at him in confusion.

"I can't do this."

Natalie smiled, a naughty, little half-smile. "Of course you can. You've done it several times, and I have always loved every minute of it."

"I have enjoyed it, too. But," he ran a hand through his already mussed hair, "I don't think I can continue this arrangement we have."

Natalie cocked her head, disappointed but not heartbroken. "Is there someone else?"

Mason hesitated and then nodded. "Maybe."

She sat up and straightened her clothes. "Well, if it does work out, she'll be a lucky lady."

Marty wanted to go find Mason Sweet and punch him right in his straight, perfect nose. How could he kiss Ellie and be with another woman in the same day?

She didn't need to rack her brain long for the answer to that one. He was a man and all men were slime. Or at least in Marty's experience.

She glanced over at Ellie. Her sister sat on the sofa, swathed from neck to toe in a pair of baggy flannel pajamas, her nose determinedly stuck in a book.

Ellie hadn't said more than three words since they saw Mason acting all cozy with the woman in the bar. In fact, Ellie was so silent on the ride home that Marty was almost afraid her sister was in shock or something.

But when they got home, Ellie went directly upstairs and dressed for bed. Then she came back down, made a cup of tea, and sat on the couch with her book as if nothing had happened.

Maybe Marty was finding the whole situation more upsetting than Ellie. Maybe Ellie didn't think it was a big deal. Maybe it wasn't a big deal. After all, Ellie had only kissed Mason. That wasn't very serious. God, if Marty got upset about every man she'd ever kissed— well, she'd be upset quite often, to say the least.

Still, there was a stiffness to the way Ellie was sitting, and she didn't actually seem to be reading. Marty couldn't remember seeing her turn a page since she picked up the book.

"Are you really okay?"

Ellie looked up, her eyes wide as if she was surprised to find Marty there. It took her a second to answer. "Yes, no bruises—just a bruised ego about being so klutzy."

"I wasn't talking about your fall. I was talking about Mason."

Ellie smiled, but Marty could see the action was forced. "Sure, I'm fine." She held the book back up in front of her face.

"I think I'll call Rod and tell him I need to stay a few more days," Marty decided.

Ellie closed her book. "No. You aren't staying for me—not about this. I'm fine. And I know you are busy and have to get back."

Marty was busy all right—busy trying to save a career and a relationship—neither of which she was really sure she wanted in the first place. "You would tell me if you wanted me to stay, right?"

Ellie nodded. "Yes."

Marty sighed. "I guess I should get back to New York. Rod has several fashion shoots lined up, and I haven't even talked to the designer who's doing the Sweden shoot."

"See, you need to take care of yourself and to stop worrying about your older sister. I can take care of myself."

Marty knew she looked dubious.

"I can," Ellie insisted. "And I'm fine, anyway, so don't worry. Please."

"Okay. Well, I might worry a little."

Ellie laughed. "Okay, but only if it makes you feel better."

"It does."

Ellie stretched and yawned. The action seemed a bit staged. She picked up her book and stood. "I'm tired. I think I'll go to bed."

Marty knew when she was being avoided, but she let her sister off the hook. "Let's get up really early and go to the old truck stop on Route 1 for some blueberry pancakes."

Ellie walked over and hugged her. "I'd like that. Good night."

"Good night." Marty listened as her sister ascended

the stairs; the third step from the top creaked loudly as it had since they were little girls. And Marty felt sad, not only for her sister, but also for herself.

Marty had just finished packing her suitcase when a loud knock sounded from the front door. She glanced at the travel alarm clock on her nightstand. It was nearly two o'clock. Who could be here at this time of night?

She rushed down the hall and down the stairs, avoiding the third step. With any luck, Ellie would stay asleep. Her room was furthest from the front door. Ellie didn't need any more drama for a while.

Marty peeked out one of the narrow side windows that framed the front door. She could make out a tall shadow. A shadow that appeared to be male.

With only slight trepidation, she opened the door. "Hello?" she greeted, keeping her voice cool and unwelcoming.

"Hey," the shadow answered, the voice male and offhanded as if it were perfectly normal to come visiting in the middle of the night.

Marty reached over to the wall switch and flicked on the porch light.

Mason stood there, disheveled and squinting against the sudden brightness.

"Is Ellie in?"

Marty leaned on the doorframe and crossed her arms over her chest. "Do you have any idea what time it is?"

Mason considered the question. "Pretty late, I guess."

"It's two o'clock. Ellie's in bed."

Mason nodded, appearing almost sheepish. "I don't suppose you'd consider waking her up?"

Marty snorted. "No, I really wouldn't."

He nodded, accepting her refusal.

Marty studied him for a moment. "Are you drunk?"

Mason straightened, the movement causing him to weave just slightly. "I'm fine."

Hearing Mason use the same phrase Ellie had kept repeating all night caused irritation to rise in her stomach. "Well, Ellie isn't. She's not some floozy who goes around kissing guys in her office every day, you know. She's a nice woman who needs a nice man, not some player."

Marty expected Mason to get mad, but instead he simply said, "I know."

"Good." Marty wasn't going to let his almost regretful expression affect her. She'd been on the receiving end of that regret many times before.

She started to close the door, but Mason put out a hand and held it open.

"Listen, I know everything you're saying is true. Ellie does need a good man. She needs someone steady. Someone who can offer her a life full of love and security." He released the door, stumbled back, and pointed at his chest. "Unfortunately, she wants me."

The statement was so honest, so self-deprecating that Marty almost laughed, but she caught herself. "I know she wants you. But Ellie doesn't have a clue how to deal with you. She's too . . . trusting. She thinks all the world's problems can be fixed with a smile and a few kind words. Do you want to be the one to destroy her beliefs?"

Mason stared at her for a moment and then looked down at his shoes.

"I didn't think so," Marty said. "So please just stay away from her."

Mason released a sigh that seemed to come from deep within him. Turning, he left the porch without looking back.

Marty watched him until he disappeared down the sidewalk.

She felt bad for meddling in her sister's life. After all, Ellie was thirty and certainly old enough to make her own decisions. But she also knew that Ellie truly believed all people were inherently good. And from years of experience, Marty knew that just wasn't true. In many ways, Ellie was very wise. But then she was also so completely naïve.

Marty wasn't necessarily wise. She'd made more than her fair share of bad choices, but she wasn't naïve either. And in this case, she was going to use her street smarts to protect Ellie.

Mason Sweet was not the type of guy any woman needed. He came with a boatload of baggage. Marty could see it in his eyes and smell it on his breath. It was meddling, but it *was* for the best.

Too bad she wasn't as astute about her own life.

Ellie ate her blueberry pancakes, but she didn't really taste them. She was too depressed, depressed about Mason and about Marty leaving. She wished she could ask Marty to stay; she had been tempted last night to accept Marty's offer to stay longer. But she knew her sister was a busy woman with many commitments. And from the sound of it, she also needed to work on her relationship with Rod.

Ellie's silly heartache wasn't as important as either of those things. Her heartache wasn't even justified. She had no right to be upset about seeing Mason with another woman. Mason wasn't hers; he could do what he pleased.

Ellie had automatically assumed, since they had kissed again and he'd said he would call, that the one-night stand was still on. Even after he'd outright refused to sleep with her. He couldn't have made his feelings much clearer on that subject, but she still hadn't gotten it. Mason probably thought she was a total nitwit.

And then there was her elegant fall in the bar. That must have made a great impression. Should he be with the poised, graceful woman sitting with him or the chubby woman rolling around on the floor?

Ellie cringed just thinking about it.

Marty was poking at her pancakes, also lost in thought, and she'd barely taken a bite.

So much for enjoying their favorite breakfast before Marty had to leave.

"I love this place," Marty said suddenly.

Ellie glanced around. The truck stop was huge, split into two separate rooms. The room they sat in was the "trucker" room. Many of the tables were actually reserved with cardboard signs that read, in black marker and crooked handwriting, "Truckers Only." Since their youth, Marty had always insisted they sit on this side.

"Are you making up stories about the truckers like you used to?" Ellie asked. "Where they're going, where they've been?"

Marty looked around, then shrugged. "I think I liked the idea of traveling a lot more when I didn't do it all the time."

"You do like seeing new things, though, right?"

"Yes, but just like these truckers, I see most of it alone. It's not quite what I'd envisioned when I created stories about hitting the open road."

Ellie knew that much of Marty's life was lonely. She was surrounded by people, photographers, and other models, but Ellie rarely heard Marty talk about close friends. She did have boyfriends, but she never seemed particularly excited about any of them. Arturo was the only one Marty had been crazy about.

"You are looking forward to going to Sweden, though," Ellie said.

Marty nodded, a slight smile on her wide lips. "Yes. I've never been there, and I hear it's beautiful."

"And Rod is going, right?"

"And then there are times when I'd rather be alone." Marty stabbed a piece of pancake, popped it in her mouth, and chewed angrily.

"I shouldn't have brought him up."

Marty reached across the table and caught Ellie's hand as she fiddled with a plastic saltshaker. "Don't be sorry; I'm just frustrated with him right now. I'm sure things will get better."

"I hope so." Ellie hesitated before she added, "You've seemed a little down since you've been home."

"Ah, I just do that to get your sympathy, so you'll make me great dinners and cookies," Marty said, waving her hand dismissively.

Ellie smiled, but she didn't believe her sister's words for a moment. More bravado. "When will you get home again?"

"In a few months, I hope. I won't be able to make it for Christmas. Stella McCartney has scheduled a New Year's fashion show for a few days after Christmas, and I'll be busy with that right through the holidays. But hopefully, the end of January, maybe."

"Well, I'll be here," Ellie said with a wry smile.

"Right here?" Marty pointed at their table.

"I might leave to use the bathroom."

Ellie drove Marty to Bangor to get a bus to Portland, where she was catching her airplane to New York. Ellie wanted to drive her to Portland, but Marty wouldn't hear of it.

"That will take up, what? Five or six hours of your day?" Marty said.

"I can take the day off. Prescott is there. And I want to spend as much time with you as possible."

Marty shook her head. "No, use a vacation day to do something fun."

"Driving with you would be fun."

Marty shook her head as she pulled her suitcase out of the truck. "I'll be fine. Go on." She looked at her watch. "If you leave now, you'll still get to work on time."

Ellie sighed with resignation. "Okay." She came up on her tiptoes to give her tall little sister a tight hug. "Call me when you get home."

"I will."

Ellie didn't rush to leave but stayed to watch Marty disappear into the bus station.

Ellie was never late for work. She was tired of being boring, predictable Ellie, and maybe being late for work was a better place to start her rebellion than jumping right into a one-night stand.

Chapter 9

"Ellie, thank God, I was starting to wonder if everything was okay," Prescott exclaimed as she walked through the front doors of the library.

Ellie checked the large circular clock hanging over the periodicals. "I'm only fifteen minutes late."

"You're never late."

Somehow Prescott's reaction made her feel even more depressed. She really had been setting her sights high aiming for an affair with Mason. Or anyone, for that matter. She couldn't even be late for work without sending everyone's perception of her into a tailspin.

"Well, I'm here, and I'm fine." She headed back to her office, then stopped, feeling guilty for her abruptness. It was hardly Prescott's fault she was dull and prompt. "I'm sorry I worried you. I took Marty to Bangor to catch her bus."

Prescott accepted her apology with an easy nod. "I bet it was hard to see her leave again. Will she be able to get back soon?"

"Maybe January."

He sighed, his sympathy genuine. "That will be the third Christmas she's missed, won't it?"

Ellie thought. "Yes, I guess it will be. The holidays always seem to be busy for her."

He nodded.

Margaret Turnbull approached the check-out desk with a list of books on her newest hobby, and Prescott hurried away to help her locate them.

Ellie was relieved. Now that Marty had mentioned Prescott's possible interest in her, their conversations seemed more significant. Either that, or she was reading more into them.

Once behind her desk, with the door closed, she tried to concentrate on her work. But the image of herself stretched over this very desk with Mason's weight pinning her there kept playing through her head like a videotape stuck on rewind.

She blushed even though she was alone. She was not that woman. Eleanor Stepp did not act that way. Chubby, plain spinsters didn't loll on desks, wantonly kissing gorgeous men. She was a shy, reserved woman. A woman that was predictable; a woman that was on time.

She was the kind of woman that stayed home in the evening and fed her cats, or Chester in her case, maybe talked to a plant or two, and possibly crocheted baby blankets for other people's children.

She rested her elbows on her desk and cupped her round cheeks in her hands. But she didn't want to be that woman. She did want to live life, experience new things. She wanted romance and love.

Mason Sweet, however, was way out of her league. She should have realized that from the moment he had made his outrageous proposal. She should have known he would come to his senses and recant.

Why had he made it in the first place? She so obviously wasn't his type. Whereas the brunette he'd been with last night—she was exactly his type. Long legs; athletic build; shiny, long hair. His ex-wife, Marla, had been that type, too. She had looked like a model.

Not a model like her sister. Marty was a waif type, like Kate Moss or Twiggy. Where Marty had graced the covers of all the biggest fashion magazines, Mason's ex-wife could have been on the cover of all the fitness magazines.

Somehow that kind of beauty made Ellie feel more insecure. Just by the reality of her height and her body type, she could never look like Marty. She'd never be a tall, willowy waif with huge eyes and pouty lips. But she could diet and exercise and achieve at least some semblance of a figure. She could be a size 8 rather than a 14.

She sighed. It wasn't going to do her an iota of good to sit around feeling sorry for herself. She knew she didn't want her life to continue on the path it was on. So, she would change her path. But she would keep the changes realistic. She'd stop waiting for her knight in shining armor. Or at least realize that her knight might only be a squire.

Someone tapped on her door.

"Come in."

Prescott poked his head into the room. "I think that Mrs. Turnbull just checked out every book we have on beer brewing. She even took some on winemaking."

Ellie laughed. "Well, maybe she'll stick with this hobby longer than she did with bird-watching and making hooked rugs."

"We can only hope. Perhaps a few drinks would make her less persnickety." Prescott smiled and left to answer the front desk bell.

Ellie stared at the closed door. Or maybe her knight in shining armor was a nice assistant librarian with auburn hair and a great smile.

"Mayor?"

Mason glanced up from the budget proposal he was reviewing. The town refuse committee had submitted it, and he couldn't make any sense of their budgeting.

Did dumps, landfills, and trash sites all need their own budget plans? Especially given the fact that, as far as Mason knew, there was only one dump in Millbrook. He'd never heard of a landfill or a trash site within the Millbrook town limits. Trash site? Wasn't that a dump? He shook his head.

"Yes, Ginny," he said, after he pressed the intercom button on his phone.

"James Howarth is here to see you."

Mason had been expecting this visit. James Howarth was the president of the board of trustees for the library.

He rose from his desk as the older gentleman entered his office. James was in his mid-seventies with a nearly bald pate and wire-rimmed glasses. His tall, thin frame was only slightly stooped, and he had an intelligent glint to his dark eyes.

"Hello, James," Mason greeted the man warmly, offering his hand. "I've been expecting you."

"I imagine you have, young man. I imagine you have." James shook his hand with a confident strength.

"Please have a seat."

James sat down in the tweed wingback chair across from him. Mason retook his seat.

"I'm assuming Everett Winslow has already spoken to you about his plan for getting the additional funds needed for a new football field over at the high school," James said.

"Yes, he has been here to rally the council for their support."

"Well, I'm firmly against it," James stated. "As is Harriet Dodge. But I can't be terribly confident about the rest of the trustees. Lou Martin has a boy on the same football team with Winslow's boy. Joseph Dunn has been a friend of Winslow's for years. And Jeanette Knight's son fishes for the Winslow Seafood Company. With all of them invested in the man one way or another, I don't think I can count on the trustees not to vote through the transfer of funds."

Mason already knew most of what James had told him. He'd had Ginny on the case. Actually, she didn't even need to be put on the case. He just asked her what she knew about the trustees, and, as always, she was a wealth of information.

"Yes, I've been afraid of that myself. I plan to make an official announcement at next week's town council meeting that I am standing with you and Ellie Stepp against taking monies from the library."

James smiled with approval. "Very good. Ellie has done wonderful things with the library. I would hate to see that destroyed."

"Me, too."

James stood smoothly, like a man fifteen years younger. "I'll be at Tuesday's meeting, front and center."

"Good. I look forward to seeing you then."

"I look forward to seeing you stop Winslow and this self-interested scheme in its tracks. And you can, young man."

Mason nodded his appreciation, but his chest constricted with doubt. He could have been confident of the town council's support a few months ago, but now . . . Well, now, he just didn't know.

After James Howarth left, he paged Ginny. "Ginny, is Charlie in?"

"Of course," Ginny said, as if it were crazy to even consider that Charles Grace, the chairman of the town council, would be out of his office. Even though Charlie also ran a real estate company.

Mason made a face at the intercom. "Thanks."

"Did you want me to page him for you?" Ginny's voice sounded tinny through the old intercom.

Mason left his desk and exited his office. "No, I think I'll go see him in person."

Ginny raised an eyebrow but said nothing.

Mason chuckled to himself as he walked down the hall to Charlie's office. Ginny could be a real pain, but she was good at her job, and in a strange way, he admired her insolence. She definitely kept him from feeling like the ruler of Millbrook.

As did Charlie but in a totally different way.

Charlie sat at his desk, the phone pressed to his ear. "Yes, your loan was approved, and I'm heading over to put a 'sold' sign out this afternoon. No, thank you. Okay, great. Great. I'll see you at the closing. Bye."

He hung up the phone, and the smile and the jovial tone he'd used with his real estate client disappeared. "Mayor, can I help you?"

Mason wanted to tell him the best way he could help him was to drop this ridiculous idea that he had about him. But he'd already done that, and Charlie wasn't going to be swayed. No more than Mason was. So he just addressed the issue at hand. "James Howarth just came to see me, and I told him that I planned to back the library against Everett Winslow's proposal."

Charles nodded, but no indication of his feelings on the subject was evident on his face.

"I think you know that Winslow has set up a situation here that is certain to split the community vote-wise. And I also think you know that it could not only affect the library's future, but it could affect my future, too. I would like to know that I have you and the other council members behind me." Mason didn't like to sound so pathetic, so unsure.

Charlie's eyes narrowed; then he finally said, "And we both know you have a bigger issue than Everett Winslow that could affect your future as mayor. And you need to address that first."

Mason gritted his teeth. Charlie was like a dog with a bone. He never let anything go. "I did make a mistake or two, but nothing that has made an impact on my abilities as mayor."

Charles raised an eyebrow. "I think passing out in your office and getting picked up for drunk driving could very easily make an impact on your position as mayor. The only reason none of the other council members know anything about either event is that Chief Peck and I are covering for you. But I won't continue to protect you unless you get some help."

Mason stared at Charlie. They had been good friends in the past. Hell, they used to go down to the Parched Dolphin for a drink or two after work. Why was he suddenly being such an arrogant teetotaler?

Sure, Mason had made a few poor choices, but he didn't have a problem. How could a friend make such an accusation?

"I guess you need to do whatever you think you need to do," Mason finally said, keeping his voice even.

"I guess so."

Mason left the office, his blood boiling. So he'd made a couple mistakes. Big mistakes. But it hadn't happened again, and it wouldn't.

He knew Nate Peck had done him a huge favor by not reporting his D.U.I. But it wasn't like he hadn't done Nate a few favors, too. Nate knew damned well he wouldn't be the chief of police without Mason's support. And Mason *had* learned his lesson. For example, last night he'd drunk too much with Natalie. But did he drive? No, he had taken a taxi.

Granted, he probably could have used better judgment on where he went in the taxi, but that wasn't the result of drinking too much. It was the result of his damned libido.

It was a very lucky thing that Ellie's sister had answered the door last night instead of Ellie herself. He could only imagine the predicament he'd be in now, if his plan had worked out.

He had fully intended to take Ellie up on her offer for a one-night stand. But Marty's protective words had been as effective as a cold shower. She had reiterated everything about Ellie that he already knew.

Ellie was too sweet and too kind. And he didn't want to be the one to hurt her. But that didn't seem to be enough to diminish this irrational desire for her. But just like his political career and Everett Winslow and everything else in his life, he'd keep his desire in control.

If Charlie had to spend even an hour in his shoes, he'd appreciate a good drink, too.

Chapter 10

With Marty gone, Ellie found her life falling back into its same dreary pattern. She left work, came home, and made dinner. As she ate, she watched the news. Then she cleaned up, went upstairs, and took a bath. She changed into her pajamas and curled up on the couch with a book. That was it. As it had been for years.

The only difference now was that she had Chester to keep her company, and that was only for a few more days. Abby and Chase would be home on Sunday, and today was Thursday.

She leaned over and kissed Chester's fluffy head. Then she'd be alone again.

Despite her depression at losing their pet, Ellie was excited to see her sister and brother-in-law. She imagined they were having a wonderful time, lounging on the beach in Saint Thomas. Drinking tall, frozen drinks and making love on the sand.

Ellie leaned her head back on the couch and closed her eyes. She tried to picture herself in the same situation with a gorgeous blond at her side. A blond with eyes gray like thunderclouds; full, sensual lips; and a low, sexy drawl.

She released a frustrated groan and opened her eyes. She wasn't going to do this. She was going to change her life. Small, reasonable steps. The first of which was to stop thinking about Mason.

It had been nearly a week since she'd seen him at the bar with the tall brunette. The only other time she'd seen him was at the town council meeting last Tuesday.

As he had promised, he did announce his decision to back the library. Throughout the meeting, Ellie had watched him, but not once did he look at her. He seemed tense, and his eyes looked tired. Afterwards, she had waited with the rest of the library staff to thank him, but he had left the meeting without speaking to anyone.

Ellie worried that something was wrong. Mason was usually very sociable and gracious. Although, his behavior wasn't really her concern.

Still, she did worry.

At work, she'd made a couple unsuccessful attempts to let Prescott know she would be interested in seeing him. Once she had mentioned a new restaurant in Bar Harbor that she'd wanted to try, but Prescott hadn't seemed to pick up on the hint.

And then, just today, she'd told him that she hadn't been to the Blue Hill Fair for years and that she thought it would be fun to go this weekend. And that she had even heard that Anne Murray was playing there on Saturday night. Prescott said he'd heard that too—and that had been the end of that.

She sighed, pulling her knees up to her chin, resting her cheek on the soft flannel of her pajamas. So much for Prescott having an unrequited crush on her.

She should have known better than to believe Marty. Marty did have a vivid imagination. She must have created the story about Prescott in the same way she'd made up exotic stories about truckers.

Ellie smiled, dropped her feet to the floor, and lifted her book to begin reading. But before she could finish the first paragraph, the phone rang.

Ellie shuffled over to it. "Hello?"

"Ellie?" It was Prescott. He sounded breathless.

"Hi, Prescott."

"Hi." There was a pause. "I was calling to see if you would be interested in going to the Blue Hill Fair with me tomorrow evening?"

Ellie smiled. Maybe Marty wasn't just a good story-teller. "I'd love to."

"Great." He sound relieved.

"Okay, well, I'll see you tomorrow."

"Great."

Normally, Ellie didn't work Saturdays, but she did have to go in the next morning for a half day to help with a children's book fair. Fortunately, Ellie was busy with the kids, because Prescott was making her feel very awkward.

Whenever she spoke to him, he just grinned at her, and she could see something in his blue eyes, something she'd never noticed before. Apparently Marty had been eerily accurate. Prescott did seem smitten.

Prescott's interest did make Ellie feel good, albeit unnerved, too. He was actually a very handsome man with thick auburn hair, pale blue eyes, and a smile that lit up a room. He was so nice, and he had a great sense of humor.

So why couldn't she just feel smitten, too? She wanted to.

But instead of lingering to talk with him at the end of the book fair, she simply told him she would see him later that afternoon and escaped home.

As she walked Chester, she tried to figure out why Prescott's interest made her uncomfortable. He wasn't an overbearing person. He wasn't even a flirt. But she did feel ill at ease.

Maybe because she didn't understand why he liked her. She couldn't imagine anyone mooning, as Marty had said, over her. She just wasn't the kind of woman men mooned over.

It was strange, but she almost felt as if there had to be something wrong with Prescott if he liked her. But she'd known Prescott for over six years, and he was just a nice guy. A "what you see is what you get" kind of guy. Of course, she'd never noticed his attraction to her until just recently, so there were potentially other things she'd never noticed, too.

She walked up the back steps to her house and opened the door. Unhooking Chester's leash, she chastised herself. Her unawareness of Prescott's interest had everything to do with her, and nothing to do with him. If anything, he was just a gentleman who hadn't made his interest known until he felt there was some interest from her.

And she was interested. Well, she would be.

Mason leaned against the side of a game booth and watched the crowd bustle by. He'd come to the Blue Hill Fair every year while growing up. It was the big to-do, officially marking the end of summer and the beginning of fall and the school year.

But this was the first time he'd been here in years. Marla had refused to set foot on the fairgrounds. She liked fancy restaurants and exclusive clubs. Cotton candy and sawdust were not her thing. But he loved it—the sounds, the smells.

He took a sip of the lemonade he'd just purchased. It would be better with a little vodka, but overall, it was hard to beat fresh-squeezed lemonade.

He smiled when he noticed a small woman struggling with a teddy bear that was nearly as tall as she. It wasn't until she shifted the cumbersome stuffed animal that he saw her tousled blond curls and pert little nose. His smile faded.

Ellie grinned up at the tall companion at her side. Even in the waning light, Mason could see her dimples deepen.

She was dressed casually in a pair of faded jeans that hugged her round little bottom and thighs. A blousy shirt dropped to a slight vee between her breasts, revealing nothing but hinting at so much. She was absolutely breathtaking.

Mason managed to tear his eyes from her to look at the recipient of that gorgeous smile. Prescott Jones.

Mason pushed away from the gaming booth and followed the couple down the midway. They stopped at different booths, watching kids play the prize games, admiring different crafts. And Mason followed a distance away like a practiced stalker.

Twice Prescott played games, and twice he won her other stuffed animals. She beamed, her arms loaded with lovely, ill-made treasures.

Finally they stopped at one of the food carts, and Prescott got drinks, fried dough, and cotton candy. They found a vacant picnic table and sat to enjoy their meal.

Mason lingered by the carousel, watching as the two talked animatedly, laughing frequently. The sight annoyed him, and he knew it had no right to. He wasn't going to pursue a relationship with Ellie.

In fact, he should feel good that Ellie had found someone nice. It was what she needed. And even though he hated to admit it, she and Prescott made an attractive couple. They looked right together. They looked happy.

Ellie pulled off a piece of pink cotton candy and popped it in her mouth. A bit of the sugary confection clung to her bottom lip. Prescott reached across the table and brushed the fluff away with a napkin.

Fool, Mason thought. If he had been sharing the candy with her, he would have leaned across that table and kissed the clinging sweetness from her pink lips.

He hardened immediately, painfully.

He watched the couple for a few moments longer, then decided he needed to leave. The charm of the fair was suddenly lost.

"Thank you," Ellie said, smiling up at Prescott as he helped her out of his beige sedan.

"It was a lot of fun," he said.

She nodded. It had been fun. In fact, she had had a wonderful time. Prescott was sweet and attentive. And she was actually looking forward to spending more time with him.

Prescott opened the back door of his car and wrestled out the several huge stuffed animals he'd won her. "Do you need help with these?"

She eyed the animals, then nodded. "Half of them are bigger than I am. Well, I mean, taller."

"This bear is nearly as big as I am," he pointed out, setting the big fella on the ground. After handing her two of the smaller ones, he picked up the bear and headed onto the porch. He waited for her to open the front door.

The house was dark, with only the light from the streetlight illuminating the porch. She left the door opened and turned back to Prescott.

"You can just set him down. I'll get him inside."

"Are you sure? I can bring him in for you."

Ellie hesitated. She should invite him in. That's what people did after a date, but she wasn't ready. For some reason, inviting him in seemed to imply more than she was ready to give.

"I'm sure."

Prescott nodded, then stood there looking down at her for a moment. Finally he nodded again. "Okay. Well, good night."

"Good night, Prescott."

He loped down the steps and waved before he got into his car. She watched as he disappeared down her street.

Turning back to the stuffed animals, she picked up several and tossed them into the house. Then she contended with the big ole bear, sliding it across the porch into the foyer.

Heaving a sigh, she shut the door and leaned against the cool wood. A small smile curved her lips. She'd had fun.

"Now see, if I'd been in Jones's position, I'd have insisted on bringing the animals in. And then I would have kissed you senseless up against that door."

Ellie jumped, a squeal echoing through the empty house. But it wasn't empty.

She reached over and flicked on the hall light.

Mason reclined on the stairs that led to the second floor, his long legs crossed, his weight braced on his elbows. A predatory smile turned up the corners of his lips.

Ellie clasped a hand to her chest. "Is this a hobby for you? Lurking in the dark?"

Mason seemed to ponder her question. "It does appear to be becoming one."

Ellie took a deep breath, trying to calm her frayed nerves. "Why are you here?"

"I wanted to see you."

"So you broke into my house?"

Mason straightened up, then rose to his feet. He swayed slightly but used the banister to steady himself. "I didn't have to break in. You left your door unlocked. That's not very safe," he informed her.

"I thought Chester would scare away any intruders."

"Well, your guard dog is snoring away on the sofa." He took a step toward her. "So did you have fun on your date?"

Ellie fought the urge to flee. "Mason, why are you here?"

He took another step toward her. "I told you, I wanted to see you."

"Why?"

Mason frowned and confusion clouded his eyes briefly. "I wish I knew."

His response wasn't overtly rude, but it stung. "Well, I—I think you should go."

Mason ignored her. "Did Prescott kiss you at the fair?"

"I don't think that is any of your—how did you know I was at the fair?"

"I saw you there." He didn't look particularly remorseful about spying on her.

Ellie opened her mouth but snapped it shut again. She had no idea what to say.

"I love you in those jeans." He stepped closer, and Ellie was caged between him, the door, and a pile of fair prizes. His hand lifted from his side and stroked slowly up the outside of her thigh.

She watched his hand, her eyes wide, unsure what to do.

"I watched you walk down the midway. Your hips swaying, the denim so damned snug. The loose flutter of your shirt teasing over your breasts and belly."

Ellie swallowed. His words frightened her, but they aroused her too.

"I wanted to touch you. Right there in the middle of the midway. Touch your thighs, those gorgeous breasts—and here." His hand slid up to cup her bottom. He used his other hand to brace himself against the door, holding his body just inches from hers.

She released a shaky breath, feeling lightheaded, scared he would continue to say and do such outrageous things, scared he'd stop.

"I want you, Ellie. God, I want you." The last words

were whispered against her trembling lips, and then his mouth captured hers.

At first she held herself rigid, confused by the whole situation, overwhelmed by him and the things he'd said. But her desire had a mind of its own, and she wound her arms around his neck, accepting all the passion he gave her.

His tongue teased over her lips until she parted them, and they tasted each other. His mouth was a wonderful mixture of spice and warmth with a hint of something strong and smoky.

He shifted away just a fraction, his lips still lightly against hers. "You still taste like cotton candy."

His lips moved over hers a few moments longer, and then he pulled away. His eyes were serious. "Ellie, please let me make love to you."

Her heart bashed painfully in her chest. She stared up at him, taking in his beautiful face, his solemn eyes. Maybe if he'd phrased it another way, she could have said no, but that was what she wanted—to make love with him.

She nodded.

He grinned, a look of triumph in his eyes. He grabbed her hand and pulled her up the stairs. She would have laughed at his eagerness, if she hadn't felt so nervous.

Oh, she wanted this. She just wished she had the first clue how to go about it.

He paused at the top, looking around with an almost humorous expression of consternation like he was looking into a maze rather than down a single hallway with a few doors. "Which is yours?"

"The last one on the left."

He tugged her toward the room, not releasing her hand until they were inside with the door closed. Then in the dark, he pulled her against him and kissed her again.

Ellie had the sensation of being pulled into a rushing current of passion. She knew at any moment she could be pulled under, but it was so thrilling, so wild.

Mason stepped away from her, and she floundered for a moment, confused by the loss of his touch.

"Ellie, are you sure you want me to make love to you?"

She nodded without hesitation. Even though his features were in shadow, she could sense his smile.

"Thank God, because I have to be inside you."

She felt electricity surge through her at his roughly muttered words. What would it be like? To feel Mason deep inside her? She thought she might pass out at the mere thought.

Then he tugged his shirt off over his head, and she found herself watching him with fascination. The slow ripple of the muscles in his shoulders and arms were silhouetted against the watery moonlight filtering through the window.

She tried to suck in a calming breath, but the air wouldn't come. So she simply stared as his fingers moved to the button of his jeans. A loud rasp of metal sounded through the room and his jeans disappeared to the floor.

Ellie felt dizzy.

He moved back to her and reached for her hand. He pressed her open palm to the hardness that strained against his boxers. She jerked her hand away as if she'd been burned.

"Am I shocking you?" he asked.

She nodded.

He chuckled and ducked his head to kiss her. His kiss was gentle and persuasive, nothing but captivating teases of lips and tongue.

Soon her anxiety was brushed aside, replaced by desire. She was simply encompassed in Mason. His hot skin, his hunger, his skilled mouth. His driving need.

It wasn't until she was already falling that she realized he had walked her backwards to her bed and had pushed her down onto the thick quilt.

Mason kneeled over her and slid his hand under her loose blouse, his palms shaped to her sides, gliding upward slowly.

"I'm going to take off your shirt, okay?"

She hesitated. She didn't want him to look at her. She didn't want him to be disappointed. "Can—can we keep the light off?"

Mason paused, then nodded. "If you want."

She suffered another moment's uncertainty, then slowly raised her arms up so he could peel the shirt off.

Mason made a noise in the back of his throat, then caught the hem and pulled the shirt over her head, tossing the garment onto the bed.

He stood silent, looking at her in the dim light.

Ellie shifted uneasily. The light from the streetlamps and the moon suddenly seemed like a spotlight. She started to wrap her arms around herself, sure that Mason was seeing the many imperfections of her body, but his hands came out and caught her wrists.

Gently he spread her arms until they were pinned out to her sides. He gazed roamed over her, and she could feel her nipples strain against the material of her plain white bra. She blushed.

His eyes moved up to hers. "Ellie," he whispered, "you are so sexy."

She knew he was being kind. Surely he was seeing exactly what she saw in the mirror every day, a little potbelly; heavy, round breasts; and arms that needed toning.

He released one of her wrists and ran his long fingers over the skin of her stomach up to cup her breast. He flicked his thumb back and forth over the peaked nipple, and Ellie released a shaky breath.

"Do you like that?" he asked, his words sounding slow and thick in his mouth.

She nodded. "Yes."

Then she found herself pulled tight against him. His fingers fiddled with the straps of her bra until her breasts were free and pressed to Mason's hard chest. He kissed her shoulder, and she mimicked the action on his shoulder.

He groaned and pushed her back down to the mattress. His fingers fumbled with the button of her jeans, then the zipper. He tried to slide her jeans down, but the denim was too close fitting and wouldn't budge.

Ellie's face burned with embarrassment, and she placed a hand on Mason's to stop his effort. "I'll do it."

He flipped over onto his back and watched as Ellie rose. She crossed an arm over her bared breasts and used the other hand to tug at her jeans. She wriggled, her hips shimmying back and forth, as she pushed awkwardly with one hand until the jeans fell to the floor. She could imagine the picture she presented, but she simply straightened back up and looked at Mason's prone body.

She waited, but Mason remained completely still.

"Mason?"

No answer.

She prayed that he wasn't so busy suppressing laughter that he couldn't speak.

She waited, both arms wrapped protectively around her.

Still no sound.

"Mason?"

This time a faint little breath that sounded distinctly like a snore greeted her.

Chapter 11

Ellie edged closer and peered down at Mason's face in the dim light. His eyes were closed.

She looked around, spotting her robe draped over a chair. Pulling it on, she approached the bed again. She reached over and turned on her bedside lamp. She studied him in the light; he was indeed asleep. Or unconscious.

She crossed to the other side of the room, then glanced back over at him. What did she do now? Was this normal? Should she call the doctor?

His arms were at his sides, and his long legs were bent at the knee over the edge of the bed. He looked like he'd just collapsed there out of sheer exhaustion.

Or he'd passed out. He didn't seem very intoxicated, not like Old Arnold Schwinn, who sat down at the docks and drank something out of a paper bag. Arnold weaved when he walked, and he muttered to himself and slurred curses at tourists.

Mason had seemed normal. Well, as normal as any man who broke into a person's house and waited for the person to come home so he could seduce her.

She edged closer again, watching him as warily as if he were a lion that could pounce at any moment. But as she got close enough to see his face, her apprehension lessened. He looked far less predatory in his sleep.

The tension that sometimes tightened his jaw was gone. He had an indentation under his lower lip that defined his chin and could have given him an almost sullen look. But his full lips just made the sullenness look sensual. Those beautiful lips were parted slightly, and his long lashes fanned out over his cheeks, glinting a burnished gold in the lamplight. His hair fell in careless waves over his forehead.

Her eyes wandered down his body. His shoulders were broad and strong, but his collarbone looked oddly delicate. She noticed for the first time that there was a smattering of hair, the same color as his lashes, covering his well-defined chest.

That must have been what had tickled her breasts when he had pulled her against him. How strange that she should feel his body before she saw it.

But she could see him now. And although she felt very naughty to peruse a man when he was unaware, she couldn't seem to tear her eyes away.

She was intrigued at how the hair on his chest tapered down to a narrow line which bisected his flat stomach and disappeared under the waistband of his boxers.

She skipped quickly over that area, only noting that his boxers were light blue cotton. Her skin heated as she recalled touching him through the thin material. She felt dizzy again.

She looked away and tried to decide what to do. He appeared to be breathing fine, and his pallor . . .

She frowned as she looked at his face. His cheeks were a bit flushed, but overall he looked good. Better than good, really.

Stop that, she admonished herself. This was only one step above being a peeping tom, and people got arrested for that kind of thing.

She looked at the alarm clock on her nightstand. It

was almost midnight. He would probably sleep through the night now.

Gingerly, she picked up his legs, noting that they were nicely muscled and covered with the same golden-brown hair as his chest. And, with a little effort, she twisted him until his whole body was on the bed.

She opened the hope chest at the foot of her bed and retrieved another quilt. Spreading it over him, he groaned and rolled over onto his side, nuzzling his cheek into her fluffy pillows.

Ellie picked up their clothes strewn around the room and folded them. She placed them on her window seat and moved quietly to her bureau to get her pajamas. She crossed to her nightstand, turned off the lamp, and headed to the bedroom door.

In the doorway, she paused and looked back to the bed. Mason's tall, broad-shouldered body made her bed seem like a children's doll bed. Somehow the scene was an appropriate ending to the surreal night.

She closed the door. Without bothering to head to the bathroom to perform her bedtime rituals, she went down the hall to Abby's old room. She threw on her p.j.s and crawled into the bed.

Staring at the ceiling, she hoped that Mason was okay. He definitely had looked tired and stressed at the town meeting. And he'd left as soon as the meeting was adjourned. Maybe he was under the weather.

She certainly didn't wish him ill, but she did like the sickness theory better than the other ideas that nudged at her brain. Like that he'd only come here because he'd had too much to drink. Or, equally as bad, he'd been so bored with their lovemaking that he'd simply fallen asleep.

Ellie rolled over and turned off the light.

Although that would be an appropriate ending to her first attempt at making love. After all, she was Ellie Stepp, the chubby, dull librarian.

* * *

Mason stretched and rolled over onto his back, trying to fall back to sleep. The rain on the roof was louder than he'd ever heard it before. Somehow the soothing sound made his bed feel incredibly comfortable this morning. The mattress seemed softer and the pillows fluffier.

He sighed. And that smell. What was it? Strange, it was like lavender mingled with bacon and eggs.

He opened one eye, then the other. He looked up at an unfamiliar ceiling. Sitting up, he surveyed a room that was as unfamiliar as the ceiling.

He was in a wrought iron bed that had been painted white. A quilt made up of different prints and shades of purple covered him. The walls were papered with satiny looking white strips and small violets. The room was extremely feminine. Even the furniture looked feminine with glossy white paint and gentle curves.

He shoved back the covers and stood. He was wearing only his boxers. The rest of his clothes were neatly folded on the window seat. Hastily, he pulled them on.

Okay, what had he done now? He headed to the door, carefully twisting the knob. The hallway was empty. He looked to his left and saw the bathroom. To his right, past a few doors, was the staircase.

Something was familiar about the hallway. *Well, it should be, you idiot. You obviously walked through it to get here.* Unless he crawled in through a window, and anything seemed feasible at this point.

He went into the bathroom. After using the toilet and splashing water on his face, he reluctantly started down the stairs. He had a pretty good idea where he was. He just hoped that something regrettable hadn't happened. Although, waking up undressed in a lady's bed . . . it seemed likely something had.

When he entered the kitchen, Ellie stood at the

stove with her back to him. She was clad in a pair of men's style flannel pajamas, although the print of little pink flowers was far from masculine. As was the way she looked in them, all curves and tousled hair.

He coughed softly, not wanting to startle her. His effort didn't work. She started, practically throwing the spatula she held up into the air. She whirled around.

"Sorry," he said. "I tried not to scare you."

Ellie smiled, a shy half smile. "That's okay, I'm just not used to anyone else being here. Can I get you a cup of coffee?"

"I can get it." He walked to the counter toward the coffee pot, then stopped, unsure where to find mugs.

"The cupboard right over the coffeemaker."

"Thanks."

"I made bacon, cheese and mushroom omelets. Nothing fancy. Can I get you a plate?"

Nothing fancy. Mason couldn't recall the last time anyone had made him breakfast. His stomach felt a little flippy, but food would probably be a good thing. "That would be great."

He poured his coffee and automatically went to the fridge to get milk. It was odd that he felt natural enough to just make himself at home. Especially given the fact he'd likely done something reprehensible.

Taking his mug and sitting at the table, he worked up the courage to ask about last night. "Did—Are you okay?"

Ellie's hand shook slightly as she placed a plate of delicious-smelling food in front of him. "I'm fine."

He felt like a total heel. She obviously wasn't fine.

"Was . . ." God, how did he ask something like this? "Was I good to you?"

Her brow wrinkled. She didn't seem to understand the question. That couldn't be good.

"Did you . . ." How did he find himself in these situations? Okay, he'd never found himself in a situation precisely like this one before. "Did you enjoy your-self?"

Ellie's eyes registered understanding. "Oh." She blushed. "I—I did."

Not exactly rave reviews.

Ellie moved back to the stove and scooped up some of the omelet for herself. Setting the plate on the table, she sat across from him.

Both ate in silence for a few moments.

The cowardly part of Mason wanted to leave things as they were, but he knew he couldn't.

Plus, there was a side of him that was more than a little irritated that he couldn't remember being with this attractive woman. Maybe if he asked more, it might jar his memory.

"Ellie? Was I gentle with you?" God, he hoped he had been. He'd wanted her so badly; he really couldn't believe he had been.

Her fork paused from scooping up some egg. After a second, she nodded.

Again, he didn't get the feeling she was too happy about the event. Damn! He was such an ass. He did God only knows what to her, and she was politely serving him breakfast.

The eggs, which had been scrumptious seconds earlier, suddenly felt like a damp sponge in his mouth.

"I—" she started so quietly that Mason almost thought he'd imagined it. And when she didn't continue right away, he was sure he had.

Then after a few moments and lots of staring at her plate, she raised her face to his and blurted out, "*You* didn't seem like you enjoyed it, though."

Mason gaped at her. Now, that wasn't something he'd expected to hear. "Why do you think that?"

She blushed to a deep, rosy pink. "Well, because you fell asleep." She said the words like he was a dolt and he realized that she didn't know that he couldn't remember anything that had happened. He did vaguely recall waiting for her to return home from her date with Prescott, but that was about all.

"I don't think that is supposed to happen," she added, although there was a measure of uncertainty in her voice.

Mason wasn't sure if he should reveal he'd forgotten, but after a little deliberation, he decided it was going to be pretty hard to act like he knew what she was talking about.

"Was that before or after we made love?"

Her eyes widened as she discovered he didn't know. "Sort of during, I guess," she murmured.

His eyes nearly widened, too. An image of himself on top of her, snoring away, whooshed through his mind. He cringed. Now that was sexual finesse.

"Exactly when did I pass—fall asleep?"

Ellie turned pinker, if it was possible. She pushed a mushroom around her plate. "When I got up to take off my jeans."

Mason let out a sigh of relief. "Thank God." If she was still in her jeans, they couldn't have actually had sex. His relief was short-lived as soon as he looked at Ellie.

Her shoulders were hunched, and she looked on the verge of tears.

"Ellie," he said in an apprehensive tone, "what is it?"

She held up a hand. "I'm fine." She gathered up her dirty dishes and put them in the sink. Then she collected the dishes from the stove. Without even glancing at him, she began filling the sink with water.

He watched her, wondering what to do.

After a few moments, she turned off the water and just stood looking out the window at the dark sky and rain pouring down.

Mason rose, pretending to just bring her his plate. But he wanted to touch her, to make sure she was okay.

When he reached her side, he saw the silent tears

that streamed down her cheeks. His stomach knotted. He must have done something worse than fall asleep to make her react this way.

He put the plate down on the counter with a clatter and reached for her arm, turning her to face him. "Ellie, please tell me what's wrong?"

She looked over his left shoulder, refusing to make eye contact with him. She made a gulping swallow in an attempt to control her tears.

"Ellie, what did I do?"

She looked at him, disbelief clear through her tears. "You didn't do anything! I'm the idiot. I'm the one that was so inexperienced, so unexciting that you fell asleep. And then the whole experience was so incredibly awful that you blocked the entire thing out. This is a nightmare."

She jerked out of his hold and started to leave the room, but he stepped forward and caught her arm again.

"No!" he said with more force than he intended. "No, it wasn't you."

She stared up at him, stunned by his fierce reaction.

"You aren't unexciting, and I can't imagine any time spent with you as being horrible."

"I bet you've never fallen asleep making love to another woman."

Mason contemplated lying, then slowly said, "No—"

"See, I knew—"

Mason leaned forward and swiftly captured her lips before she could continue her thought process, thoughts that he knew would be self-belittling.

His intent had been to merely stop her, but as soon as he tasted her, he was lost. He loved the softness of her lips and the salty taste from the bacon she'd eaten—and her tears. He loved how her mouth clung to his with timid need.

He could have easily kissed this sweet woman all day

long, but unfortunately, they had things they had to straighten out.

"Last night was not your fault," he vowed after he ended the kiss.

She blinked up at him, her eyes dazed by her passion. He had a hard time not kissing her again.

"I had a couple drinks before I came over last night," he told her, "and I shouldn't have, because I've been getting over a—a cold, and I guess they affected me more than I realized."

She nodded and some of the dreamy softness left her face. Again, she moved away from him, but she didn't attempt to leave the room. She did, however, situate herself so the table was between them, and he'd keep his hands off her.

"I thought it might be something like that," she said quietly.

Mason nodded, glad that she finally understood that last night's events had nothing to do with some inadequacy in her.

"I couldn't imagine that you really meant all the things you said," she said with a sad little smile.

Mason almost groaned. "What did I say?"

She blushed again. "You said you liked the jeans I was wearing."

Mason remembered the jeans. He really did like those.

"You said you wanted to touch me . . . all over."

He still wanted to.

"You said you wanted—you wanted to be inside me." The words were whispered, but their effect was loud and clear. His cock rocketed to stiffness.

She smiled wider, her dimples peeking out briefly, but there was still unhappiness in her eyes. "I know you wouldn't have said those things if you were feeling yourself."

"I believe," he pointed out, "I had already said all

those things in one variation or another. Why would you doubt that I'd say them again?

Ellie sighed, wrapping her arms around her middle. "Because I've seen your ex-wife. I saw the woman you were with the other night. I'm not in their league."

Mason frowned. "What league?"

"Tall, gorgeous . . . thin."

Anger ripped through him. How could this woman not see how beautiful she was? He stomped around the table and grabbed her wrist, being careful not to squeeze her delicate bones too roughly. "Come with me."

She followed behind him passively as he led her upstairs to where he knew there was a full-length mirror—her bedroom.

He positioned her in front of him before the mirror. She looked up at his reflection, bewilderment clear in her blue eyes.

"Look at yourself."

Ellie shook her head and let out a self-conscious noise, trying to turn away. "No."

Mason placed his hands gently on her upper arms and held her steady. "Well, I'm going to tell you what I see when I look at you." He moved a hand up to her chin, gently holding her face toward the mirror. "I see such an adorable face with big blue eyes the color of periwinkles in the spring and lips the color of peonies. And when those lips smile, I see your dimples, and I feel like I've just been given this precious gift."

His hand moved to touch the curls framing her face. "Your hair is like swirls of pale sunlight, and I love how the curls are always tousled as if I've just run my fingers through them."

He moved his fingers down to the column of her neck.

She stood perfectly still, helplessly watching him in

the glass. Her eyes were wide, but there was awareness in them.

Awareness that spurred him on. He knew he should stop, but he couldn't. He wanted to touch her so damned badly.

Leisurely, he stroked her delicate skin at the base of her throat with his thumb. "Your skin is creamy and flawless."

He moved both hands down the outside of her arms until he reached her fingers just peeking out of the ends of her sleeves. "Your hands are so small with dainty little fingers." He pressed his palms to hers, and his fingers extended over an inch past her fingertips.

Next, he shifted his touch to her hips, spanning them with his fingers. "Your hips are round and womanly and sway so enchantingly when you walk."

His fingers slid slowly over her belly, the small curve fitting pleasingly against his palm.

She wiggled slightly, whether from distress or desire he wasn't sure.

"Your belly is smooth and soft, and I want to nestle my head there and kiss your little bellybutton."

Very, very unhurriedly he let his hands slide up her torso, watching her watching him in the mirror.

She shifted again, and this time there was no mistaking the passion darkening her eyes.

He was aroused, too, agonizingly so, and he wished he wasn't just stroking her through fuzzy flannel.

His hands reached her breasts, and the weight of them filled his palms. Her head dropped back against his chest, just under his chin, and her eyes drifted closed. "Your breasts are perfection. Soft and supple," he murmured.

His thumbs ran back and forth over her hardened nipples. "And your eager little nipples beg me to touch them." He swirled them between his thumbs and forefingers, using just a little pressure.

Ellie's mouth parted, and she made a ragged noise in the back of her throat.

With one hand, he continued to rub her breast, while the other slid back down her belly toward the junction of her legs. Their height difference forced him to curl his body around her so he could reach her there. Moist heat radiated through the flannel, and he reveled in the knowledge his touch had excited her so.

Gently, he pressed his fingers to her, massaging her sensitive core.

She gasped but didn't pull away. Instead, she nestled in against him, unintentionally, he was sure, rubbing her curvy little bottom against his erection.

He released a shaky breath of his own, then whispered against her ear, "I haven't had the joy of seeing this part of your body, but I can imagine how exquisite you would look. And how it would feel to be surrounded by your heat."

Again, she wriggled against him, and a breathy moan escaped her parted lips.

He watched the two of them in the mirror, his hands touching her, Ellie quivering with each stroke.

This was a foolish and dangerous way to deal with their situation. How was walking away now going to prove she was attractive?

Reluctantly, he moved both of his hands back to her waist and held her against him.

"That's the Ellie I see," he murmured, nuzzling her ear. "A beautiful, sexy woman."

She opened her eyes and found his in the mirror. She was flushed and her eyes clouded with unsatisfied longing.

She gazed at him for a few unbearable moments, then whispered, "So why won't you make love to me?"

Chapter 12

Mason knew that was going to be Ellie's question. And he had many valid and chivalrous reasons. He really did. Reasons she'd heard before. Reasons that were beginning to sound like excuses, even to his ears.

But he had to try to make her understand.

"Ellie, I told you before, I won't have a relationship with you, and you won't be happy with what I can give you." He knew his voice was beseeching, but he didn't think he could say no much longer.

"I think I'm the one who should decide what will make me happy," she said.

"But you don't understand how little I can give."

"I want whatever you are willing to offer."

"Even if it's nothing more than sex now and then, a quickie a couple times a week?" He tried to make the arrangement sound as coarse as possible.

Ellie did flinch, but then her eyes locked with his, and he saw determination mingled with vulnerability in their blue depths. "Maybe that's all I want, too."

He knew that her claim was nothing but pluck. But he also knew he was lost.

Ellie waited with bated breath for him to answer. She was telling him the truth. She would be satisfied with anything he could give her. If it was only—sex, then so be it. She should be happy with that. A woman like her couldn't hope for anything more from a man like Mason.

He *had* made her feel beautiful earlier. But she knew the way he saw her right now was enhanced by lust. And she knew that lust didn't last. It eventually played itself out. Or at least that's what happened in books.

Only love lasted.

And she would never expect love from Mason.

Despite his reaction downstairs, she knew that when he fell in love again, it would be a long-legged, svelte beauty with flowing hair and a million-dollar smile.

So she was going to enjoy what she could get. Dissatisfaction only happened when a person expected more.

"Ellie." Again his voice had an almost pleading quality. "You don't know what you're getting into."

Ellie took a deep breath. "I know that I want you to get into me." She couldn't believe she had said something so . . . so naughty.

Her skin burned, and her heart clattered unevenly against her ribcage. If he turned her down after that, she would have to give up. She didn't think she could get any bolder.

But he didn't turn her down. Instead a wicked smile curled the corners of his full lips and he pulled her even tighter against him. She could feel the muscles of his chest against her back and the strength in his arms around her waist.

"Now?" he said in a low voice that sent warm shivers down her spine.

It took her a moment to understand what he was asking. Did she want him now? Oh dear, was she ready? Could she go through with it? Now that she had made such a brazen offer?

She met his gaze in the mirror. His smoky eyes

appeared sleepy, but his slight smile was very aware . . . and hungry like a wolf.

Even though her heart was threatening to pound right out of her chest, she nodded, the movement minute.

But Mason saw it, and his smile widened.

Ellie knew she had just given this wolf permission to devour her whole.

His hands moved from her middle and slid up her arms to her chest.

Once there, he unfastened the first button of her pajamas, then the next. The flannel parted to reveal the deep valley between her breasts.

The next button was flicked open, and then the next. The worn flannel separated more, hinting at the curves of her breasts and a thin strip of pale belly. Ellie fought the urge to pull it closed. But she wanted this. She wanted Mason.

He unfastened the last plastic, pearlized button, and with excruciating slowness, he peeled the pajamas open until her breasts and belly were bared. To both of them.

Ellie's face blazed as she looked at herself in the mirror. Reluctantly she looked up to Mason.

He stared at her, his expression unreadable.

When she would have jerked the pajamas shut, he released a shuddering breath and said in a low voice, "God, Ellie, you are amazing."

Her nipples puckered to rigid peaks, the hunger in his voice as substantial as touch. Then his hands touched the distended peaks, and she decided that his voice, while amazing, didn't compare to his fingers touching her. He cupped her breasts, and absently she noted that her breasts almost looked small against his large hands.

"So, so beautiful," he murmured as he began to kiss her neck and knead the sensitive flesh of her breasts.

Ellie's head fell back against his solid chest, and she lost herself to the heat he generated inside her. The movement of his lips over her skin, the caress of his hands built a fire deep in her belly. But the fire was a low, teasing smolder. And she wanted more. She needed more.

She squirmed against him, unsure what to do to make the pleasurable burning more intense.

He groaned, and one of his hands left her breasts and skimmed down her stomach and under the waistband of both her pajama pants and her panties. He cupped her there.

She started, unnerved. Even though he'd just touched her there, it had been through her pajama bottoms. This sensation was decidedly different.

"Is this okay?" Mason murmured near her ear. The resonance of his deep drawl tickled her earlobe.

She nodded.

"Good." One of his fingers parted the curls to touch her. With that one small stroke, the smoldering in her belly leapt like a match sizzling to life.

She gasped and squeezed her legs together.

"No, angel, keep your legs apart," Mason said.

"It's too—too much."

Mason chuckled, the sound warm, rippling over her heated flesh. "I'll be very gentle."

Still unsure, she complied.

He brushed her again, the touch light and fleeting. Again the embers flared to flames. She gasped, but determinedly kept her legs apart.

"You are like warm, slick honey," he said. His fingertip swirled again.

She bit back a cry.

He circled, then circled again.

Her head twisted against his chest, a small whimper escaping her.

Then he was rubbing her continuously, relentlessly.

The fire within her spread, engulfing her, with no re-
prieve from the heat. She began to shake.

"That's it, angel," he encouraged.

His words seemed far away, barely audible over the
roar of the fire now consuming her.

Then he pressed the pad of his finger hard against
her, and the fire exploded. Sparks scattered throughout her whole body, and she cried out with the
intensity of the experience.

She leaned heavily into Mason, feeling warm and
boneless.

But Mason didn't allow her respite, twisting her to
face him. He wore a grin rich with smug satisfaction,
and Ellie agreed he did indeed deserve to feel smug.
What he'd done had been absolutely amazing.

Mason gazed at the delightful woman in front of
him. Ellie was the picture of shameless satisfaction.
Her cheeks burned pink. Her lips were damp and
parted. Her eyes were heavy and hazed with fulfill-
ment.

She didn't seem to realize her pajama top still hung
open, one rose-tipped breast peeking out at him so
enticingly.

His cock twitched, hoping for the same freedom.

God, he wanted to be buried in her responsive little body. And she was responsive. He couldn't ever
remember a woman reacting so strongly, so quickly.
He'd barely touched her and she'd come.

He stepped away from her, and she swayed slightly
but then managed to muster her balance. She
watched him, her blue eyes drowsy, but as he tugged
off his shirt, she became more alert, more intrigued.

He pushed down his jeans and boxers, and straightened. Ellie's eyes widened, all traces of languidness

gone as she saw him in his full naked and aroused glory.

She couldn't seem to tear her eyes away from his engorged penis. Her rapt curiosity was thrilling. His penis jerked impatiently.

Mason groaned. "Angel, are you going to make me embarrass myself before I even get inside you?"

She blinked up at him. "Sorry," she mumbled, although it was obvious she had no idea what he meant.

He smiled. She was truly the most charming combination of wanton and innocent.

He approached her and caught her hand. He led her to the bed. "You first," he said.

She started to crawl onto the mattress, but he caught her hips, stopping her.

"I don't think you'll be needing the jammies."

She blushed. After much uncertainty, she let her top slide from her shoulders. Then she reached for the waistband of her bottoms. Wiggling them over her hips, she let them fall to the floor.

Embarrassment clear on her face, she stood up.

He was speechless. Her legs were lovely—smooth pale thighs, cute little knees, and nicely shaped calves. At the apex of her thighs was a neat little triangle of tight curls.

"I was wrong," he said, softly.

Ellie gave him a look rich with doubt and worry.

"Exquisite doesn't do you justice." He reached out to brush his fingers between her thighs. "You are perfect—absolutely perfect."

He was pleased to see her worry disappear as his fingers held her spellbound.

"Now, get in bed," he said with mock severity. "I want to touch all of you."

She scampered in, whether out of eagerness for more of his touch or the desire to cover herself, he wasn't sure. She did pull the quilt up to her chin, regarding him with bashful eyes.

He followed her under the covers and pulled her to him. Despite her obvious shyness, she came to him willingly. Wrapping her arms around his neck, she pressed her whole sweet body tightly against his. She was warm and soft, her skin smooth like velvet.

He kissed her, feeling a measure of timidity on her lips. But as his lips teased hers, licked her, she started to respond, tasting him back with the same need.

He rolled her underneath him, deepening their kiss and running his hand over her velvety skin.

He left her mouth, needing to taste her rosy breasts.

She gasped when he sucked one of her peaked nipples between his lips, drawing firmly on the little bud. He suckled her for a few seconds before shifting his attention to the other breast.

As he lavished that breast with attention, he slipped his hand down her soft belly to find the little folds between her thighs. She was hot, damp.

He groaned. She was amazing.

Gently, he slid a finger inside her. She stiffened slightly, her muscles clenching his finger.

"Relax," he whispered against her breast and cautiously began to move his finger.

She gripped his back, and he raised his head to look at her.

Her eyes were wide with uneasiness and, he thought, fear.

"Angel, am I hurting you?"

She shook her head.

"Do you want me to stop?"

Again she shook her head.

"Then why do you look so scared?"

She looked away from him for a moment, and then

back with such a look of misery that he was suddenly scared, too.

"Your fingers . . . and well—all of you is big."

He stared at her for a moment, and then he laughed.

Ellie frowned, almost petulantly. "I don't see how that is so funny. I think it's a valid concern."

Mason stopped laughing and placed a quick kiss on her serious mouth. "Oh, Ellie, it will work. I promise."

She regarded him with doubt but nodded.

He smiled before returning his lips to hers. He kissed her like he was content to do nothing more all day. With the same leisurely pace, he began to caress her again, paying special attention to the places where he already knew she liked to be touched, her neck, her breasts, and the taut little bud between her thighs.

Soon, Ellie was shivering with need and Mason was utterly astounded by how reactive she was. She was on fire.

But so was he, his own desire building right along with hers.

"Do you feel good?"

She nodded, her eyes closed, her mouth parted.

He had to be inside her, and he told her so.

She nodded adamantly, clutching his back and spreading her legs wide to cradle him.

Mason released a low groan. If that wasn't the most awe-inspiring invitation, he didn't know what was.

Positioning himself, he gently pushed, entering her inch by slow, excruciating inch.

She gazed up at him, her eyes trusting, and no indication on her face that he was hurting her.

When he was buried fully inside her, he remained perfectly still.

"Are you all right?" he asked, his voice strained, sweat beading on his brow.

"Yes," she nodded, with a tremulous smile. "You feel wonderful."

He growled. "My God, Ellie, you feel incredible." She was so hot, so wet and so unbelievably tight. "I've got to move."

Again she nodded, and Mason began to thrust, trying to keep his movements smooth and steady. But Ellie clung to him, her lips against his, her arms and legs around his body, her moist heat encircling him, driving him mad.

"Ellie," he breathed, overwhelmed, "I want you, deeper, harder." He demonstrated his need, surging into her.

She gasped, and he immediately pulled back, afraid he'd hurt her, but she grasped him.

"Please, Mason, don't stop." She pushed up against him, imitating his grinding movement.

He groaned and began to move again. His desire escalated uncontrollably, consuming him, devouring him whole.

Only by sheer willpower did he stay focused long enough to be sure he felt Ellie's shuddering release. Then he shouted out his own climax and collapsed on her, spent.

Chapter 13

Mason had no idea how long he slept, but when he woke, the room was shadowy. Rain still pattered against the roof, and Ellie was sound asleep curled against his side. Her small hand rested on his stomach, and her steady, even breaths tickled across his chest.

Suddenly, he felt like his own breath was stuck in his throat. What had he done?

Not only had he slept with a woman who he knew was completely wrong for him, but he had also taken her virginity.

He'd suspected Ellie was a virgin. Then he felt the truth for himself when he'd discovered her incredible tightness, but had the truth stopped him? No. He hadn't even considered stopping. No chance. *Damned greedy bastard.*

He lifted his head to better see her face. Her lashes brushed against her cheeks, golden and spiky. Her lips, though a bit puffy from his kisses, formed a perfect bow. And her loose blond curls surrounded her face like a halo. She did look like an angel.

Great, you defiled an angel. Now you're really going to hell, you horny, selfish ass.

Carefully, he lifted her hand from his stomach and eased out of bed. He froze as she stirred, but she only curled further onto her side with a contented sigh.

In hasty, quiet movements, he gathered his clothes

and was starting toward the door when a quiet voice said, "You're leaving?"

Mason spun around, holding his bunched-up clothes in front of him. He wasn't sure why; he'd never been a modest person. Maybe it was the directness of Ellie's gaze. She seemed to see right through him. Right through to his black soul.

"Yeah, I thought—I need to get going." He gestured toward the door.

Mason could see the hurt in her eyes, those eyes that not only looked straight through him but also revealed everything within her, too. But she didn't say anything; she simply nodded.

"I'm just going to use your bathroom before I go." Another nod.

He hurried away from her and into the bathroom, closing the door tightly against Ellie and her damned expressive eyes.

He quickly pulled on his clothes and went to the sink to splash water on his face. His breathing came in rapid, shallow puffs, and he actually felt like he was going to hyperventilate.

What was he doing? He couldn't continue this. But how was he going to tell Ellie that he couldn't see her again?

Hey, babe, thanks for your virginity and all, but now I gotta run. God, he needed a drink.

After scooping several handfuls of ice-cold water onto his face, he ran his hands through his hair and looked at himself in the medicine cabinet mirror. Outside of the bloodshot eyes, he looked normal. He took a deep breath.

Everything was okay. He'd made a poor choice. He would apologize. He'd tell her their arrangement could not continue but that he'd always treasure what she'd given him.

He cringed at the lame explanation. She'd either laugh or punch him. Maybe both.

"Okay, stay focused," he told his image. "Ellie," he said in an earnest voice, "I want you, but things are too out of control. And I need to step back and think about everything."

He nodded. That wasn't half bad. And certainly not a lie. Unfortunately, it did leave the situation open-ended. But once he didn't get in touch with her again after a week or so, then she'd get the point and realize she was better off without him.

His stomach churned. He really disliked the idea that Ellie would always remember the loss of her virginity as an unpleasant event—lost to a self-indulgent weasel. But she'd feel even worse if things continued and more emotions were invested.

Deciding his bad plan was the only plan, he headed back to her bedroom, prepared to break the news. The room was empty.

Her departure left him feeling a bit shaken. But he gathered his wits and headed downstairs.

Ellie was in the kitchen. She had dressed. Baggy cords rode low on her hips, and her t-shirt hugged her torso. Her curls were piled loosely on her head, held in place by things that looked distinctly like chopsticks. Bare feet appeared out of the frayed cuffs, and he couldn't help noticing that she had the teeniest little toes.

He coughed, and this time, she didn't jump. She looked up from scraping the remains of his breakfast plate into Chester's food dish.

She smiled shyly. "Are you okay?"

"I think I should be the one asking that question."

Her smile widened, her dimples peeping out at him. "I feel wonderful."

His heart swelled, but his gladness and pride were

immediately followed by a wave of guilt. "Good." He hesitated. "Listen, Ellie—"

His sentence was cut off as the back door flew open, and a soaked Chase and Abby dashed into the room with their jackets over their heads, laughing.

Then all mayhem broke loose. Chester began bounding around, barking. Abby rushed forward, greeting and hugging Ellie. Then Chase greeted and hugged Ellie. All three greeted Chester, who was happy to see everyone.

It was several seconds before Chase and Abby even noticed Mason, leaning in the kitchen doorway.

"Hey, Mason," Chase said with his usual easy smile, "what are you doing here?"

Taking your sister-in-law's virginity. So how was your honeymoon?

Somehow Mason didn't think Chase would still be smiling if he announced that.

"He's here to help me with the library," Ellie said, before he formulated an excuse for himself.

Abby frowned. "Why? What's happened at the library?"

Ellie told them about Everett Winslow's plan. "And Mason is being wonderful and really showing his support for the library," she said as she finished the story with a cheery smile toward Mason. A smile he really, really didn't deserve.

Abby also gave him an undeserved smile. "That's great. I guess we must have walked in just after you. We should let you two have your discussion."

Mason frowned, confused by her assumption.

Abby pointed at his damp hair. "The downpour got you, too."

Mason nodded. "Oh yeah. Yes. But I think Ellie and I sorted out everything we needed to. I should let you visit."

"You could stay," Ellie said quickly, "and I could make dinner for everyone. We could all visit."

Mason didn't miss the hopeful quality to her voice. He couldn't stay.

"That's a great idea," Chase agreed.

"I have the makings for lasagna," Ellie said, going to look in the refrigerator, "and salad."

"I think we have garlic bread and cheesecake in the freezer at our place," Abby recalled. "I'll just run across the street and get them."

"I really should go," Mason insisted.

Chase clapped a hand on Mason's back. "You may as well settle in for the evening, my friend. When Ellie decides to feed you, you aren't going anywhere. And she is the best cook in Millbrook. If you leave, your dinner's going to be what? Frozen pizza or a bowl of cereal?"

"It sounds like you have my culinary skills," Abby said to Mason with a measure of approval.

"Yes, my dear wife considers a home-cooked meal a can of soup and maybe a ham sandwich," Chase told Mason with a good-natured grin.

"If you're lucky," Abby stated. "But you didn't marry me for my cooking skills, now did you?"

Chase caught Abby around the waist and pulled her against him. "No, I did not." He placed a quick kiss on her lips. "If I had, I would starve to death," he added with a sly grin.

Abby cuffed his arm playfully. "Come with me to get the bread and cake. I think we have a couple bottles of wine, too."

"We'll be right back," Chase said, before disappearing into the rain.

Ellie smiled until the door closed; then she gave Mason an apprehensive look. "You will stay, won't you?"

"Ellie, I don't think it's a good idea."

"But it would be even stranger if you left while they were out."

Ellie had him there. Chase was his best friend. Why wouldn't he want to visit with a friend he hadn't seen in a couple weeks?

"I won't bite," Ellie added with an innocent smile.

Images of Ellie nipping his bare flesh appeared in his mind, and he felt his penis begin to stir. He cursed under his breath.

"Ellie, I don't think Chase and Abby need to know about our arrangement." The arrangement he intended to end.

She nodded solemnly. "You're right. That is our business and our business alone."

Mason was surprised by her adamancy.

"So you'll stay?" she asked.

"Where's the lettuce? I'll make the salad."

Ellie rewarded him with a huge dimpled smile that seemed to warm his whole body.

Ellie tried not to openly stare at Mason, but it was nearly impossible. She had to keep looking at him, just to convince herself that he was here and everything they'd shared had really happened.

She felt so happy, so jubilant, and he was the cause. He'd made love to her. He'd touched her whole body. He'd been patient and gentle. And he'd given her pleasure beyond her wildest dreams. She hadn't even been self-conscious, well, not too much, anyway. Her cheeks warmed; she thought she'd brought him pleasure, too.

And then he had stayed. She knew he'd been uncomfortable when he woke up with her. At first, she'd been afraid that he was going to tell her he wanted to end things. But then he'd helped her prepare the dinner. They had talked and laughed and everything had been right with the world. Okay, he, Chase, and Abby had done most of the talking, but Ellie still thought everything was going well.

Under her lashes, she watched him as he talked with Chase. His posture was relaxed, a dazzling smile on his face. He finished his glass of wine and refilled it. Then he laughed at something Chase told him, and the sound filled the room with rich, cheery warmth.

Ellie wondered if this was what it would be like to be married to Mason.

No, she would not think like that. Not even in her private little daydreams. She had to remain practical. She wanted to enjoy what she had. Catalog every moment, store every detail.

She would remember every minute facet of today. His touch, his mouth on her breasts, the full, heavy feeling of him inside her.

She almost giggled. There was something so— naughty about only she and Mason knowing what they'd done earlier.

"Why are you looking so smug?"

Ellie turned to Abby, surprised by her comment. "I don't look smug."

"You do."

Ellie shrugged, trying to look unconcerned. "I didn't mean to."

Abby studied her for a moment, then let the subject drop, taking a drink of her wine.

Ellie took a sip of her wine, too. Even though she usually passed on the spirits, tonight was different; she was celebrating. Three empty bottles sat in the center of the table; everyone was celebrating.

"Abby, I hear you had Chase here cutting the rug every night in Saint Thomas," Mason said with a sly grin.

"I'm married to a dancing queen," Chase said, shaking his head woefully.

Abby made a face at her husband. "It wasn't as bad as that." She shot an amused look toward Ellie. "Plus, no one would guess, but my little sister is the dancing queen."

Wincing at Abby's revelation, Ellie blushed.

"So Ellie likes to dance, too, huh?" Chase said.

Abby laughed. "She used to dance in front of her bedroom mirror for hours."

Ellie covered her face, mortified. "Abby, that was years and years ago. I was only about ten years old."

Abby gave her a rueful look; then a huge smile curved her lips as if she was driven to reveal more. "She watched reruns of *The Partridge Family*, and she danced in front of the television."

"Abby!" Ellie exclaimed.

"And she loved disco!" Abby added.

Ellie reached over and clapped a hand over her sister's mouth. "Abby, you're terrible."

Ellie was embarrassed, but she knew Abby wasn't exposing the silly secrets of her past to humiliate her.

"I'm sorry," Abby said honestly, even though she was still laughing. "I get loose lips after a couple glasses of wine."

"She just gets loose in general," Chase said with a lecherous grin.

Abby threw a napkin at him. "Now who's terrible?"

Chase pushed out of his chair and came around to Abby, pulling her up against him. "Shall we dance?"

"Please."

Chase whirled Abby around the kitchen and into the living room.

Ellie laughed at their antics, feeling warm and happy. Suddenly, another kind of warmness brushed over her, a warmth filled with awareness.

Mason watched her. Speculation filled his gray eyes.

"What?" she asked with a slight smile.

"Nothing," he said as he rose from his chair and came around the table, his gait unhurried and loose.

When he reached her, he held out his hand. "Would you like to dance?"

Ellie could feel the intensity in his eyes stroking over her, tingling across her skin. She placed her hand in his, and he pulled her against him.

They touched from chest to hip, his large hand splayed across her lower back, holding her firmly against him. He swayed her back and forth. The gentle movement rubbed her breasts against his chest. She could feel the friction throughout her body.

"So, *The Partridge Family*, huh?" The intensity faded, replaced by an amused grin, and she half wondered if she had imagined his attentiveness.

Ellie sighed with a smile. "Yes," she admitted, rolling her eyes. "I get the distinct feeling I'm never going to live this down."

From the living room, the beginning notes of "Dancing Queen" began to play. Ellie heard Abby's delighted laugh.

"I still like disco."

"Nothing wrong with a little disco," Mason agreed. He sped up his pace to match the music.

The delicious friction increased.

"So back to *The Partridge Family*. Did you have a crush on David Cassidy?"

Ellie felt herself blush. "Yes, I did," she stated with pride. "Is this 'embarrass Ellie' day?"

Mason smiled, a devious glint in his eyes. "David Cassidy, huh? So have you always liked the nice boy who has a bad boy streak?"

Ellie considered his question. "Maybe. Is that how you would describe yourself? Because I like you."

Ellie didn't intend her response to make Mason uncomfortable, but his teasing expression disappeared, and she wished she could take back her last sentence. Although, she did like him. Liking him wasn't overstepping the bounds of their arrangement, was it?

Silently, they circled around the kitchen.

"And you used to dance in front of your bedroom mirror?" Mason asked, and Ellie thought the awkwardness of the moment had passed.

"I'm afraid so," she admitted.

"And now I've made you come in front of that mirror. Which did you enjoy more?"

Mason felt Ellie stiffen against him. His question had the effect he wanted; it shocked her.

He wanted to scandalize her, to offend her, to stop her from liking him. A person like Ellie had no business liking a person like him.

He could control this situation if it was only about sex, no emotions other than lust involved. And somewhere over the course of the evening, he had decided he very much wanted their situation to continue.

But no emotions, only great, mind-blowing sex.

All night, he'd watched her. Her adorable, infectious smile. The way her lips sometimes moved, too, when someone told her a story. As if she was trying to memorize every detail. The way she bustled around the kitchen, making sure everyone had enough to eat. Even the way she ate herself, in small, delicate bites.

And he'd listened to her. Her voice, soft and lilting. And the way she quietly said such subtly witty things, making him laugh out loud. And her own laughter, which was musical and enchanting like the gentle tinkle of wind chimes.

Mason wanted her and knew he couldn't let her go—not yet.

He knew he was treading in dangerous waters. An affair with Ellie was going to be tricky. He didn't want anyone to discover their tryst.

He didn't want to upset Chase and Abby, and he had a feeling they wouldn't be too pleased with him, if they knew. But more importantly, Ellie's reputation would be in shambles if people found out.

Plenty of women had affairs but not women like Ellie. And not in a small town where everyone felt like they knew her. To the folks of Millbrook, Ellie was the model of propriety and respectability. She worked with children. She read to the elderly. Everyone knew Ellie Stepp, and they knew she was a good girl.

Only Mason knew there was a hot, sexy woman hidden under her proper exterior. The fact that he alone knew her secret thrilled him and aroused him beyond reason.

No, everything about Ellie aroused him beyond reason. Otherwise, he would never have let his lust get so out of control in the first place.

He pulled her closer, letting his fingers stray down to the curve of her bottom.

She regarded him with wide, uncertain eyes.

He hated her wariness, but he hoped if she was unsure of him, she wouldn't care for him. He couldn't allow her to think they were sharing anything more than fantastic sex.

"So you haven't answered me; which did you like better?"

Ellie's eyes moved to a point over his shoulder. "I liked . . . what you did."

"Do you want me to make you come again?"

She eyes shot back to his. There was a long pause before she answered, "Yes . . . please."

Mason nearly groaned. She was so damned sweet.

"I'll be over tomorrow, late. Leave the back door unlocked, and wear something sexy.

Chapter 14

Ellie hadn't felt any shame about what happened with Mason, not even a slight twinge, until she stepped into the library on Monday morning. And there stood Prescott, welcoming her with a huge smile and a cup of her favorite French vanilla latte from the new coffee shop on Main Street.

Then she felt terrible. Absolutely terrible.

"So did he get into the house okay?" Prescott asked, and Ellie nearly choked on a sip of piping hot coffee.

"Excuse me?" Did Prescott know Mason had been waiting for her?

"The teddy bear, did you get him inside okay? I thought he might be too wide for the front door."

"Oh, yes. Yes, he's still sitting in the foyer." Forgotten. Like her date with Prescott. She was an awful person.

"I really had a great time," Prescott said, his voice rich with meaning.

Ellie smiled weakly. "Me, too." An awful, awful, self-centered person. "I should get to my office," she pointed toward the back of the library. "I need to—to check on something. Thanks—for the coffee."

Prescott seemed to accept her flimsy excuse without question, and she made her escape. Unfortunately, she couldn't escape the guilt, which sat heavily in the dead center of her chest.

How could she forget her date with Prescott? The date she'd angled to get. And they both saw it as a date; she couldn't very well play it off like she thought it was anything less.

She dropped her head into her hands and tried to think of something to tell him. She couldn't tell him the truth. But she hated lies. She wasn't good at lies.

Yet, here she sat, poised on the precipice of a mountain of them. Just by agreeing to keep the affair with Mason a secret, she was going to have to lie to everyone. Abby and Chase. Prescott. Marty. Heck, even herself.

No, she wouldn't lie. She would withhold information. That was different from lying, wasn't it? Unfortunately, withholding facts from Prescott wasn't going to be enough. She needed to give him a reason why she couldn't see him anymore. She was going to have to tell him something—something that could hurt him.

"Ellie?"

Ellie's head snapped up.

Prescott stood in the doorway, a concerned look on his face. "I'm sorry to disturb you, but you have a call on line two."

She straightened, forcing a smile. "Oh, thanks."

She picked up her phone and said hello. Prescott remained in the doorway.

"Hey," Mason said in his lazy drawl.

"Oh, hi." She hadn't expected to hear from Mason until tonight.

"I just wanted to call and tell you that I'm looking forward to tonight." His sexy, languorous voice stole through the telephone line and stroked over her sensitive flesh. Her toes curled in her mary janes.

"Me, too," she said softly, and with less enthusiasm than she was feeling, because the focus of her tremendous guilt was still standing in the doorway.

"Have you been thinking about me?"

"Yes."

"I've been thinking about you, too. In great detail. All the places I'm going to touch you. Kiss you."

Heat poured directly from the phone receiver into Ellie's veins. She shifted in her chair, suddenly feeling very, very warm. She shot a quick glance at Prescott.

He watched her but didn't seem to notice anything improper. Oh, if he could hear Mason.

"Can I do that, angel? Kiss you? Wherever I want?"

Heat pooled between her legs. She tried to remain unflustered, but she found the feat nearly impossible. Images of Mason licking her in various interesting places flashed through her mind. A shiver of pure desire ran down her spine.

It took her several moments to formulate an appropriately vague response. "Yes. That would be fine."

There was pause; then Mason chuckled. "My proper little librarian isn't alone, is she?"

"No, not at the moment."

Mason laughed again. "Then I will let you go. See you tonight."

"Yes."

The line clicked dead, but Ellie held onto the receiver for a moment longer, trying to collect herself. After a few breaths, which did very little to calm the desire tingling through her skin, she looked over to Prescott.

His brow was creased with concern. "That was Mayor Sweet, wasn't it?"

Ellie nodded, still not trusting her voice to be steady.

"Did he have any news?"

He certainly did. Again a flash of heat flared inside her. "He had a few ideas." There, her first official half lie. The landslide had begun.

"He hasn't decided to withdraw his support, has he?"

"No," she said slowly, "but I do think things are

getting a bit more—more complicated." Again, she managed another "not quite" lie. It was appallingly easy. She'd never been a deceitful person, but she seemed to be taking to the way of life like a pro. Faint stirrings of nausea replaced the heat in her stomach.

"I think you may be right," Prescott agreed.

At first his response didn't make sense to her. And given she had been alternately fixating on her fine lying abilities and her mounting queasiness, she thought she must have missed something, but Prescott's next sentence made his meaning clear.

"I heard Ginny talking at the diner this morning, and it seems Charlie Grace is undecided on whether to side with Mayor Sweet on the library issue."

As Prescott's words sank in, the guilt and the queasiness faded to the back of her mind. That would make the library's problems more complicated. The information surprised her. "Charlie has always backed Mason."

"Well, I get the feeling that something is not quite right at city hall. And if Charlie ends up supporting Everett Winslow and his football field, then a lot of other folks might vote that way, too."

Ellie didn't need Prescott to tell her the potential outcome. She knew this could be detrimental to the library. But she had a hard time believing Charlie Grace wouldn't side with Mason. Charlie had been one of Mason's biggest supporters during his mayoral campaigns.

None of this made sense to her.

"I'm sure that's just gossip," Ellie finally stated. It had to be. "Mason would have told me if he thought there were any real concerns about Charlie Grace."

Prescott gave her a speculative look. "Do you talk with Mayor Sweet often?"

Ellie's guilt returned with sickening intensity. "We

talk some. Since the whole thing with Everett." Fudging the truth was frightfully easy, she realized with dismay.

He nodded. "Well, I'm sure you're right. After all, I did hear it from Ginny. And she is quite a gossip."

"Right. I'm sure things are fine." She smiled encouragingly and waited, hoping he was done and would leave. But he didn't; instead he broached the subject she had hoped to avoid, at least for a while longer.

"Actually I was wondering if you are free tonight. I thought maybe we could go out to dinner."

The nausea returned with amazing speed. "I—I can't. I actually already have plans."

"Oh, how about tomorrow?"

Ellie pretended to ponder her schedule, trying to think of an excuse that wouldn't be too obvious, too invented. "I—" She couldn't do this. She couldn't lie to him. Hurt him. "I think I'm free."

Prescott grinned, obviously very pleased. "Great, how about that new restaurant you mentioned in Bar Harbor?"

She nodded, her mind awhirl.

"Great." He grinned even wider and then bowed out of her office.

Ellie stared at the empty doorway. A few days ago she would have been thrilled. Now she was too busy trying to figure out how she was going to juggle two men.

Ellie Stepp, juggling men. She would have found the situation laughable if she hadn't felt like she was going to vomit.

Mason squinted at his watch. It was just a little after ten. Earlier than he had intended to arrive at Ellie's place, but he wanted to see her. Touch her.

He'd parked on the street behind her house. That

way, Chase and Abby wouldn't see his car. It was shifty. His conscience niggled him, but his doubts were quickly squelched by longing and excitement.

He hadn't intended to call Ellie today, but he had to hear her voice and know that she wasn't having second thoughts.

After work, he'd headed to the Parched Dolphin to get some broiled scallops and a beer or two. He'd hoped a couple drinks would temper his need. Make him a bit more sensible. Alas, it didn't. If anything, he was itching to see Ellie more.

Carefully he got out of his car, trying to push the door shut as quietly as possible. He didn't think anyone would be outside to hear him, but he still felt the need to be cautious.

With the stealth of a thief, he made his way down the edge of the Holmeses' yard, hugging shadows created by the apple trees that lined their driveway. He seemed to recall the Holmeses' had a dog, but he thought it was a small breed and that it was a little deaf. So he should be safe.

Still, he was relieved to reach Ellie's backyard. Lilac bushes and gray dogwoods surrounded the perimeter of her lawn, making it impossible for the neighbors to see him. He crept up her back steps.

Testing the door, he found that the knob turned easily in his hand, and he stepped into the dark kitchen. A faint light from the hallway signaled where he would find Ellie. In her bedroom.

His heart thumped as he imagined her lounging on the bed in something silky and scant. His pace quickened to match the speed of his heart, and in several bounds, he was upstairs.

Ellie's door was open, and a soft glow emanated invitingly from inside. Again, he visualized her in a few scraps of lace, her milky skin bathed in soft, golden light.

When he reached the door, however, he didn't discover Ellie sprawled alluringly across the bed. Instead, she sat on her window seat with her legs curled underneath her, bundled in flannel and chewing fretfully on her fingernail.

She looked up as he came into the room. No surprise, none of the anticipation he was feeling. Just a look of anxiety and self-reproach.

Mason's heart continued to race, although his eagerness was replaced by foreboding.

"Hi." His voice sounded uncertain. He did not like to feel uncertain.

"Hi," she said back, and a tremulous smile touched her lips.

Somehow, the tiny smile made him feel better.

"What are you doing?"

"Waiting for you."

Now, those were the words he wanted to hear.

"And feeling awful."

Those words—not so much.

Mason crossed over to the bed and dropped onto its softness. "What are you feeling awful about?" *Please, please don't let it be me.* He immediately rebuked himself. This was an affair; it was temporary. He'd be disappointed if Ellie ended it, but only because he hadn't had his fill of her delectable body yet. That was all.

"Prescott."

The name stopped him. For a moment he was confused. Why would she be worried about her goody-two-shoes assistant?

"After what we did, I completely forgot about him and our date."

"Well," Mason said with a slight smile, "if you hadn't forgotten, then I'd have been doing something wrong."

Ellie colored the same shade of pink as the flowers on her pajamas. "It was selfish of me. I should have at least considered his feelings before beginning the arrangement with you."

Mason didn't see what difference it made whether she had considered Prescott Jones's feeling or not. Ellie had made her choice; it was as simple as that. "Just tell him you're not interested."

Ellie shook her head. "I don't want to hurt him." She lifted a finger to her mouth again, gnawing on her nail. Finally, she said slowly, "I was the one that pursued him. I can't just tell him I'm not interested now."

Mason raised an eyebrow at her admission. Ellie had pursued Prescott. That was interesting.

"So I told him I would go to dinner with him tomorrow," she told him. "I figured it was okay since we're not really dating or anything."

So prim little Ellie was considering seeing two men at once. Mason was almost proud of her, proud to see a more daring and assertive woman underneath the shyness. Almost. He had absolutely no intentions of sharing her with anyone while they were together. Especially poor Prescott Jones. Ellie was Mason's, plain and simple—until the affair ended.

"No. No dinners. No dates, not until we decide to end this."

Ellie seemed a bit surprised. "But we're not dating; we just . . ."

"Doing the nasty? Knocking boots? Screwing?"

Ellie blushed, and she looked down at her hands folded in her lap. "Yes," she said softly.

"Well, I guess I should have stated the rules right off the bat. Number one rule, no seeing other guys while you're seeing me. I don't share."

Ellie stared at her hands for a moment longer, then raised her head. Her chin jutted out just slightly. "Neither do I."

Mason suppressed the proud grin that threatened to curve his lips. Hot damn! Shy, unassuming Ellie was making some demands of her own. He liked it—he liked it a lot. But instead of revealing his approval, he only said, "Fair enough. Now, come here." He patted the bed.

Ellie hesitated only a fraction of a second before she uncurled from her seat and came to him.

Once she was nestled by his side, he kissed her lingeringly like he'd been wanting to all day. After several enjoyable seconds, he ended the kiss and grinned at her. "So, I take it I need to buy you some lingerie."

She glanced down at her pajamas, then regarded him with troubled eyes.

He immediately wished he could take the comment back. He was just teasing her, but he had to remember she took teasing very seriously. And actually, he rather liked her jammies. They were modest and cute and hid that gorgeous, voluptuous body that was only his to see.

"Don't look like that. You could wear a potato sack, and I'd think you were sexy as hell."

Disbelief shadowed her eyes.

"Am I going to have to get a potato sack just to prove my point? This is Maine. You know I can rustle one up from somewhere."

A reluctant smile curved her lips.

He couldn't resist leaning forward and tasting the tiny adorable grin.

When they parted, she looked more relaxed, less anxious, but there was still worry shadowing her eyes.

"Okay," he sighed, realizing she was going to fixate on this Prescott thing until they found a solution. "Tell Prescott that you aren't comfortable dating a coworker. It might hurt his feelings a bit, but it's not like you're rejecting him personally."

Ellie considered the idea. "I guess I could tell him that. I just hate to lie."

"So don't lie. It's just good business practice not to mix up your private and your professional lives."

"Is that what happened between you and Charlie Grace? Did something at work hurt your friendship with him?"

Mason stopped stroking his fingers back and forth over her flannel-covered knee. "What?"

"I—I heard that Charlie might not side with you on the library issue."

Mason ground his back teeth. *Damn it! Damn small towns.* Charlie hadn't made any formal statement either way. As far as Mason knew, even the other council members weren't exactly sure where Charlie stood on Winslow's proposal.

"He hasn't made his decision yet," Mason said curtly. He didn't want to discuss this. He didn't even want to think about it.

"If he did decide to back Everett Winslow, that could lose the library the necessary votes, couldn't it?"

"It's not going to happen." Even as he said the words, he knew he couldn't guarantee that fact. He didn't know what Charlie was going to do. He didn't know much anymore.

"But if it did—"

Mason stood and crossed the room. He didn't come here for this. He came here to get laid. To forget everything but Ellie.

He'd think about the town's problems later. Shit. He'd think about everyone else later.

"You know," he said as he turned back to Ellie, "you are just like everyone else in my life. You want something. You want the benefits of my success. And when things don't go exactly how you think they should, you complain. You lose faith."

Ellie's eyes widened, filled with shock and confusion.

"I—"

He raised a hand to stop her. "You know what? I don't need more shit. Just screw this. Screw it."

He left her room, her house. He needed to get away from the doubt in her eyes. The disappointment. The confusion.

This time he wasn't stealthy going across her yard. He strode to his car in quick, angry steps, his only thought to get home. To get a drink.

Not until he'd reached his library and downed a full highball glass of whiskey did he allow himself to think. And to regret his reaction.

Why had he lost it? Ellie had just been asking questions, exhibiting valid concerns. Instead of discussing her worries with her, he'd gone on the defensive.

But he had a right to feel defensive. People did expect too much. His father had expected perfection. His ex-wife had expected political success and power. Charlie Grace expected . . .

Grabbing the bottle of whiskey and the glass, he sank into the leather chair behind his large oak desk. He shoved the keyboard to his computer out of the way with his heel and propped his feet on the desk, then poured himself another drink.

So what did Ellie expect?

She expected him to do what he said he would. She expected him to make his best effort to save the library. She didn't demand perfection or power or success. She didn't demand anything.

She just hoped he could help her. But instead, he shouted at her and made her feel guilty about asking for his help when he was the one who should feel guilty because he might not be able to help her or the library.

He picked up his glass. For the first time in a long time, the liquor tasted acidic, burning his throat, nearly gagging him. He slammed down the glass, the sound unbearably loud in the empty house.

He didn't want booze. He didn't want to be alone in this gigantic house. He wanted Ellie. He wanted her warmth. Her sweetness. He wanted the trust he saw in her eyes.

Twisting the chair to the small table behind him, he picked up the phone. His finger was poised over the buttons to dial when he realized he didn't know Ellie's home number.

He really was an ass. He slept with the lady, he planned to keep sleeping with the lady, but he didn't know her number.

Rummaging under his desk, he found a phone book and looked up her number. On the third ring, Ellie answered.

"Hi," he said with none of the casual cockiness he'd used when he'd called her at the library earlier.

"Hi." Even in that one brief word, he could hear her discomfort.

What did he say now? He had no idea. He needed to say something suave, something so charming that she couldn't help forgiving him, something persuasive.

"I need you." So much for suave, charming and persuasive. Needy was all he'd managed.

There was silence on the other end.

"Will you come here?" More neediness.

There was a brief pause, then a simple, "Yes."

Apparently needy worked, Mason thought with relief as he hung up the phone.

Chapter 15

When Ellie arrived at Mason's house this time, he wasn't lurking in the shadows of his porch. Instead, he waited in the doorway, his body silhouetted against the foyer lights, a cold wind off the Atlantic ruffling his hair.

"Thank God," Mason muttered as she stepped onto the porch. He grabbed her wrist and pulled her inside. Before she even had a chance to speak, he was kissing her. Kissing her like he was dying of thirst and she was a cold drink.

She clutched him with the same need. Thankful and thrilled to touch him and taste him.

When he'd gotten so angry and stormed out of her house, she'd thought everything was over. She truly believed it. And she wasn't ready for that. It was too soon, too abrupt. She wasn't going to ruin this second chance to be with him.

"Thank you," he whispered, his forehead against hers. "Thank you for coming."

Ellie smiled, relief flooding through her. "I'm so sorry. I should—"

Mason kissed her soundly. "No," he stated, when he pulled back. "I'm the one who's sorry. "I shouldn't have lost my temper. Work has been—tough lately."

Ellie noticed he did look tired. His complexion was a little pale and his features drawn. She should have

There was moment of silence, and then he murmured, "I've died and gone to heaven."

She didn't respond, determinedly leading him up the curved staircase. Once they reached the top landing, he moved forward to steer her toward his room.

She followed, chanting silently over and over to herself that she could do this. She could. But the chant stopped dead on her lips as soon as she stepped into his bedroom.

Maybe it was the floral wallpaper in deep pinks and blues. Or the enormous four-poster bed carved with vines and flowers. Or even the curtains with ribbon tiebacks. Or maybe it was all of it put together, but her boldness deserted her.

She tried to concentrate on the signs of Mason's presence in the room. His clothes piled on the winged-back chair in the corner. A pair of his shoes kicked off near the wardrobe. Several sports magazines scattered on the nightstand. A set of weights lined against the wall near the dresser.

There were indications of Mason everywhere, but she couldn't see him. This was a woman's room. His ex-wife's room, decorated to her taste.

Her eyes strayed back to the huge bed. Mason had slept with Marla there. They had made love under that pink ruffled duvet.

Did he lie in bed at night and long for her to be back beside him? Would he pretend she was Marla?

"I—I can't do this." The words were choked out, painful.

Mason was at her side, turning her to face him. "Ellie, what's wrong?" Concern creased his brow.

"I can't be with you here."

"What? Why?"

She cast a look around the room. "This was your wife's room."

Mason glanced around the room, too. "No, this is

my room. Yes, I did share it with Marla. But that was nearly two years ago."

Ellie shook her head. "I just can't."

He considered her for a second. "Ellie," he said, touching her hair, "I want to be with you." Then he chuckled grimly. "No, that's an understatement. I am absolutely dying to be with you. I don't care where. If you aren't comfortable here, then you pick a place."

Ellie hesitated, then caught his hand again. She led him back into the hallway. With care, she deliberated at the doorway of each of the three guestrooms. Finally, she returned to a room done in pale blues, except for the gray velvet duvet on the bed, which reminded her of Mason's eye color.

"Have you ever—slept with anyone in that bed?"

Mason promptly shook his head. "I think the only person who's ever slept in there was my cousin Neil. And I swear I only shared a tent with him at Boy Scout camp."

She smiled slightly, then looked back into the room. "Okay, I pick this room."

Mason quickly scooted her inside. "Thank God. I was starting to think I had the hots for Goldilocks." He tweaked one of her blonde curls, then twirled her around so she was facing him. "Now, I believe you were planning to seduce me."

Ellie would have laughed at his eager expression, except she was still feeling nervous about—well, everything. But she did manage to ask in her best attempt at coyness, "Where did you get that idea?"

"Let me see—I think it might have been when you grabbed my hand, dragged me upstairs, and told me you were going to make me forget everything."

"Maybe I thought a nice conversation would do the trick," she suggested, stalling for time, hoping to get her wishy-washy determination under control.

"Well," he leaned closer, "we could have just as easily had a conversation downstairs."

He had her there. And she was finding that his closeness was sending her nerve endings into overdrive. So much for getting a chance to gather herself.

"But just out of curiosity," he said, "what topic of conversation did you think would make me forget everything?"

He was toying with her, but she didn't care. She needed a few moments to attempt to calm down. Mason's bedroom had shaken her—badly.

"I thought we could talk about—" She glanced around the room, looking for something, anything to talk about.

A picture of Mason in college sat on the corner of the bureau. His hair was cut shorter than the style he wore now, and he had on a football jersey. "We could talk about your college days."

He raised his eyebrow. "And you think this will be a good distraction, say, over great sex?"

Ellie gave him a weak smile, her heart battering against her breastbone. "I would feel better if we could just talk for a few minutes."

He stared directly into her eyes, then pulled her toward the bed. He motioned for her to sit down. He sat, too, moving back to lean against the headboard. "Okay, let's talk about college life."

She hadn't really expected him to agree to the chat. She must look every bit as stressed as she felt. "Did—did you enjoy college?"

"Sure." He shrugged. "It was a pretty good gig. I went to Yale."

Ellie already knew that, of course. She could still recall seeing him in front of his locker at Millbrook High the day after he'd received his acceptance letter. He'd been laughing and excited and telling all his

friends how great it was going to be. And Ellie remembered thinking she'd never see him again.

"Why did you come back here after college?"

Mason stretched out his long legs and crossed them
at the ankles, considering the question. "I liked living
in a city. I liked the fast-paced life, but there are some
things you just can't find anywhere but a small town."

Ellie twisted to face him, her knee almost touching
his thigh. "Like what?"

He folded his arms over his chest, and Ellie admired the way the crisp, white cotton of his dress shirt
pulled taut over the muscles of his broad shoulders
and upper arms.

"Hmm. Well, the way neighbors help neighbors.
The way kids can still play in their front yards and ride
their bikes and be safe. The slower pace of life."

"I like that, too. Not that I've ever experienced life
anywhere else," she qualified.

"You didn't go away for college?"

Ellie shook her head. "I commuted to the University of Maine. My grandmother wasn't well, and I
couldn't leave her."

"Abby and Marty left."

"They always had bigger plans than I did." Ellie
shrugged one shoulder. "I didn't mind staying with
Grammy. I liked it."

Mason studied her, and she shifted, feeling like he
was looking right into her soul.

"You aren't comfortable doing things just for yourself, are you?"

Ellie frowned, perplexed by his question. "I don't
know. I never thought about it, really."

He watched her a moment. "You want me to make
love to you, don't you?"

His question caught her off guard. She looked
back toward the picture of him in college. He was
smiling, a huge, genuinely happy grin. A grin she

couldn't remember seeing on his face, not since high school, anyway. "Yes," she murmured, heat burning her face.

"But I'm not talking about us just having sex," he stated. "I'm talking about me pleasuring you—the way you want me to. You in control. Setting your own pace. Telling me what you want. Where to touch you."

She turned her head back toward him, but she couldn't meet his eyes. After a few moments, she nodded her assent.

"So why don't you?"

She hesitated. "I can't."

"Why?"

"I feel—ridiculous."

Her response obviously surprised him. "Ridiculous? Why?"

Ellie struggled for the right words. "I feel out of my depths with you. Embarrassed."

"What would make you feel less embarrassed?" he asked, no judgment, no impatience in his voice.

"Well, being thirty pounds lighter with long legs and perky breasts would be a good start." The words were out of her mouth before she could stop them. She fought the urge to clap her hand over her big mouth.

Mason sat up, the movement bringing his face closer to hers. "But that's something you think *I* want." He touched her cheek. The caress was barely there, a feathery whisper of his fingertips, but she could feel it to the soles of her feet. "And I think you are perfect just the way you are."

His fingers brushed down the column of her neck, leaving a tickling, tingling path in their wake. "In fact, I can't imagine you being more perfect. More gorgeous."

He moved forward and placed a kiss to the sensitive spot just below her earlobe. Her skin hummed and quivered, snapping all the nerve endings to attention.

"So what would make you feel more confident?" he asked.

She didn't know. But his lips on her throat, his hot breath like rushes of flame on her flesh, they were certainly doing a wonderful job of taking her mind off most of her inhibitions.

He gently bit the delicate skin where her neck met her shoulder. She gasped, pleasure rippling through her.

"I think," he whispered in between kisses that meandered back up her neck, "I know something that might help you feel more self-assured."

"Mmm," she answered, but her attention was really focused on his moist suckling kisses.

"I think we should talk."

His suggestion, and the loss of his lips against her skin, managed to catch her notice. She blinked up at him. "Talk?"

He nodded, guilelessly. "You did say that talking would help you feel less nervous, right?"

She eyed him. "Yes."

"Well, let's keep talking."

Chapter 16

Ellie regarded him closely. He looked the picture of innocence.

"All right," she agreed, but she could not quite keep the skepticism out her voice.

His grin widened at her agreement. "But this conversation is going to be a bit different."

"How did I guess that?"

Mason raised an eyebrow. "Is my sweet, agreeable little Ellie getting snippy?"

Ellie grimaced, but she actually felt like grinning foolishly. Was she really his Ellie? Warmth spread throughout her body. "I'll try to be less snippy."

"See that you do."

She stuck out her tongue, and Mason leaned in to kiss her.

"Okay," he said after he straightened away from her. "We're going to talk about things we like."

That sounded harmless enough.

"Or rather, things we'd like to have done to us. And more specifically what you would like me to do to you. And of course, what I'd like you to do to me."

Ellie's stomach sank. "How is this going to make me feel less nervous? We haven't even said anything yet, and I'm a wreck."

"We'll start slow." He reclined back against the headboard, looking very relaxed. Ellie fought the urge to cuff his leg. How dare he look so at ease when she felt like she might pass out?

"Do you want to go first?" he asked, his voice overly polite.

Ellie's fingers twitched with the impulse to swat him again, but she controlled her newly discovered violent side and kept her hands to herself. She shook her head no.

"Okay, I'll go. Let's see. I'd like . . ." He rubbed his chin in thought. "I'd like you to take off your top."

Ellie frowned and tried to ignore the heat rising in her cheeks. "I thought you were supposed to be telling me something you'd like done to you?"

Mason eyed her, his gaze roaming for a minute to her breasts. "Oh, I think seeing your lovely breasts would most definitely do something to me."

Ellie shook her head. Like she'd said, she was way out of her depths with Mason Sweet.

"Your turn."

She looked at her hands folded on her lap. What did she want him to do to her? She had fantasized so many things, but she couldn't possibly say them aloud. To him.

"I'd like," she began slowly, "I'd like you to kiss me."

He grinned. "I can do that." He leaned forward and pressed his lips to hers, a kiss rich with tenderness and leisurely persuasion.

He pulled away, staring into her eyes. "I'd like you to take off your pants."

The abruptness of his statement in comparison to his slow, thorough kiss caused a startled laugh to escape her. "That *isn't* something being done to you," she insisted.

"Okay, okay. I'd like you to take off my shirt."

Her breath caught in her throat. He returned to lounging against the pillows. His dress shirt was taut over his torso, and she could see the muscular definition of his chest and shoulders and the flatness of his belly.

"I'd like that, too," she whispered.

"Well, I did fulfill your request of a kiss," he remarked.

She eyed the row of buttons that disappeared into the waistband of his black trousers. The buttons were tiny. She'd never get her hands and her mind synchronized enough to unfasten them. But she did very much want to see his muscular bare chest.

She slid up the edge of the bed so her bottom was beside his hip. Timidly, she reached for the button at his neck, relieved to see the first two were already undone.

With clumsy fingers, she worked the buttons. As more golden skin appeared, her fingers seemed to grow surer. When the last button was undone, he sat up so she could push the shirt off of him. As the material slipped away, she let her hands brush over the sinew of his shoulders and sides before she moved away.

"So what would you like me to do to you?" His voice sounded uneven, but she wasn't sure if it was just a distortion caused by the deafening beat of her own heart.

Fantasies whirred through her mind. Things she'd imagined Mason doing to her. Things she'd imagined doing to him. Yet she still couldn't form the words.

She focused on him. He watched her in return, his eyes dark and intense. She saw need there. Desire. She could see the rapid rise and fall of his perfect chest. She could see the bulge in his trousers.

He was aroused—because of her. It was intoxicating to know her touch made him burn.

Like a strong wine, his desire went straight to her head and gave her more courage than she could have imagined. "I—I want you to touch me."

"Where?"

"Everywhere."

He groaned, the sound pained. "I want that, too, but I want you to be specific. I want to know exactly how you want me to please you."

She gave him a helpless look. She couldn't do this. "Where do you want to be touched first?" he pressed gently.

Ellie stared into his eyes and centered on the hunger she saw there. "My—my breasts," she found herself murmuring.

He groaned again and moved his hands to the buttons of her blouse. His hands seemed as shaky as hers had been. But he managed to undo them and push the shirt apart.

"God," he murmured, "this is so much better than lacy lingerie."

Ellie hadn't bothered to put on a bra when she'd changed out of her pajamas to come to his house. She had been in too much of a hurry to get to him. Apparently her omission had been a good thing.

"You are so beautiful," he whispered, brushing his fingertips lightly over her breasts.

The feathery touch sent shivers through her.

"Perfect." He pinched one of the tightened nipples. An immediate and violent rush of desire shot through her veins like her blood had come to a sudden boil.

"Do you like that?" he asked, tweaking the nipple again.

"Yes." Her answer was more of a gasp than an actual word.

He continued to stroke her, his fingers twirling and squeezing, her pleasure becoming almost painful in its intensity.

"Should I move on?"

She nodded, only half aware of his question. The turbulent rush within her muted every other sense but touch. She closed her eyes, giving in to those intense swells of sensation coursing through her.

"Where?" he pondered. "What part of you is desperate to be caressed?" His hands left her breasts. Her nipples strained and tingled greedily.

She shifted. She knew exactly where she wanted him to touch her—the focal point where all the heat and need in her body was gathering.

She wanted his hand between her legs, but the words clung to the back of her tongue. "I—I think it's your turn to tell me what you want," she said instead.

A wonderfully wicked smile turned up the corners of his lips. "Is it? Well, what should I ask you to do?" He thought for a moment. "I'd like you to take off my pants."

Her eyes flashed to his black dress pants and his clearly outlined erection. The temptation to press her hand to the hardness was too strong to ignore. She desperately wanted to explore his perfect body.

With hands that trembled out of both need and nerves, she reached for the button of his trousers. The button slipped open, and she found the zipper. With more bravery than she had thought she possessed, she slowly tugged the metal tab down, letting her knuckles graze the hardness underneath.

Mason hissed, and his penis jerked under the faint touch. He stood, and with great impatience, started to push down his pants. Then he stopped to shove his hand in his pocket.

Ellie watched as he pulled out foil packets and tossed them on the bed.

"As you can see, I was a very good boy scout," he said.

Ellie frowned, not finding any correlation between condoms and scouts.

"Always be prepared," he said and wiggled his eyebrows, a slightly lascivious curve to his lips.

Judging from the number of condoms, he was very

prepared, and he was expecting it to be a long, very amazing night.

Ellie's gaze immediately returned to the heavy erection, which prodded at the material of his boxers.

Unable to stop herself, she reached out and traced a fingertip down the length of the swollen shaft. It leapt again under the soft cotton. And Mason released another ragged hiss.

"Lie back," he said, his voice as impatient as the rest of him, but he was gentle as he pushed her back onto the velvet duvet.

She went willingly, eager for more, too.

His hands returned to her breasts, cupping them, shaping them against his palms; then his palms trailed downward. "So where should I touch next? Here, maybe?" He swirled a fingertip around her deep little navel.

She squirmed. "No, it tickles."

He chuckled, the sound like a whisper of warmth across her over-sensitized skin. His fingers continued down her stomach to the top of her khakis.

She moaned with need and eagerness. She wanted his fingers on her, in her.

There was a small tug as he untied the drawstring at the waist. "Here?" His hand slipped into her pants and brushed the edge of her panties.

She nodded adamantly, her heart pounding with anticipation.

He fondled her through the cotton of her panties and she dug her fingers into the velvet duvet.

"Do you want me to take off your panties?"

She couldn't answer; her breath came in short bursts and her blood thrummed through her. She wanted it all.

"Ellie, tell me what you want. I will do anything you ask."

It was too much. Too tempting. Too wonderful.

"Just tell me." He leaned over her, his mouth near her ear, his breath tickling her skin and his fingers pressing against her so deliciously. Taunting her, teasing her, driving her toward the brink, but not quite over the edge.

"Make love to me. Now!" she told him, desperation making her greedy, demanding.

Mason smiled, a supremely pleased grin. But then he did as he was told.

Mason slid up beside her and held her against him as the aftershocks of another climax rippled through her limbs. She must feel like a rag doll, limp in his arms. She felt boneless, satisfied beyond anything her vivid imagination could have conceived.

Gradually her body calmed, and she felt sleepy.

Mason stroked her back and bottom, the warm, rhythmic touch lulling her into a state between wake and sleep. A wonderful, blissful place.

"I didn't seduce you," she murmured, curling into him, drowsily looking up at his incredibly handsome face.

He smiled, and she thought she saw something akin to adoration flash through his eyes, but it was quickly replaced by his usual look of arrogance. "You've been seducing me from the moment you walked into this house."

"I have?"

He nodded, resting his head on his arm, his other hand still stroking her bare skin. "You seduce me with your dimpled smiles and your shy glances."

"Well, I guess I'm lucky you are so easily seduced." She laughed, but her laughter faded as she realized he was still serious.

"No one has ever had this effect on me. I could

spend hours just holding you. I want you more than I've ever wanted anyone."

Ellie found that hard to believe, but she wanted to. She wanted him to feel as overwhelmed by her as she did by him. She wanted him to love her—as she did him.

No, she wasn't going to think things like that. She told herself she wouldn't.

Mason lifted his head and pressed a slow, sweet kiss to her mouth, and she returned it with all the emotion she had.

The emotion that was dangerously close to love.

Mason could get used to this—having a warm, soft, very, very responsive woman in bed with him.

No, strike that. Not just any woman would do; it was definitely Ellie that he wanted beside him.

He watched her as she slept, cuddled against him. Her legs twined with his, her hand curled on his chest.

Last night had been amazing. He had spent hours touching, tasting, and kissing Ellie. He'd wanted to make the whole night only about her. About learning to be selfish and fulfill her own needs. And most importantly, making her understand that she was incredibly beautiful, no matter what other silly beliefs she had about herself.

But in truth, the night had been as much of an ego trip for him as it had been for her. Ellie responded so honestly and with such abandon that he couldn't help feeling somewhat arrogant. He also couldn't help finding his own release—twice. Although, he could proudly say that she had found satisfaction far more than twice.

Of course, her reaction was probably how she would have been with any man. Especially given the fact she had waited thirty years to take a lover. For someone as sensual and alive as Ellie, that must have been quite a feat. In fact, he couldn't begin to understand how she'd managed to remain a virgin for so long. Or why.

Of course, he couldn't deny that he was pretty damned pleased that he'd been her first. And frankly, the idea of her with another man made his blood boil.

He didn't contemplate his reaction too deeply, but he assumed he wouldn't feel so possessive of her once his lust waned. But right now, he wasn't ready to let her go, and he definitely wasn't going to share. It was a good thing that rule had now been established.

Ellie stretched beside him, her lovely, full breasts rubbing against his side. She blinked up at him with a sweet, sleepy smile. "Hi."

"Hi there yourself, beautiful."

She stretched again. "Mmm, I feel like I've run a marathon," she said; then a content little noise rumbled in her throat.

He smiled. "I hope it was a bit more fun than a marathon."

Ellie propped her chin on his chest. "It was wonderful."

His smile broadened. It had been. Last night had been as close to perfect as he could have imagined. And this morning, he felt better and more tranquil than he had in . . . possibly ever.

This was exactly what he needed. A genuine and generous woman. A person to keep him focused, grounded. How he felt this morning proved Charlie Grace and Nate Peck didn't know what they were talking about. He didn't have a drinking problem. He just needed a little warmth in his life. A little affection.

He moved his hands to catch Ellie under her arms and pulled her up his chest so he could kiss her.

"Mmm," she moaned against his lips, her fingers slipping into his hair. "I have morning breath."

"So do I." He kissed her again, more soundly. "Actually, I guess it would be more like noontime breath."

Ellie pulled away, her eyes wide with alarm. "It's noon?"

He looked at his wristwatch. "Well, quarter of, really."

Ellie jumped up from the bed, dragging a blanket with her. "Oh no. Oh no. I'm over two hours late."

Mason rolled over on his side, his head resting on his hand, watching her scurry around the room, collecting her clothes. "Since you're late already, why not call in sick? We can play hooky."

She paused, blowing an unruly curl out of her face. "I can't do that."

"Sure you can. Ole Prescott is there. He can handle things."

"But don't you need to go to work, too?"

Mason shrugged. "Ginny could run this town with a hand tied behind her back."

"Ginny? She's just your . . ." Then she nodded. "I suppose if anyone could, it would be Ginny."

"She is in the know," he agreed. "So, come on, take the day off."

She stood in the center of the room, a blanket clutched to her chest with one hand, a shoe in the other, looking so endearingly undecided. Finally she shook her head. "I want to, but I can't. We're receiving a shipment today. I need to go in."

"Okay." Mason sighed. "You're lucky, because half of what I like about you is your goodness and conscientiousness."

She stopped trying to wiggle into her panties while still holding the blanket modestly over her chest. "What's the other half?"

"Your modesty." He said, eyeing her blanket with a wry grin.

"You!" She picked up his boxers and threw them at him.

He easily caught them.

Despite his teasing, or maybe because of it, she did manage to don her clothes without revealing more than quick flashes of skin and then came to the bed.

"I would love to stay."

Mason took pity on her, although he wanted nothing more than to haul her back into bed and take off all the clothes she had just struggled into. "I'll come over to your house tonight."

That seemed to please her. "Good, I'll make dinner."

He hesitated. "Well, it'll be late. But I'd love dessert." He gave her a lascivious look.

She smiled, although the happiness in her eyes seemed to dull a bit. "Okay."

She started to rise from the bed, but he caught her and pulled her down to him for a deep kiss.

After a few delicious moments, she pulled away. "I do have to go."

He released her, but when she reached the bedroom door, he had to stop her just once more. "Ellie." Even he could hear the slightly desperate quality to his voice.

She turned back, questioning with her eyes.

"Do you want to go away on Columbus Day weekend?" He hadn't known he was going to ask that until the words were out of his mouth.

"With you?"

"No, with Prescott. Yes, most definitely with me."

A huge dimpled smile lit her face. "Sure."

A wave of relief washed over him. "Okay, good."

Chapter 17

For someone who had spent the entirety of her adult life being punctual, Ellie was really ruining her perfect record in a very short amount of time.

She pulled into her space in the library's parking lot and flipped off the engine. Angling the rearview mirror, she inspected herself. There were dark circles under her eyes. But she couldn't care; the bags had been worth every moment. In fact, she could probably forgo a good night's sleep for quite a while to repeat what she'd done with Mason.

Her night had been incredible—far beyond anything in her favorite romance novels. She should have been exhausted, but she felt so totally alive.

She dug through her purse and located a barrette. With her fingers, she combed out the worst of the snarls in her hair and clipped the jumble back. Several unruly curls sprang free, but overall, the barrette did make it look a bit tidier.

She foraged through her purse again and found a wet nap packet. She ripped the foil open and wiped her face with the lemon-scented cloth. The alcohol-based solution made her skin burn a bit, more so around her lips. She peered into the mirror, noticing a slight pinkness there. Whisker burn from Mason.

She studied it again and decided the marks weren't

too noticeable. Wiping her face one last time, she grabbed a tin of mints from where she kept them in her unused ashtray and popped one in her mouth.

She surveyed herself in the mirror. She craned her head a bit, trying to see as much of herself as she could in the small rectangle. Then she buttoned the dark blue cardigan that she'd found in the car almost up to the neck. Thank goodness she'd had it; the bulky knit would disguise the fact that she didn't have on a bra. She felt her cheeks heat. She was *never* late, and she *always* wore a bra to work. She was turning into a tardy trollop.

She looked in the mirror again, tilting it to see the sweater. A little—tousled, but overall, she was fairly presentable. She paused. What was that? She angled her head so she could see her neck in the mirror.

Oh my gosh! She had a hickey! Not a huge, purple, ugly thing like the teenage checkout girl at the local grocery store often had. But it was a hickey. Right on the side of her neck!

She scavenged through her pocketbook, but she had nothing. Not even a Band-Aid. She turned to look in her backseat. Nothing. Then her glove box. More nothing.

This was awful. She was arriving to work extremely late. She was supposed to tell Prescott that she couldn't go out to dinner with him. Because she had decided it was a bad idea to mix business and pleasure. All the while with a glaring hickey on her neck.

How did she get herself into this situation?

She looked back in the mirror. If she angled her head just right, it hid the mark. She looked like she was doing a rather good impression of Igor from *Frankenstein*, but it might hide the blotch long enough for her to get to her office and look for a Band-Aid or something.

Taking a deep breath, she got out of her car and

headed up the walkway. At the door she slanted her head, then entered the library.

She'd been reasonably prepared for Prescott to be waiting and worried. She had *not* been prepared for Abby and Chase to be waiting with him.

"My God, Ellie! Where have you been?" Abby rushed toward her, a distraught look on her face. "Prescott called me at work around ten to say you weren't here yet. And he wanted to know if I'd seen you. I told him that your car was gone when I left at 8:30. I couldn't imagine where you—what's wrong with your neck?"

Ellie blinked, dazed by Abby's worried, rapid-fire greeting. She tilted her head tighter to her shoulder. "I—I slept on it wrong."

Abby frowned. "Did you go to the doctor or something? Does it hurt that badly?"

"No. I mean, yes, it does hurt, but I didn't go to the doctor." Ellie said slowly, trying to come up with some plausible excuse. Frankly, anything would probably seem more plausible than the truth. "I stopped by Miss Limeburner's to see if she wanted me to bring her any books. And, well, you know how she is. She just got talking about this and that, and I couldn't get away." That was true enough. It hadn't actually happened today, but the story was true enough. Ellie had been stuck in Miss Limeburner's living room many, many times.

Abby's frown deepened. "I don't remember seeing your car there."

"It was," Ellie assured her, hating every moment of the lies.

Abby considered her for a moment, then shrugged. "Well, thank goodness you're okay. I was scared witless."

"Sorry." Ellie smiled apologetically. She tried to

direct the smile to both Chase and Prescott, but the bent angle of her head made the gesture difficult.

"Okay," Abby said, going back to the front desk to retrieve her purse and give Chase a quick kiss. "I have to head back to the lab. I have a thousand things to get done before I go to Boston University next week." She hugged Ellie tightly before dashing from the library, looking very much like a mad scientist.

Chase, however, still leaned on the desk and regarded Ellie with a curious expression. "So you have a crick in your neck, huh?"

Ellie nodded her head as much as the odd angle would allow. "It's the strangest thing."

Chase nodded, too, a peculiar smile causing the dimple in his left cheek to appear. "Well, these things happen."

Ellie frowned and for just a moment forgot to keep her head tilted. What an odd conversation. Had Chase seen something?

"Well, I need to get going, too." He came over and gave her a brief hug.

When they parted, Ellie could swear there was still a mysterious glint to his eyes, but the look disappeared as he asked, "Hey, do you want to come over for dinner after we get back from Boston?"

"Is Abby cooking?"

Chase raised his eyebrow. "What do you think?"

"Okay."

"Great, say that Monday. It's Columbus Day. Do you have it off?"

"No," she said a bit too quickly. "I mean, yes, I have it off, but I—I actually think I might have something going on." For just a fleeting moment, she thought she saw that strange twinkle return to his pale eyes, but once more it vanished before she could decide if she'd really seen anything or not.

"Hmm. Well, Tuesday, maybe. I plan to drive up to

Machias that day to get some barn boards this old fella is selling, and I should be home early—to do the cooking." He winked. "How's Tuesday for you?"

"Great."

Chase hugged her once more. "Glad you didn't go missing on us. See you later."

She smiled, watching him leave the library. She adored her new brother-in-law. He was such a nice guy.

And so was the guy who'd been standing quietly behind the checkout desk. And with Chase gone, Ellie couldn't avoid Prescott any longer. And she did need to talk with him. Even if the topic made her feel horribly guilty and slightly nauseous.

"Sorry I called Abby," he said as soon as she turned to face him. "I didn't think she would leave work. Or call Chase."

"That's not your fault. I should have let you know I'd be late."

"Your neck looks sore."

Ellie froze. Had he seen the hickey?

"Are you sure you're going to feel up to going out to dinner this evening?"

Ellie released a grateful breath. He hadn't seen the mark, *and* he'd just given her the out she needed. Her alleged stiff neck wasn't a permanent solution, but it would buy her some time so she could—well, so she could work up the nerve to give him another excuse.

"You know, I do think maybe I should take it easy tonight."

He gave her an understanding look, and guilt ripped through her. She should just tell him—well, okay, the truth wasn't really an option. But she should at least tell him that she didn't think she could date him right now. She owed Prescott that much.

"I'll be in my office." She was a liar and a chicken. But even as she berated herself as the worst kind of coward, she made her way to the back of the library. To hide and to look for a scarf.

"Hey," Mason greeted Chase as he walked across the marbled linoleum floor of Eddie's Diner. He was a little surprised to see his friend.

"Hey, what are you doing here?" Chase was obviously surprised to see Mason, too. "I stopped by your office earlier, but Ginny said you were out for the day."

The worn red vinyl squeaked as Mason took a seat across from Chase and reached for the menu that his friend wasn't using. "I had something personal come up this morning, so I'm only working half a day. What are you doing in town, anyway? I thought you're still working on that Congregational church out in Ludlow."

"I was, but I got a call from Abby. She was in a panic because Prescott had called and said that Ellie hadn't shown up for work, and I thought I'd better come back to make sure everything was okay."

A flutter of satisfaction warmed Mason as he recalled where Ellie had been to make her late and why. But the contented feeling fled as he realized that her lateness had caused people to worry. Of course, who would have thought that Prescott would sound the alarm at the woman being less than three hours late?

"So did she show up?" Mason asked casually.

"Yeah." Chase nodded, then chuckled. "She gave this lame excuse about stopping at Millie Limeburner's, but . . ." he leaned forward and lowered his voice, "I think she's seeing someone."

Mason tried to look surprised. "Really? Why do you think that?"

"She had a hickey. On her neck."

"Really?" Now Mason was shocked. How had he missed that this morning? He didn't think he'd done anything that would cause a hickey. But Ellie did have delicate skin, smooth and soft like a baby's.

"Yeah." Chase laughed again. "You should've seen her. She walked into the library with her head cocked to one side like her ear was attached to her shoulder. But I caught a glimpse when she first walked in."

Mason could picture his bashful Ellie trying desperately to hide the incriminating mark.

"The thing I don't get is why she would feel the need to lie to us."

Mason focused back on the conversation. "She must have her reasons. Maybe she's embarrassed."

Chase shrugged. "I guess. But I'd be happy to see her find someone, and I know Abby would be too. Ellie has spent a long time alone. She really deserves to find a nice guy."

Mason shifted in his seat and was relieved to see Sandy, the diner's oldest and loudest waitress, approach the table. "Hello, honey-sweeties. What can I get you, dears?"

Chase ordered his usual, and Mason scanned the menu quickly and picked the first thing that sounded good.

As Sandy wrote down their orders, she smacked her gum and muttered to herself, occasionally scratching her head with the end of her pen. "All right, honeys, I'll be right back with that."

Chase shook his head after she'd wandered away. "I bet she loses pens in that hair. Do you think it's real?"

Mason glanced at the waitress. She looked like she'd walked straight out of a sixties girls' group, just as she had for the last thirty years. "I hope not."

Mason wanted to keep his thoughts on Sandy. He wanted to think about the questionable authenticity of her hair. He wanted to think about anything but what Chase had just said about Ellie. Unfortunately, Chase's words couldn't be kept at bay. Ellie did deserve a nice guy. She deserved a lot of things—a lot of things that Mason was not.

Chase stopped watching Sandy and sighed. "The thing is, if Ellie is seeing someone, she obviously feels the need to keep the relationship a secret. And that makes me suspicious."

Mason began fiddling the condiments. "Why?"

"Well, Ellie is such a romantic. God, she devours romance novels like candy. So if she was interested in some guy, I'd think she'd be thrilled to introduce us to him. That makes me think this guy is asking her to keep the relationship quiet."

"If she is seeing anyone."

Chase nodded. "I really think she is, and I don't like the idea of her seeing someone that is just using her."

"Using her?"

"Yeah, for a good time or whatever. Ellie isn't that type."

"So I've been told."

Chase frowned at him. "What?"

Mason stopped lining the condiments in a straight row between himself and Chase like a barricade and glanced at his friend. "I just meant that everyone knows Ellie isn't the type to have an affair. She's too respectable."

Chase regarded him for a second. "Yes, she is. And I bet this guy knows that, too. So if he is asking her to hide the relationship, it's because he intends to just have an affair. Why would Ellie even be interested in such a lowlife?"

Mason's hand paused from pushing the mustard to the other side of the relish. "I have no idea."

Fortunately Chase decided to let the theory of Ellie and her lowlife lover drop. Mason pretended to follow Chase's other topics of conversation, but his mind was still stuck on Ellie. And the lowlife she was seeing.

Damn, he was that, all right. A lowlife of the lowest

order. He had her lying to her sister and her brother-in-law—his best friend. To everyone. He still believed their secrecy was the best way to keep her reputation unsullied, but it wasn't fair to her.

He should be dating her. Going out like normal people. But he couldn't offer her that, even though he knew it was the right thing. She would see that as a sign that their relationship went beyond a fun fling. That he was considering more than a brief affair. And he wasn't. He had no intention of marrying again. His first marriage, even though it had ended, would last him a lifetime.

He just wanted to have fun. And he wanted Ellie to have fun, too. Although he had his doubts that she could really be enjoying herself when she was sneaking around and lying.

"Hello? Mason?"

Mason blinked to see Chase waving a hand in front of his face.

"Man, you were miles away." Chase smiled. "Any place good?"

Mason snorted. "Not really. Just thinking about how complicated life can be."

"Well, don't look now, but here comes someone who threatens to make it even more complicated."

Mason glanced at the front door in time to see Everett Winslow enter the diner and start toward their table.

"Great," Mason muttered under his breath, and Chase chuckled.

"Mayor, how nice to see you," Everett said in an overly affable voice. "Chase." He nodded in the other man's direction.

Chase returned his greeting with a similar nod, then continued to eat his lunch.

"Well, this was a stroke of luck. I was just over at Town Hall, and I actually stopped by your office, but

Ginny told me you were out today." Even though the words were said pleasantly enough, there was an underlying note to them.

Mason nodded. "Actually, I'm taking a half day. I had some personal things to attend to this morning. How can I help you, Everett?"

"Oh, I don't need any help. I just wanted to stop by and say hello."

Mason frowned. What was Winslow up to now? "So you didn't go to Town Hall to speak with me about something in particular?"

A small, shrewd smile curved the older man's mouth. "Oh, I was actually meeting with Charles Grace. It seems that he is quite interested in the new football field."

Mason shifted, the tension in his spine pulling him ramrod straight. "I know he was considering all the pros and cons."

"Indeed he is."

Mason tried to decide if there was more to Winslow's words other than the hope they would make Mason nervous. Did Charlie tell Winslow his concerns about Mason's drinking? He didn't think his old friend would do something like that. Unless Charlie was planning to go over to Winslow's camp for the next election, which was a possibility.

"And has Charlie come to any decisions?" Mason hated to ask. He shouldn't have to ask. Charlie should be talking to him, not this angling, underhanded snake.

The snake's smile widened. "I'd say he's close. Very close."

Mason nodded, keeping his face stoic, calm. "Well, I know Charlie will make the right choice."

"Yes," Winslow agreed, his face equally unreadable. "I believe he will."

* * *

Ellie left work late. Since she had to spend a majority of the day hiding in her office alone with her hickey, she hadn't been able to get all her work done. So she'd hung around until Prescott had left and she could venture out again. None of her evening staff knew she was supposed to have a stiff neck. And they hadn't even questioned the Scooby-Doo Band-Aid on her neck, much to her relief.

The sky was already inky black when she pulled into her driveway. A huge, orange autumn moon hung over her house, looking like it was balanced on the shingled roof.

She walked up the path toward her back door, admiring the breathtaking night and thinking how content she felt. Suddenly, a dark form came out from behind one of her grandmother's lilac bushes in front of her.

She managed a small squeak before she was pulled against the form's hard body. Lips came down on hers, and she sank against the solid shadow, all at once very aware of who the shadow was.

"You have the strangest ways of showing up at my house," she murmured against Mason's lips. She could feel him smile.

"I find myself doing the strangest things when it comes to you. Lurking, breaking and entering, making lots and lots of lewd and inappropriate propositions."

"They'd be inappropriate only if they offended me, and so far, I've found all your propositions quite agreeable. Even if they are sometimes a bit lewd."

She couldn't see his face, but Ellie could tell Mason had grown solemn. Then he asked, his tone as somber as his posture, "You are okay with our arrangement, aren't you?"

Ellie became serious, too. Was she okay with it? She wanted to be. She wanted to listen to her head instead of her heart. She wanted to simply enjoy the time she had with Mason and not think about the future. But her thoughts wouldn't obey. Questions kept sneaking in, about how long they would last and how she would recover when he decided to end things.

But she couldn't tell him that, not without the risk of his feeling uncomfortable or pressured. So she said how she felt that moment. "When I'm with you, things couldn't be more okay. They are wonderful, in fact."

He seemed almost relieved by her response as he ducked to kiss her again. Then he caught her hand and led her up the back steps. She fumbled to unlock the door, and Mason stood behind her, his hands caressing her.

She turned to scold him, trying hard to keep her voice stern. "Stop that. Do you want to spend the night on the back stoop?"

He tried to look repentant, shaking his head, but as soon as she turned back to the door, his hands snaked around her waist again, then slid up to cup her breasts.

Finally, after several attempts, several pauses, and several small gasps, she got the door open.

Before she could even flip on a light or take off her coat, Mason was dragging her toward the staircase to her bedroom.

"Don't you want some dinner? Or something to drink?" Personally, she didn't want food or a beverage, not when she could have Mason. But even at times like this, good manners were deeply ingrained in her makeup.

"I think I'll have dessert first tonight," he said in his low drawl that sent shivers shimmying throughout her body.

Ellie had always been a big fan of the philosophy of "dessert first."

Chapter 18

Mason sat up from where he relaxed against a pile of flowery pillows as Ellie entered the room. On one hand she balanced a platter stacked high with sandwiches, while in the other she managed to carry a bag of chips and two cans of diet soda.

He threw back the quilt and started out of the bed, but Ellie stopped him. "Stay put."

Reluctantly, he leaned back against the headboard. He felt like a sultan basking on cushions as he waited for his concubine to serve him.

Rather than making him feel pampered and decadent, Ellie's attention made him ill at ease. Mason would readily admit that he had many foibles, but expecting a woman to wait on him wasn't one of them.

He'd offered to help make the sandwiches, but Ellie had adamantly refused. She said she could tell he was tense, and he should just rest. In truth, he had been tense, but Ellie had done wondrous things for him in that department.

Ellie set the platter onto the jumbled bedding, then crawled onto the bed herself.

Mason noticed her grimace slightly as she situated herself across from him. Another flash of guilt assaulted him.

"Are you okay?"

Ellie stopped from attempting to tug the bag of chips open. "I'm great. Why?"

"I was a little—single-minded when I first got here."

Ellie blushed. She looked amazingly cute sitting with her legs crossed, decked out in another of her seemingly endless supply of flannel pajamas. Although this time, she wore only the top, which still managed to hide most of her. But it was a start.

"Are you sure I wasn't too rough?" He knew he had been. He'd been desperate for her and had taken her with more intensity, more force than he'd intended. But all reason had left his brain as soon as he had touched her lush body.

Her pink cheeks darkened. "You were—just right."

"You are my little Goldilocks, aren't you?" He reached over to tug one of her messy curls. "Well, I'm glad I'm 'just right.'"

"Not too hard. And definitely not too soft."

Her comment caught him off guard, and he paused from lifting one of the sandwich halves to his mouth. Then a true laugh escaped him. His Ellie could really surprise him at times. "That was downright naughty, Miss Stepp."

She grinned back at him, obviously pleased with her own audacity. "Just telling the truth, Mayor Sweet."

They fell into an easy silence, munching on their dinner and lounging in the stillness. Both satisfied. Both happy.

Ellie did constantly surprise him, Mason realized. He'd expected her to be shocked, maybe even a bit frightened by the force of his need for her tonight. But she hadn't been, not in the slightest. In fact, she had responded in kind, giving back everything he gave her. The encounter had been frenzied and mad, and possibly the most earth-shattering sex Mason had ever experienced. Ellie was extraordinary and so, so sensual.

Again, he wondered how had such a responsive and

clearly sexual woman managed to remain a virgin for so damned long?

He was about to ask her when Ellie said, "I would have made a nicer dinner, but you said you weren't going to get here until late."

"I hadn't planned to, but I couldn't stay away. I needed to see you." The truth was out before he could temper it, make it seem like his decision was just a casual change of plans, rather than a serious necessity. Serious wasn't the impression he intended to give her of their relationship.

"I'm glad." She gave him such an open, warm smile that another twinge of guilt tugged at him.

After his conversations with Chase and Everett Winslow today, he'd been convinced he had to tell Ellie things were getting too complicated—and that they needed to end. Then back at work, alone in his office and able to think, he realized that being with Ellie was all he wanted. It was the one thing that he looked forward to, and he wasn't giving that up. Not for a while.

"I was going to go get something to eat at the Parched Dolphin. But then I decided I'd rather be with you."

"I'd rather you be with me, too."

"I saw Everett Winslow today." Again his mouth seemed to work without any interaction with his brain.

"You did?" The sandwich that she'd been about to take a bite of lay forgotten in her hand. "Did you say anything about the library?"

"He said he'd talked with Charlie, and Winslow thought Charlie was close to making a decision."

"Do you know Charlie's decision?"

Mason shook his head. "Charlie isn't really talking to me about this issue."

"Why?" As soon as Ellie asked, she looked contrite.

She was probably remembering his reaction when she had questioned him about Charlie the other day.

But Mason wanted to talk to Ellie, wanted her on his side. And he knew she would be.

"Charlie is—angry with me. He thinks I have a problem."

Ellie frowned. "What sort of problem?"

"He thinks I have a drinking problem." Mason watched her reaction and saw no judgment in her clear blue eyes, so he continued, "I was drinking quite heavily after Marla and I split. And I made some dumb choices, which Charlie saw. He's insisting that I go to AA and get help. I'm not an alcoholic. Unfortunately, I can't seem to get Charlie to see that."

Ellie was quiet for a moment. "Well, a marriage ending is a very traumatic thing. Surely Charlie knows that."

"You'd think."

Ellie's spine straightened. "So he's planning to vote against you if you don't get help?"

"He hasn't said so, but I get the distinct feeling that is his plan."

Ellie bristled. "That's terrible! Can you talk to him? Make him see that you're fine now?"

"I've tried, but for whatever reason, Charlie has his mind made up about this."

"Well, that's crazy," she stated with all the righteous outrage he'd expected.

Warmth spread through his chest. It was good to know someone believed in him. He knew he could count on Ellie.

"I know you'll be able to save the library, even without Charlie's support. People in this town respect you."

Some of the warmth faded. There wasn't any guarantee that he could control the vote. But he was going to try.

"I will do everything I can, Ellie."

"Of course you will," she acknowledged readily, and some of the warmness returned.

"I also saw Chase today."

"Did you?"

He nodded, a slow grin across his lips. "He said you had a problem with your neck."

Her hand flew up to the Scooby-Doo Band-Aid on her neck. "Oh, I forgot I had this on." She quickly pulled the bandage off to reveal a small scarlet mark the size of a dime. "Did he think I was acting strange?"

Mason couldn't help smiling a little wider; then he said as sincerely as he could, "No, he didn't notice a thing."

"Good." She let out a sigh of relief.

"But I'll have to remember to be more careful. Your skin is so delicate." He reached forward to stroke the bare knee that poked out from under the flannel top. He ran his hand up toward her thigh, then back down again.

Her lips parted, and she watched him touching her.

He repeated the action once more, loving how she reacted to even the smallest touch.

"I should probably shave more often, too. I'm sure I give you whisker burn."

"I like the feel of your whiskers."

Mason raised an eyebrow, giving her a dubious look.

"I do," she insisted. "It's very—sexy."

His eyes widened. "Did my pure little Ellie just say 'sexy'?"

Ellie smiled, shaking her head. "I'm not that pure."

"Mmm," he said, the sound filled with disbelief.

They were silent again, nibbling at the food.

Ellie lifted her soda can, taking a sip. The liquid left her lips damp, and they glistened in the lamplight.

Mason leaned forward to taste them. The sweetness

of the soda clung to her, but it was overshadowed by the sweetness of Ellie herself.

"You know, I'm becoming a big fan of flannel jammies. Especially ones with little yellow ducks on them."

She made a face at him.

"Seriously, Ellie, you are gorgeous," he murmured, staring into her eyes.

She looked away, obviously uncomfortable with the compliment.

"I have a question for you."

She looked at him inquiringly.

"How did you manage to remain a virgin this long?"

Her eyes widened. "You knew?"

Mason hid his smile. "Yeah, I knew."

"Oh." She didn't seem disappointed, but she didn't seem particularly pleased either. And she also didn't appear to be planning to answer his question. But the question was too intriguing for him to leave alone.

"So, how did you pull off such a feat?"

"I—I never met anyone that I wanted to be with." Her explanation seemed awkward, stilted. "And of course, I didn't really have men beating down my door, either."

Mason watched her for a moment.

She picked crumbs off the bedding, placing them in her napkin. She curled the chip bag closed and then finished her soda. She wasn't waiting for an objection to her last comment. She wasn't expecting it.

That made Mason angry. Didn't she realize she was incredibly beautiful? Everything that a man could possibly want. "I think the guys you've known must have been stupid and blind."

She blinked up at him from clearing the remainder of their dinner onto the hope chest at the foot of the bed. "What?"

"I just can't believe that men haven't been trying to go out with you for years."

"Well, they haven't." She shrugged.

"Well, they should have." He leaned in and kissed her. She responded with her usual relish, and although he didn't want her to think she was unattractive, he was glad that other men had somehow missed this absolutely wonderful woman. A possessive feeling pulled at his chest.

And he had every intention of showing her how remarkable she was as he pushed her down onto the mattress and began to remove the little yellow ducks.

Ellie lay curled against Mason's side. He was asleep, his breathing deep and even. She lightly stroked his chest and savored how the sprinkling of coarse hair tickled her fingertips. His heart thumped just under her palm, and she couldn't help wishing his heart were hers. That she had his love as well as his body. But thoughts like that were just greedy and pointless.

When he had asked her about her virginity, she'd almost told him the truth—she'd been waiting for him. But she quickly realized she couldn't. So she told him something that was as close to the truth as he would want to hear. The truth seemed to always be just out of reach these days.

Determined not to think about the pretenses of her relationship, she concentrated on the reality. Mason was here with her. Warm and cozy. She snuggled against him, breathing in his masculine scent. She loved how he smelled. It was a combination of bergamot, citrus, and a rich scent that she couldn't quite place and that she had finally decided was simply Mason.

She glanced at the clock. The bright digital numbers read well after 1 A.M. By all rights, she should be exhausted. She'd barely gotten any sleep the night before. And Mason had been very demanding tonight. But despite her body's fulfilled languidness, her mind was still restless.

She wanted to believe that Mason was starting to think of her as more than a bed buddy. He'd made plans for them to go away almost two weeks from now. So he thought their affair would last at least a couple more weeks. He'd come to her much earlier than he'd said he would because he'd wanted to see her. He'd confided in her about Charlie Grace.

She was surprised by his disclosure about Charlie. Ellie had always found Charlie to be a nice, level-headed man. He certainly didn't seem like the type to make random accusations about the mayor who was also his good friend. But she didn't think Mason would have even brought the subject up if he'd really had a problem.

The night he'd passed out suddenly came to mind, and for a half a second, she wondered. Mason had said that he'd had a couple drinks and a cold. That was the reason he'd had such a bad reaction. Ellie hadn't had any cause to doubt him. She didn't drink often enough to know much about it. His excuse sounded plausible. It still seemed plausible.

She lifted her head up and looked at Mason's face. He looked so handsome, so perfect. She couldn't doubt him. She didn't want to. She liked Charlie Grace just fine, but she loved Mason Sweet.

Chapter 19

"We could have gone to my house," Ellie hesitated at the bottom of the steps to Mason's place. She knew she was being silly, but she didn't feel comfortable in his house. It was magnificent. She loved the style, the layout, the gorgeous view, but it felt like Marla's house to her. And she didn't enjoy comparing herself to Mason's ex-wife. Ellie always fell short.

"We've been to your house every night for the past week. And to be honest, I want you in my house." He grabbed her hand and pulled her up the stairs.

The past week had been wonderful. When Mason had originally tried to dissuade her from starting an affair with him, he'd asked her if a couple quickies a week would be enough for her. Well, so far, she still didn't really understand what he'd meant. Mason had been to her house every evening, usually by seven if not earlier. They had dinner together. They talked. Sometimes they watched television, which was apparently an aphrodisiac for Mason because he never made it through a whole show without starting to kiss her and touch her.

And as far as their lovemaking, she didn't know what Mason's definition of a 'quickie' was, but if they were having them, she didn't think she could survive a 'longie.' He was a wonderful and attentive lover, and all that attention had given her more confidence.

For all practical purposes, they were a real couple. Except no one knew they were. And even though Ellie tried to squash down her feelings of dissatisfaction, she couldn't quite get them to obey.

But at least in her house, she could feel like he was truly hers, even if it was only for the hours they were there. But in his house, she was constantly reminded that he wasn't really hers. He was on loan until someone better came along. Someone like his ex.

When Mason pushed open the front door, Ellie was greeted by the delicious scent of something cooking.

"What is that?" she asked. "It smells great."

""I decided to make you dinner, for a change."

"Really?" Ellie was surprised and thrilled. "You can cook?"

His pleased expression became a bit sheepish. "I can reheat. I actually picked up dinner from that restaurant in Bar Harbor you've mentioned you wanted to try."

Ellie's pleasure dampened a bit. Why couldn't he just bring her to the restaurant? No, that was not fair. He was trying to create a romantic evening, and she was being ungrateful.

"I got you the seafood-stuffed portabella."

"Mmm, I love mushrooms."

"I know."

A warm feeling skipped through her. Mason listened to her, even the humdrum stuff like the fact she liked mushrooms. It made her feel good. It almost made up for the secrecy. Almost.

He led her into the dining room. The long rectangular table was set for two with a dozen candles casting warm, flickering light around the room.

"This is gorgeous." Ellie released his hand and wandered inside. She'd never been in this room before. The furniture and the decorations still declared Marla, but Ellie didn't focus on them, instead keeping

her attention on the romantic setting Mason had created for her.

"Sit," he said, pulling out a chair for her. Once she
was seated, he poured her a glass of champagne.
"Relax. I'll be right back." He placed a kiss on the side
of her neck and then disappeared into the kitchen.

Ellie sipped her drink. Wrinkling her nose at the
bubbles and the flavor, she set the glass aside. She
hoped he hadn't spent a lot of money on the champagne, because she had no taste for it. But it did help
create the scene.

The table looked great, and she especially liked that
he had set the place settings beside each other, one at
the end of the table and the other to the right, rather
than across from one another. Even though the table
was large, it created a sense of intimacy.

Mason returned, carrying a plate in each hand.
Reaching over her, his chest brushed her back and
she could feel his breath stir her hair as he set the dish
in front of her.

The plate was arranged with a delicious-looking
green salad, but Ellie's mind wasn't on dinner, not
when Mason was so close.

Mason sat down beside her, his knee bumping hers
under the table. He watched her, and it took her a moment to realize he was waiting for her to taste the food.

She picked up the fork and speared some of the
mixed greens. As elegantly as possible, she sampled
them. "Mmm, very good." She didn't know good
champagne, but she did know a good salad. "I'm a bit
of a connoisseur when it comes to salads. They've
been a staple of my diet for . . . well, most of my life."

Mason frowned. "Well, I hope you're eating them
because you happen to be crazy about raw vegetables.
Because if you're eating them for any other reason,
there is no point."

"You're telling me," she said with good-natured self-derision.

His frown deepened to something akin to a scowl. "Ellie, I swear I'm eventually going to convince you that you are perfect just the way you are."

Then why don't you want to have a real relationship with me? Why can't we be seen together? But instead of speaking the questions aloud, she just smiled. "It is good," she said again, stabbing more of the leaves.

"So, what do you want to do on our weekend away?" Mason asked, reaching to refill his glass with more of the fizzy golden liquid.

"We can do anything?" The change of subject to their Columbus Day weekend excursion lifted her spirits.

Mason nodded. "Anything."

"Then I would like to go to Portland and see the new exhibit at the Museum of Art. It's the American Masters."

Mason nodded readily. "That would be fun. And I know a great inn in Cape Elizabeth."

"Did you stay there with Marla?" The question popped out of her mouth before she could stop it.

Mason smiled with indulgent amusement. "You are hung up on this whole 'who I've had sex with and where' thing, aren't you?"

Ellie blushed, annoyed with herself that she couldn't control her mouth, especially on this particular matter. "I shouldn't have asked that."

"Well, at the risk of ruining this studly image you seem to have of me, I haven't had sex with anyone there. I actually threw my parents' thirtieth anniversary party there."

Ellie heated with more embarrassment. She was pathetic. She took another bite of her salad.

"Okay, my jealous little angel, I think I'd better serve the main course before it all shrivels into a dry mess." He rose, then leaned down to kiss her. The champagne tasted infinitely better on him.

"You don't have to worry about the other women I've been with. I can't remember a single one of them when I'm with you."

Ellie knew his claim probably wasn't true, but he said it with such sincerity and even a touch of bemusement that she almost believed him.

He returned with two more plates heaped with scrumptious-looking mushrooms stuffed with lobster, shrimp, and scallops.

He set the plate down with great flourish, and then he reached into his pants pockets and pulled out a can of diet soda and a fresh glass. Like an accomplished waiter, he cracked the can open and poured it into the wine flute. Setting the glass beside her plate, he bowed. "For my lady."

Ellie laughed. "Thank you." She took a sip of the soda with exaggerated appreciation, caught up in his silliness.

Mason returned to his seat, once again filling his glass with sparkling wine. "I figured the champagne wasn't really your thing. Don't like the taste?"

Ellie shook her head regretfully. "But it was a lovely gesture. And it does taste better on you."

"Hmm," he wiggled his eyebrows in a suggestive way, "I'll remember that." He picked up his glass and polished it off.

She picked up her knife and fork and cut into the huge portabella. Closing her eyes, she savored the wonderful flavor. She made an appreciative sound, then opened her eyes.

Mason watched her with a pleased expression of his own. "I love to watch you eat."

Ellie grimaced, then picked up her napkin and wiped her lips. "I can't imagine why."

"Because you eat like you do everything else, with a sparkle."

Ellie made a face. "I think the champagne has gone to your head."

"Maybe, but all I know is that I love to just watch you. The animation on your face. The enthusiasm in your reactions. And you are just so damned adorable, sometimes it takes my breath away."

Ellie blushed, enchanted by his description and amazed that the man whom she had always considered dazzling seemed to see her the same way. It was unbelievable.

"You know," he said with a lascivious smile she knew well, "I've never had sex with anyone on this table."

Ellie bit back a laugh. "Is that so?"

He nodded, giving her an endearingly earnest look, and she did laugh.

"Well, I suppose—"

He shook his head. "No, finish dinner. I have a bad habit of interrupting your meals."

"And *Jeopardy*."

"Well, I have to do that. Otherwise you'd always win."

The remainder of the meal, they continued to banter, most of the comments filled with lots of innuendo.

Ellie loved that she was comfortable enough to flirt with him. She'd never flirted with any man in her life. She supposed it only made sense that she could flirt with the man she was sleeping with, but she still felt very audacious. In some ways, it also made her feel closer to him. It showed her that they were friends as well as lovers.

She took the last bite of her dinner and had barely put down her silverware when Mason reached for her.

"Come here."

She allowed him to pull her over to his chair and into his lap, but she couldn't relax against him.

He sensed her qualms immediately. "Don't you even say it," he warned.

"What?"

"That you're too heavy. Or my legs will fall asleep, or some other silly thing. You're tiny."

She made a sound at that. But the dubious snort turned into a squeal as he stood, taking her with him.

Her arms flew around his neck, clinging to him, afraid he'd drop her.

"I won't let go," he assured her as he left the dining room and strode down the hall to the staircase.

"I really can walk," she said nervously as he started climbing the steps.

"I know you can walk. You sure do make it damned hard to be romantic. Geesh!" he said with such exasperation that Ellie couldn't help but laugh. Although she was still fairly certain they were going to tumble backwards down the stairs to their deaths.

"You like to give a man a hard time, don't you?" he said, shaking his head once he reached the landing.

She tried to look contrite, but she couldn't quite keep the smile off her face. "I was sure you were going to drop me." But he hadn't; he hadn't even broken a sweat.

He grimaced at her. "You need to learn to trust me."

She sobered. "I do trust you."

He stared into her eyes, and she thought she saw a flash of something in his gray irises, but he kissed her before she could identify the emotion.

She was so absorbed in the strength of his lips and his arms that she didn't realize they had moved until he lifted his head.

They were outside his bedroom door.

Ellie didn't want to ruin the moment, but she still didn't think she could make love with him in a bed that he'd shared with another woman. A woman whom he'd once loved.

"Mason," she said, slowly, "can't we go to the other—"

He cut short her question with another kiss, a gentle, coaxing kiss she was helpless to ignore.

She vaguely felt him nudge the bedroom door open and walk into the room, but she couldn't break the kiss. She didn't want to.

After a few more moments, Mason was the one to end their kiss, but he stayed close, staring into her eyes. "We don't have to stay in here, but I'd like to."

She hesitated, then nodded. When it came to this man, she couldn't seem to deny him anything.

He grinned and set her on her feet, her body sliding down his, the friction, even with clothes on, heady.

She continued to stare up at him, hoping he would kiss her again and give her the confidence to ignore her doubts.

Instead he watched her expectantly.

She suppressed a frown, then looked away from him, unsure what he wanted her to do. Then she blinked. And blinked again.

This wasn't the bedroom she'd seen before. Except it was.

"Mason," she whispered, turning away from him to scan the room. The heavy, carved wood furniture was gone, replaced by unfussy mission-style pieces. The curtains with ribbon tiebacks were also gone. In their place were simple white shades. The pink and blue floral wallpaper had disappeared, too; the walls were now coated with paint, a soft blue, subtle and serene. Even the ruffled pink duvet had vanished. A thick white duvet with narrow indigo-blue stripes and plump king-sized pillows graced the new bed.

This was Mason's room. His style. His taste.

"So, what do you think?"

She glanced at him and saw he was watching her intently. Like her reaction mattered. Like maybe he hadn't done this just for himself, but for her, too.

"It looks terrific," Ellie said, reaching out a hand to touch the polished wood of the dresser. "I love it."

He came up behind her and wrapped his arms around her waist. "I thought you would. I've been meaning to change things. To make them . . . more mine."

Ellie continued looking around the room, feeling the apprehension leave her body. She knew it was silly that furniture and curtains and a few coats of paint could make her feel better. But it did. Marla's presence wasn't here now. Or at least not so vividly, not such a ready reminder for comparison.

"You know," Mason said, resting his chin on her shoulder, his lips close to her ear. "I've never had sex with anyone in that bed."

"Really?" She feigned surprise.

"Nope, and I really think we should do something about that."

Ellie sighed. "Yes, I suppose we should."

Chapter 20

"You really do like it?" Mason said teasingly as he fell back against the pillows and pulled the sheet over them. Then he cuddled Ellie close. She snuggled against him with a weary nod of her head against his shoulder.

Even though the question was posed as a joke, it had been important to him that she liked the room. That she felt comfortable in his home.

He couldn't give her much, but he wanted to give her that. He wanted her to understand she was important to him. Even if this was just an affair, she was very special to him.

He nuzzled his nose in her unruly curls, breathing in the scent of lavender. Ellie made him feel like he wanted to be a better man than he'd been in . . . since before he and Marla fell apart. Before he realized that most of his life had been a charade.

Ellie was everything Marla hadn't been. The two women were polar opposites: Marla had been cool and aloof; Ellie was warm and approachable. She was generous and open; Marla didn't do anything that didn't fit into her own agenda.

Marla had been polished. Dressing like she was going to a country club, even when she'd only been running down to the Millbrook General Store.

Ellie dressed comfy and cute. He could remember

that he had once thought of her style as frumpy. Now he wondered where he had gotten that idea. Her clothes were actually rather hip, just not designer brands or severe styles. Ellie didn't need to look urbane; she looked natural, real, and beautiful.

It was strange. Ellie even slept differently from Marla. Marla didn't like to cuddle. She liked her space, saying she felt claustrophobic when he held her. Marla also slept in the same position all night, as if moving too much might muss her hair or wrinkle her nightgown.

As a test for himself, he pulled Ellie tighter against him. She snuggled in willingly, as she always did. She wiggled a bit so her bare back and bottom were aligned with his chest and crotch. She fit perfectly.

He couldn't even think of a single area where Ellie and Marla were similar. So why was he unwilling to consider something long-term with Ellie? Wasn't his reluctance based on the reservation that he might end up in another sham of a relationship?

He moved his hand from around Ellie's waist to run his palm over her hip, to shape the rounded curve.

God, he loved how this woman felt. All soft, silky skin. There was nothing fake about Ellie. Nothing false. But still he hesitated. Why?

He knew if he allowed himself to, he could love Ellie. He was being to think he was half in love with her already. Why couldn't he just tell Ellie he wanted something beyond an affair? Hell, they already had something far beyond an affair. So what held him back?

It wasn't Marla. Not totally. So what was it?

His hand moved up and down her hip, each pass taking his fingers closer to her belly and the tight curls below. He let his hand stray there, gently brushing over her.

She shifted, her legs falling apart just slightly.

He touched her again, this time his fingers threading into the curls, tracing the plump folds.

Her legs spread a bit wider.

He lifted his head to watch her. Her eyes were still closed, her lips parted. But he could tell she was aware of his touch even in her sleep.

Slowly, gently, he continued to touch her.

She moved then, squirming against his fingertip. Her eyes blinked open. Then she smiled up at him, her eyes dazed with sleep and budding yearning.

"Hi, angel," he whispered, pressing a kiss to her parted mouth.

She kissed him back, a hand coming up to caress his face, then tangle in his hair.

"Can I make love to you again?" he whispered, his finger still swirling languidly, lightly.

She nodded. "Yes, please."

He then proceeded to make love to her with all the emotion he couldn't seem to give voice to any other way.

"Oh, Mason," Ellie exclaimed as they pulled up to the inn where they were spending the weekend. The Victorian building with porches and turrets rose from the cliffs of the Atlantic Ocean overlooking a rocky beach. She got out of the car to better see the view. The autumn sea air was chilly, but she didn't care, lifting her face toward the sky, breathing in deeply.

"You like it?"

She turned to him with a huge smile. "It's perfect." And it was. The whole thing. Mason, a weekend away with him, the inn. The whole thing was more than she could have ever imagined.

She breathed deeply again, glad to be out of Mason's speedy sports car. She had actually started to feel a bit ill on the curvy roads leading to the inn. For just a moment, she felt a slight pang of sadness. Somehow, her motion sickness seemed like another difference between them. Another way that she wasn't suited to him. Then she brushed the silly thought aside. She wasn't going to think about anything except enjoying herself.

Mason came over and caught her hand. "Let's go check in; then I'll come back and get our stuff."

She nodded, linking her fingers with his and heading up the walkway toward the inn. The outside of the building was decorated for fall. Cornstalks and pumpkins were arranged on either side of the front entrance, and inside mums in yellows, oranges, and reddish purple were arranged everywhere. The place was lovely.

Ellie released Mason's hand to cross over to look at a series of old pictures lining one wall of the front hall. The pictures were actually tintypes of Mainers from the area during the 1900s. Ellie was leaning forward, studying a photo of three young women, when she heard flirty feminine laughter followed by Mason's deep chuckle.

She walked to the end of the entryway to see a tall, willowy redhead smiling at Mason. And there was no missing the interest in her dark eyes.

Ellie remained where she was, watching them. Listening.

"Are you from this area?" the redhead asked.

"No, from a small town outside of Bar Harbor," Mason told her. He wasn't looking at the woman but was instead writing something.

"Mmm, I love Bar Harbor."

Mason glanced up at the woman and nodded. "It's a nice part of Maine."

The redhead smiled at him, and although Ellie couldn't see Mason's face, she imagined he was grinning back. His dazzling, breathtaking smile.

They both stared at each other for a moment until Mason finally said, "Do I need a key?"

The woman released a startled laugh. "I'm sorry. Yes, of course." She turned away from him.

Mason also turned, leaning against the desk and casting a look around the lobby. Ellie ducked back into the hallway.

"Here you go," the redhead said. "Room 24. It's up those stairs." She pointed to a staircase that exited from a small sitting area to her left. "It has one of the best views."

"Thanks."

Ellie peeked back at them. Mason was walking away from the desk, but the redhead spoke again, stopping him. "So are you staying here alone?"

"I wasn't, but I appear to have lost my girlfriend," Mason said with a slight laugh. Ellie's heart thumped madly in her chest, and the woman behind the desk looked very disappointed.

"Thanks," Mason said again and headed back toward the front entrance. Ellie spun around and pretended to still be absorbed in the tintypes.

"Hey, there you are," he said. "I thought you had left me."

Ellie couldn't contain herself. She flung her arms around his neck, pressing her lips to his.

"What was that for?" he asked, a pleased smile on his lips when they parted.

"I'm just so happy."

He laughed. "Good. Me, too." He hugged her against him briefly before saying, "Okay, I'm going to get our stuff. Here's the key, if you want to go to the room. Room 24."

She took the key. "You don't need any help?"

"Nah."

She grinned as she watched him head outside. Then she turned back to the lobby. She stepped out of the hallway into the lobby. The redhead looked up as soon as she entered.

"May I help you?" she asked with a polite smile.

"No, thank you. I'm all set," Ellie said.

"Have you checked in?" The woman frowned. The inn was small enough that she must have realized she didn't recognize Ellie.

"No, well, yes, you just checked in my—boyfriend." As absurd as it was, referring to Mason that way made her feel almost giddy.

The redhead's frown deepened, and then a dawning realization widened her eyes. "Oh, yes." She smiled politely, but Ellie could tell the woman was assessing her. And Ellie could tell the redhead found her lacking. A strange match for a gorgeous man like Mason.

Some of her happiness faded, but she didn't look at the redhead again, instead climbing the stairs to find Room 24.

She located the room easily, inserted the key, and disappeared inside. She suddenly wished they had just stayed home. Here, she'd thought she wanted to be seen on Mason's arm, but now she wasn't so sure. She sat on the edge of the bed, feeling dejected.

There was a knock on the door, and she rose to answer it. Mason stood on the other side, his small overnight bag in one hand and her enormous tapestry suitcase in the other.

"What the heck do you have in here?" he asked good-naturedly as he struggled through the narrow doorway.

"I couldn't decide what to bring, so I brought a little of everything." She shrugged.

He shook his head with an indulgent smile. "Who knew flannel jammies weighed so much?"

He loved to rib her about her wide array of flannel pajamas. And normally she didn't mind. In fact, she thought he'd gained an appreciation for baggy flannels. She'd even bought him a pair, which he wore around the house, although he only wore the bottoms. She had to admit it was a very, very good look.

Then she thought of the svelte redhead downstairs. She bet that woman didn't wear dowdy old flannels to bed. And especially not when she had a magnificent hunk like Mason waiting for her.

"I like my pajamas," Ellie said defensively.

"I know you do."

"They are comfortable. They are warm. They are a very reasonable thing to wear to bed in Maine."

Mason nodded. "You get no argument here." His eyebrows drew together as he considered her. "Did I miss something? What happened to the very happy woman I left downstairs?"

Ellie sat back down on the bed. "Which woman, me or the redhead?"

Mason's frown deepened. "What?"

"That redhead was hitting on you."

"Okay, I definitely did miss something. What redhead?" He shook his head, confused. "What hitting on?"

Ellie sighed. "Nothing. It's nothing. Just forget it."

"No, what the hell happened? Did I do something to upset you?"

She immediately felt terrible. Mason had done nothing to upset her. In fact, he had acted just the way she would have hoped he would. She was the one making a big deal out of nothing. "I'm sorry, I guess I'm just more tired than I realized, and being unreasonable."

He came over and sat beside her, the bed dipping under his weight. Her shoulder bumped his. "Ellie, did someone say something to you? To upset you?"

She forced a smile. "No, I—I'm being silly." She sighed. "I watched you with the front desk clerk.

When you were checking in. She was interested in you."

Mason seemed puzzled. "She was?"

She nodded, embarrassed to be so insecure.

He shrugged. "I didn't notice. I was too busy wondering where I had lost this phenomenal blonde with whom I was supposed to spend the entire weekend."

Again she forced another smile, then looked down at her hands in her lap.

He turned so his body was facing hers and caught her chin between his forefinger and thumb. Gently, he brought her face up to look at his. "Angel, I didn't even notice that woman because I was thinking about you. Don't you understand that I'm not interested in anyone else? I want to be with you."

She fought the urge to blurt out, *For how long?* and *Why can't we just be a real couple?* But she simply stared into his eyes, trying to see inside his head. Trying to understand what he was really thinking. But she couldn't, of course.

"You do look tired," he said softly, tucking a curl behind her ear.

She felt tired. She felt old. This wasn't how love was supposed to make her feel. It was like being on a roller coaster of emotions. Except this roller coaster ran in the pitch dark, and she couldn't even prepare for the rises and the plunges because she couldn't see them.

"Maybe you should take a nap," Mason suggested. "You actually look a little pale."

"No, we just got here," she said. "I wanted to—do something."

"Do something, huh?" He gave her a suggestive look, but he grew serious. "We can do something later. Why don't you just rest."

She glanced at the pillows and the thick comforter. She did feel very tired. "Are you sure?"

He stood and pulled down the covers. "Come on, crawl in."

She toed off her mary janes and slipped under the blankets. The cool sheets and the weight of the covers felt good. She closed her eyes briefly, then opened them to find Mason. He still stood by the edge of the bed.

"What are you going to do?"

"I think I'll lie down with you, if that's okay?"

Ellie nodded. Despite her fatigue, her confusion, her doubts, there was still nothing she wanted more than this man beside her.

He slid under the sheet, pulling her against him so she could rest her head on his shoulder. They were both quiet. And even though Ellie thought it would take a while, she quickly drifted off into a deep sleep.

Chapter 21

Mason watched day fade into night and continued to hold Ellie. He carefully turned his head to look at the clock on the bedside table. It was nearly nine. She had been asleep for nearly four hours. Four hours that he'd just stayed beside her and thought.

He thought about her earlier reaction to the woman downstairs. He honestly hadn't even noticed the woman, but obviously whatever Ellie thought she saw shook her. He wished Ellie would understand and truly believe she was a beautiful woman. But he couldn't seem to convince her of that fact.

Of course, if he stopped the whole affair scenario, that might be a start. It was pretty damned hard for her to believe she was amazing when the man she was seeing didn't want a real relationship with her. But he did, and he knew she did, too. In fact, he was fairly sure she thought she was in love with him.

Actually, he knew she did. Ellie wore her heart on her sleeve. She couldn't hide a feeling to save her life. Her big blue eyes revealed everything, everything in her head—and in her heart. And he saw love there. The idea that she could love him was humbling; it was amazing.

She stirred beside him, squinting around the room. "It's dark. How long did I sleep?"

"A little over four hours."

She sat up. "My gosh, I'm sorry. I didn't mean to sleep that long."

Mason pushed upright, too, flipping on the lamp on the nightstand. "You needed it. Besides, I like just lying with you."

She gave him a dubious look.

"I do," he insisted. "What? Do you think I'm just a sex-fiend?"

She laughed. "No, I wouldn't say *fiend*."

He smirked back, but a wave of relief spread through him. She did look much better than she had earlier. Her cheeks were rosy, her eyes sparkling. "Are you hungry?"

She thought about it, then nodded. "Starving, actually."

"Well, let's go find a nice place to eat."

The Old Port was abuzz. The cobblestone streets were crowded with people, young and old, out for a good time on a Friday night. Ellie held Mason's hand as they walked up Cottage Street searching for a restaurant that looked interesting.

"How about this one?" Mason pointed to a tapas bar on the corner. The building itself was painted in yellows, oranges, and reds and looked very intriguing.

Ellie peered in the front window. The interior was done in polished wood, brick, and the same warm colors as the outside. The lighting was mellow with flickering candles on the tables. It looked inviting and fun. "Yes, this looks really neat."

Mason placed a hand on her lower back and ushered her toward the door. Warmth and the wonderful scents of different foods assailed them as they stepped into the restaurant. The place was busy, but a hostess seated them right away.

Once at their table, Ellie slipped off her long black

sweatercoat. She could feel Mason's eyes on her. She smiled at him. "What?"

"I love that dress," he stated.

She loved her dress, too. It was short and black with a ruffled hemline that swished when she moved and a bias-cut bodice that made her look curvy rather than stout.

"And I love when you do your hair that way."

She almost laughed about that. He had complimented her before when she had worn her hair up in her chopsticks. He seemed to find the tousled effect very attractive. She found it the easiest thing to do with the unruly mess. But if he liked it, all the better. "Thank you. You look great, too."

And he did. He looked fantastic. The V-neck, black cashmere sweater he wore accentuated his broad shoulders and lean frame. And his jeans fit him to a tee. He looked—well, yummy.

"Hello, folks. Can I start you off with a drink?" asked the waiter, holding out a wine menu.

"Wine?" Mason asked.

She shook her head. "I think I'll stick with a diet cola."

Mason seemed to hesitate, then said, "I'll take a beer."

"Thanks for coming this weekend," Mason said, once the waiter was gone.

"I wouldn't be anywhere else."

He studied her for a moment, and she had a feeling there was something on the tip of his tongue. But instead he smiled and said, "This place reminds me of you."

Ellie glanced around, taking in the restaurant's cool and unique décor. "Really?"

"The wood and bricks are classic, but the bright colors make it more alive, more interesting. It's cozy, but still very groovy."

She was captivated. Did he really see her that way? Ellie Stepp, classic, alive, interesting, cozy, and groovy. Did he see her as that complex? That remarkable?

She could feel her cheeks burn. "That's a wonderful compliment." The best compliment she'd ever gotten because his description was exactly what she wanted to be.

She reached across the table and squeezed his hand.

"Mason, is that you?"

They both turned to see an older couple approaching their table.

Mason immediately stood. "Mr. Edwards. Mrs. Edwards. How are you?"

Mr. Edwards grasped Mason's hand and shook it in a no-nonsense fashion. "How are you, son?"

"Fine, sir. And you two?"

"Not too bad. Never happy to see the cold weather coming. It really cuts into my golfing," Mr. Edwards said.

"Until we head to Florida after the holidays," Mrs. Edwards added long-sufferingly. "I can't keep this man off the links."

"How's Jim?" Mr. Edwards asked, not even acknowledging his wife's comment. "I heard he's still busy with the hotels and such."

Mason nodded. "My father shows no signs of stopping."

"I miss spending the afternoons with Elizabeth at the club," Mrs. Edwards said.

Mason nodded again.

"Now, who is this young lady?" Mrs. Edwards asked, smiling down at Ellie.

"This is Ellie Stepp, my girlfriend."

Ellie hadn't expected Mason to say that, to his parents' friends, no less. She was so surprised that it took her a moment to offer the older woman her hand.

Mrs. Edwards accepted it. "Are you from Millbrook, too?"

"Yes."

"We lived there . . . let's see, I guess it must have been almost ten years ago now."

"Stepp?" Mr. Edwards pondered the name. "Did your father own the shipyard in West Harbor?"

"No, my dad was a schoolteacher. History," Ellie said.

Mr. Edwards frowned like schoolteacher wasn't a career he'd ever heard of. He turned back to Mason. "So when am I going to see you on the ballot for governor? I expected it years ago, quite frankly."

Mason smiled, and Ellie could tell the gesture was forced. "Well, I'm pretty content where I am."

"Hmpf, I'm sure Jim is disappointed. As I recall, he had you slotted for the Senate by age thirty-five."

Mason's forced smile widened into something closer to a grimace. "Well, I'm sure my father has been disappointed with me in many aspects of my life, sir."

Mr. Edwards suddenly seemed to realize he had overstepped his bounds. Mrs. Edwards shifted uncomfortably.

"Well, Mason, it was nice to see you." Mr. Edwards looked over to Ellie. "Nice to meet you, as well."

"Please give your parents our best," Mrs. Edwards added as she scurried after her husband, who had already reached the restaurant door.

Mason watched them leave before he sat down again. The cheerful atmosphere was gone. Mason looked grim, his gray eyes like cold granite. He was silent for a few seconds; then he blinked over at her as if he were coming back from somewhere very far away. "I'm sorry. That was . . ."

"Unpleasant," Ellie finished for him and immediately flushed with remorse. That wasn't fair. She'd barely met them, but she hadn't liked the things they'd said to Mason. He didn't deserve to be treated as though he wasn't a success. He was mayor. A good mayor.

He seemed startled at her response, but then a smile crossed his lips and some of the coldness left his eyes. "Yeah. Yeah, that was unpleasant."

Ellie started to reach across the table to hold his hand, but the waiter returned with their drinks.

Mason downed half his beer before she even got her straw out of the wrapper.

"Let's just forget that even happened," Mason declared, then polished off the remainder of his beer.

Ellie watched him, concerned. But when he lowered his glass, she asked brightly, "Are you hungry?" She opened her menu, but she didn't think either of them was particularly hungry anymore.

However, dinner did go better than she had expected. Mason drank four beers in rapid succession, but once he started to eat, he slowed down. She supposed he had a right to drink a bit. What Mr. Edwards had said was inexcusably rude, and she got the feeling that it had hit a little too close to home for Mason.

Mason didn't mention his parents very often. She knew they lived out on Whitford Road, where all the wealthy residents of Millbrook lived. She knew that Mason's dad owned several hotels up and down the Maine coast. But other than that, Ellie didn't know much about them.

"So," Mason said, reaching for one of the delicious stuffed mussels, "I bet you are wondering what my parents are like if they have such pleasant friends."

She paused from nibbling the spinach empanada she'd just picked up. "No," she said too quickly, discomfited that he had guessed exactly what she was thinking about.

"My mother is a wonderful person. We're close, or

pretty close. She'd tell you I don't visit enough," he said with an enchanting smile that Ellie was sure he used on his mother when she scolded him for that exact infraction. "But my father, well, he's like Mr. Edwards. Aggressive, opinionated, controlling. We get along, but he makes no bones about the fact that I have been a big disappointment to him."

"I can't believe that," Ellie said. "You got excellent grades in school. You were the quarterback. You went to Yale. You're Millbrook's mayor. How can he not be proud?"

His charming smile withered to little more than a sardonic twist of his lips. "Because I wasn't valedictorian. I didn't get any scouts out to look at my football playing. I did not get into Harvard. And I'm not a senator." He reached for his beer.

Ellie was stunned. She couldn't imagine not being proud of a son like Mason. Millbrook had always considered him their 'golden boy.' She could remember that, in high school, a lot of the businesses in town would close early during football season when there was a home game. That had been because of Mason. And when he had decided to run for mayor, he had won by a landslide. People in Millbrook saw it as the town's golden boy coming home to do good. And he was a good mayor.

In his five years in office, he'd gotten the financing to restore the waterfront, which had been in a terrible state. That one move had increased the town's revenue immeasurably, not only by helping the commercial fishing, but also by building up the tourist industry. He'd put more focus on education. He'd reworked several areas of the town budget so there were more monies for children's programs. He did care about his hometown.

"But doesn't your father see all the good you've done for Millbrook? You've made such a tremendous difference." Ellie shook her head. How could his father not see that?

"My dad measures success by how much power you have. And how many people know your name."

"All of Millbrook knows your name."

He smiled, cynicism still there, but not as much. "Yeah, but all of Maine could. And better yet, all of Washington, D.C., could."

"Well, I'm proud of you," she stated. "And I think you are extremely successful."

Mason studied Ellie. Her cheeks were pink, and her eyes glittered. She chomped on her food as if she'd like to be chewing out his father. His Ellie always jumping to his defense. It felt good.

She looked at him, frowning. "I just don't understand how a father couldn't be proud of his child. Even if my child was a ditchdigger, if he was a hard worker and honest, I would be as proud as if he were the president."

"Well, it would be great if you were my father." Then he paused and gave her a horrified look. "No, wait, if you were my father, our relationship would definitely be very bizarre, and just way too creepy."

She shook her head and laughed. "I think it's best we don't even go there."

"Agreed." He was happy to see her smile, and some of the distress had left her eyes. Although he liked her support, he liked seeing her having fun much better.

"Did you try this one?" he asked, picking up a small piece of toast with a meat spread and a sprig of parsley on it.

She eyed it suspiciously. "Isn't that the anchovy thing?"

He nodded, holding the bread out to her. "Yes, it's delicious. Try it."

She shook her head. "I really don't like anchovies."

"It doesn't even taste like anchovies."

She shook her head again.

"Chicken." He popped it into his mouth.

"Yep," she said, quite agreeably, and he had to smile.

"So where would you like to go after this?" Mason asked.

She looked at him almost coyly. Definitely coy for Ellie. "I think I'd like to go back to the inn."

He gave her a speculative look. "Are you sure? This is your weekend."

"Well, if this is my weekend, then I definitely want to go back to the inn."

Damn, he adored this woman.

When they got back to their room, Ellie disappeared into the bathroom. Mason undressed, pulling on the pajama bottoms Ellie had given him. She did have a point; flannel was very comfortable. Then he sprawled on the bed to wait for her.

Fifteen minutes later he was still waiting. He set down the room service menu he'd been reading to kill time and got up. Crossing over to the bathroom door, he listened. The room was silent. He knocked softly. "Ellie, are you okay?"

There was another moment of silence; then the door opened, and Ellie peeked out. She looked like she was on the verge of tears.

Alarmed, he asked, "What's wrong?"

She turned a brilliant shade of crimson right before his eyes. "I—I bought lingerie for tonight."

He nodded, now torn between concern and anticipation.

"And I—I can't figure out how to put it on," she

blurted out. She thrust a scrap of lace, silk, ties, and straps at him.

He looked at it, pulling at first one strap, then another. He tugged one of the straps, and the silky material wadded into a tight ball. He shrugged. "I have no idea. It's like origami for the sexually frustrated."

That seemed to be the right thing to say because she began to giggle. "I hope you aren't disappointed that I'll be wearing my usual flannel."

"Are you kidding? Flannel is like an aphrodisiac for me now. My own pajamas turn me on."

She giggled, giving his p.j. bottoms a significant look. "Okay, then I guess I'd better hurry." She closed the door again, but she opened it right back up. "I was wondering . . ." Her cheeks started to turn pink again. "Have you ever had sex in a shower?"

He'd had sex in a shower several times, but there was no way in hell he was telling her that. Not if it meant he couldn't have sex with her in the shower now. "Nope, never."

She smiled, her dimples deepening. "Good." She opened the door, and he quickly stepped inside.

Much later, they crawled into bed, squeaky clean and very, very satisfied.

Mason flipped off the bedside lamp, but the light from the bathroom cast a dim, indirect light throughout the room.

Ellie cuddled against him and stroked his chest, brushing her fingers over the smattering of hair.

He caressed the smooth skin of her back, tracing the length of her spine.

She shivered.

He smiled.

"Are you sure you've never had sex in a shower before?" she asked suddenly.

His hand paused. "Not with you."

"I thought you had." She didn't sound hurt, just smug that she'd guessed right.

"I've never, never enjoyed it like that before, though." He could say that with all honesty.

"Not even with Marla."

Mason's hand stilled again. He was taken off guard. Ellie hadn't asked anything specific about his ex-wife. Not about his feelings for Marla, anyway.

"Actually, I honestly never did have sex with Marla in a shower. Or any place outside of a bed, for that matter."

"Really?" Ellie sounded astounded.

Of course, given the variety of places they'd made love, it must seem a bit strange to her. "Marla didn't like things . . . unusual."

"Unusual? Is it unusual to make love in a shower?"

"No, but Marla would have thought so. She was a standard bed/missionary-position type gal. She was very conservative, very controlled."

"I wouldn't have guessed that."

"Why?"

"I just can't picture you with someone like that."

"Well, we *are* divorced."

Ellie continued to run her fingers lightly up and down his chest. "Did you divorce because the two of you were too different?"

Mason's first reaction was to steer the conversation toward a less personal subject. That is what he always did. But he realized he wanted to tell Ellie about his marriage. He wanted her to understand.

"I met Marla at Yale. My freshman year. But we didn't start dating until our sophomore year." He hesitated, knowing that Ellie might be uncomfortable with his disclosures, but he felt she deserved to understand exactly how things had been with Marla. "I'll admit I was quite taken with her. She was different from the girls I'd known in Millbrook. She was refined, cultured. She had this drive and decisive attitude that I found appealing. And she had this way about her that just made a person want to please her. I was no different."

Ellie's hand stopped moving over his chest. "So you fell in love right away."

He smiled; leave it to his Ellie to want to turn this story into a great romance, even at the expense of her own emotions. "No." He shook his head. "I mean, I guess I thought I was in love. It's hard for me to tell now. But I don't think Marla was ever in love with me. She just thought we were a good match."

Ellie sat up, frowning down at him. "How could she possibly think you were a good match if she didn't love you?"

He smiled again, amazed at how simply Ellie saw the world. She really did believe that "love was all you need." He brushed a wayward curl from her cheek and continued, "I was pre-law. I was considering a career in politics. I was from a wealthy family. Marla liked that. But more importantly, our families liked the match."

Again, she seemed confused.

"I was on my way to becoming a successful attorney. My father, and Marla's father for that matter, were definitely pushing me toward politics."

"But what did Marla want?"

Mason snorted. "To be the next Jackie Kennedy."

"Didn't she want a career of her own?"

"Marla considered being a politician's wife a perfect career. Chairing committees, organizing service groups."

"But I don't recall her doing anything like that in Millbrook."

He laughed humorlessly. "With Marla, it wasn't

about actually getting into the nitty-gritty and helping the community. It was about being recognized, receiving adulation. Who of importance was going to see her good deeds in Millbrook?"

Ellie looked appalled.

"Marla, just like my father, expected that I was going to be in D.C. by my thirties. You can imagine her dismay when I finally agreed to go into politics only to realize that I really loved small town government."

"So she just left?"

He nodded. "I heard she's already engaged to a senator from New York. So to answer your initial question, we did divorce because we were too different. We were too different, and we were living a charade."

She shook her head, perplexed, then laid her head on his chest. "Was any of your marriage happy?"

He thought about it. "I guess. It's funny, but now it all seems a bit like a dream. We spent so many years not actually seeing each other but seeing what we wanted each other to be. I don't know."

She lifted her head. "I can't imagine wanting anything more than this. Being able to just lie here with you."

Tightness squeezed his chest, and he knew he had to tell her that he wanted more from her than an affair. But the words stuck in his throat.

Instead, he cupped a hand around the back of her head, tangling his fingers in her curls, and kissed her.

When they parted, she put her head back on his chest. After a few moments of silence, she said in a very matter-of-fact voice, "She'd die if she knew we did it on her antique credenza."

He laughed, hugging her.

Chapter 22

The next morning Ellie woke up several times, only to roll over and fall back asleep. When she finally managed to struggle out of the overwhelming tiredness that seemed to weight her limbs, she was shocked to see it was after noon. How had she slept so late?

Mason wasn't in bed. She listened and heard him in the bathroom. Water was running, and he was humming—just slightly off-key.

She leaned back on the pillows, feeling content. Her eyes started to drift shut again when Mason stuck his head out of the bathroom door.

"Hey, sleepyhead, you up?"

She blinked at him, nodding.

He grinned at her, his cheeks and chin covered with shaving cream. "Come in here and keep me company."

She crawled off the bed and trundled into the bathroom, settling on the closed toilet seat.

Mason returned to the mirror and began shaving, each stroke revealing more of his sharp jawline and sullen chin.

She watched, fascinated.

"So, what's the plan for today?" he asked between swipes of the razor.

"I'm up for anything."

He caught her gaze in the mirror. "Are you sure?

You look a little pale again today. Do you feel all right?"

"I feel fine." She did. Now that she was up, the exhaustion seemed to be fading, and she felt . . . "Actually, I'm starving."

"Okay, want to just eat here, then head to the museum for the afternoon?"

"Sounds perfect."

"Okay," Mason said, looking at the map of the museum. "Do you want to walk through or go straight to the new exhibit?"

Ellie turned from admiring a painting by Andrew Wyeth. "Let's walk; I haven't been here in years."

He nodded, more than willing to take a leisurely pace and enjoy the artwork.

They wandered hand in hand, talking quietly about the paintings. Occasionally they would just pause and admire a piece, neither of them feeling the need to say anything. And he couldn't help but notice that Ellie was just as beautiful as the artwork. He loved watching her expressions as she looked at the different pieces. And again, he found himself wanting to ask her if she would consider having a real relationship with him.

"Look at this," she exclaimed as she approached a marble sculpture of a young man washed ashore, a diver's net draped over his nude body. "That's remarkable."

She circled around the statue, studying it with amazement clear in her eyes. "I feel like I could touch him, and he would be alive, his skin warm."

Even though he knew it was ridiculous, he actually felt a pang of jealousy at the way she admired the carved man. "Well, he would actually be cold," he informed her. "He's titled *The Dead Pearl Diver.*"

Ellie frowned. "Oh, that's awful. I don't want to think of him as dead. He's too beautiful."

Mason caught her hand and tugged her against him, leading her away from the marble figure. "Okay, that's enough looking at him."

She glanced up at him, confused. Then a dawning smile curved her lips. "You're jealous," she said with incredulity.

He grimaced at her. "No."

She stopped, beaming up at him. "You are! You're jealous of a marble sculpture."

He shrugged. "Maybe."

"Oh, poor baby," she murmured and rose up onto her tiptoes to kiss him.

When they parted, they simply stood grinning at each other like fools.

"Mason?"

He turned abruptly at the sound of a familiar voice.

Natalie came toward them, a surprised smile on her face. "Mason, that is you." She gave him a quick hug.

"Natalie," he said stiffly, a sinking feeling in his stomach. "How are you? What are you doing here?"

"I'm here with my folks." She glanced over his shoulder at Ellie. "Who's your friend?"

"Oh." He turned back to Ellie, who regarded Natalie with wide, troubled eyes. "This is Ellie Stepp."

"Hi," Ellie said, hesitating before offering the other woman her hand.

"Hi, nice—" Natalie paused, recognition crossing her face. "Wait, you're the woman from the Bear's Den. Mason, you told me you didn't know her."

Ellie's eyes snapped to Mason's, and he saw pain darkening their blue depths.

"Excuse me," she said in a shaky voice, pivoted on her heel and headed toward the front entrance of the museum.

Natalie gave him a bewildered look. "I didn't mean to offend her."

"You didn't. I did," he assured her quickly. "Listen, I've got to go." He started after Ellie before he even saw Natalie's reaction. He wasn't worried about Natalie. He was, however, definitely worried about Ellie.

He rushed through the museum, garnering a suspicious look from the security guard. He darted out onto the sidewalk and looked around. The street was busy, and it took several seconds to locate Ellie, sitting on a park bench.

She looked pale and drawn into herself.

"Ellie," he said softly as he took slow steps toward her. He half expected her to flee again, but she remained seated, staring straight ahead. "It isn't like you think."

She continued to stare as if she hadn't heard him.

"I don't know why I told—"

Ellie stood up. "I just want to go home."

"But Ellie—"

She held up a hand, regarding him with hurt, resentful eyes. "I don't want to talk about it. Not right now. Please."

He nodded, hoping that if he gave her a chance to sort through her thoughts, then she would let him tell her . . .

What? The truth? He didn't even understand why he'd denied knowing her. But he had to make her understand that the stupid comment had never been meant to hurt her.

She started walking in the direction of his car, and he fell into step beside her, but not getting too close. She needed space. He understood that.

Ellie didn't even realize they were back at the inn until Mason parked the car and came around to open her door. Her head had been too cluttered with terrible thoughts, painful thoughts. Mason had told Natalie he didn't know her. Why? All the obvious answers were just too hurtful. Too humiliating.

She ignored the hand he offered as she got out of his car. She also refused to look at his eyes. If she did, she might cry. She wasn't going to cry. Even though tears were strangling her, making it nearly impossible to breathe.

With more strength than she knew she had, she simply strode into the inn, never acknowledging him.

Once in the room they'd shared, she struggled her suitcase onto the bed and began gathering her things.

Mason, who had been waiting by the door, stepped forward and flipped the suitcase closed. "Ellie, we have to talk about this."

She remained rooted in the center of the room, toiletries clutched in her hands. "I think we should just go home."

He caught her hands, taking her items from her numb fingers. He tossed them on the bed. Then he took her hands again. "Please, Ellie, tell me what you're thinking."

Why should she have to tell him? Why should she have to give voice to all her uncertainties, all her worst fears? "Why don't you tell me what *you* were thinking?" She glared up at him.

He hesitated.

The brief pause was enough to snap something inside her. She jerked her hands out of his. "Just keeping your options open, right? I guess you knew Natalie would have enough self-esteem not to sleep with you if she thought you were interested in another woman. Unlike me." She snorted, furious with herself, angry that she was so—so pathetic.

"I'm not interested in anyone but you." His gray eyes were pleading. "You have to believe that."

Ellie crossed her arms over her chest, feeling the

need to shield herself from the sincerity she saw on his face. She didn't want to submit to him, to those eyes. Not again.

"Just tell me the truth. Just one truth," she said as she crossed to the other side of the room, needing to put space between them.

He nodded, waiting for her to continue.

"You don't want people in Millbrook to know about us because you're ashamed of me, aren't you?" Tears threatened to suffocate her again.

"What?" He seemed taken aback and then outraged. "No!"

She gave him a disbelieving look. "Please," she whispered, "just admit it."

"No!" he insisted. "Why would I be ashamed of you?"

She stared at him, and then she threw her arms out to her sides. "Because I'm overweight. Because I'm frumpy. Because I'm boring."

"How can you think that?" He appeared honestly staggered. "You have to know I think you are beautiful. Damn it, Ellie, I'm half out of my mind every time I'm around you. I want you more than any woman I've ever met." He moved so he was close to her again, but he didn't try to touch her.

She was thankful he didn't, afraid she would break down. Her mind warred between wanting to believe him and still not having the answers she needed. "There is a difference between finding me attractive, alone in a room, and admitting it to other people."

"Is that really what you think?"

She looked down at the floor, then nodded her head slightly.

"Oh, Ellie," he sounded as devastated as she felt. "I never, never meant for you to feel that way." This time he did touch her, cupping his large hand to her cheek. "Ellie, angel, I didn't want people to know about us because I was offering you a fling, and I didn't want your reputation to be ruined."

She blinked up at him, irritated that tears had started to blur her vision. "It's my reputation. I think I should be the one who decides how to handle it."

He stroked his thumb over her cheek, then nodded. "You're right. But you have to believe me—you are the most gorgeous, amazing woman in the world. And embarrassment was definitely *not* the reason why I told Natalie I didn't know you. Nor was it to keep my options open. From the first time I kissed you, my options were limited to just one person." He leaned forward and brushed his lips against hers. "Please forgive me."

Ellie accepted the gentle kiss, but instead of feeling comforted, she felt like she was going to splinter. It was all becoming too much. Too painful.

She pulled away. "Mason, I feel—I don't feel well. Please, I just need to rest. Please."

He looked like he was going to argue, but then he nodded. He placed her suitcase on the floor beside his. Then he scooped up her scattered toiletries and threw them on the closed case.

She sank onto the edge of the bed and shrugged out of her coat, then tugged off her shoes, feeling totally drained.

The sun was already beginning to set. She lay back against the pillows and closed her eyes. Maybe after she rested, her jumbled emotions would untangle and her thoughts would become clearer.

Mason sat in a chair across from the bed, watching Ellie. He could tell by the rise and fall of her chest that she was sleeping. But without that faint movement, she would have looked like the statue she'd admired earlier today.

Was that only today? It seemed like eons ago that

she'd been smiling and laughing. Now she just looked exhausted, depleted. Her skin appeared almost gray in the waning light.

He ran a hand over his eyes, pinching the bridge of his nose. What the hell was he doing?

He knew he'd been selfish starting this affair with her, but he truly didn't know the toll it had been taking on her. Not until now.

He looked back over at her. He'd realized Ellie was insecure about her looks. But he'd never once considered that she would think his reason for secrecy was that he was ashamed of her. And he got the distinct feeling she still believed that was his real reasoning. Or at least part of it.

His Ellie, who was so generous, so trusting, so beautiful, inside and out. How could he ever be ashamed of her?

He sighed. He wanted to crawl into bed and hold her, but he knew she didn't want him near her right now. Maybe she was going to decide she didn't want him anymore, period. Could he blame her?

He looked at the bedside clock. It was almost six. The inn's bar had to be open.

A noise woke Ellie. She blinked into the darkness, making out a dark figure looming at the foot of the bed. "Mason?"

He shifted. "Yeah, it's me." His voice sounded funny, thick as if he had cotton in his mouth, nothing like his usual smooth drawl.

She sat up. "Are you okay?" She glanced at the clock. It was after one in the morning.

"No." He moved again, but this time she realized he was swaying.

"Are you sick?"

"No. Well, maybe." He came around the side of the

bed, using his hands, one over the other on the mattress to steady himself. When he reached the head of the bed, he collapsed beside her.

He rolled over so he was facing her, and he reached up to graze his fingers over her hair. Then he touched her face, cupping his hand to her cheek. "Ah, angel, how am I ever going to convince you how beautiful you are? How much you mean to me?"

She accepted his caress, pressing her face against his palm. He slipped his hand around to the back of her head, tangling his fingers into her curls, and pulled her mouth to his.

She could taste a smoky tang on his lips, a flavor she'd tasted on him before, but until now she'd never realized what it was. Never realized it was liquor.

She started to pull away, but he held her. His lips still lightly against hers, he whispered, "I need you. God, Ellie, how I need you."

He kissed her again, and this time she responded, trying to tell him she was there for him. That she needed him, too.

He broke the kiss and fell back on the pillows, watching her through barely open eyes. He touched her face again. "Forgive me?"

"Of course," she answered immediately, but she didn't think he heard her.

His hand left her cheek, dropping heavily on the mattress as he fell into unconsciousness.

She pulled up her knees and rested her head on them, watching his dark form.

He remained motionless. The faint scent of alcohol reached her nose. She buried her face into the sleeve of her shirt.

She was still hurt and overwhelmed by Mason and their relationship, but she was beginning to understand that things in his past had injured him, too.

She turned her face back to him. In the faint

moonlight, she could see his shadowed features. She was also beginning to realize that Charlie Grace's concern for Mason might be justified.

Chapter 23

The trip home from Portland was very quiet and more than a little awkward. Ellie didn't talk much, mostly looking out the window or dozing, which was fine. Mason had a raging headache and didn't think he could talk much anyway. It was hard enough to concentrate on the road at the moment. But he did intend to talk to her about their situation, once he didn't feel quite so awful.

Of course, it would be easier to talk with her if he could remember anything that had happened. All he remembered was heading to the bar, and sitting there and having a few whiskey and waters, but he had no idea how he'd gotten back to the room.

Ellie hadn't asked about where he'd been last night, but he supposed she knew. He was relieved Ellie hadn't made a big deal about it this morning, though. He didn't feel like having to explain himself to yet another person.

She didn't even seem upset when he asked her if she minded cutting the trip short. She actually looked a little relieved.

The relaxed, happy atmosphere of the trip was gone, and he thought they both needed to do a little reflecting about their situation. Not that he wanted their relationship to end, but he did have to consider what he could realistically give Ellie. And if what he could give her would really be enough.

But he'd decide that once his head stopped pounding.

"Do you want me to come in?" she asked as they pulled up his driveway and parked next to her car.

"I think I could actually use a little sleep."

She nodded, her smile kind, but her eyes clouded with uncertainty.

He was such a selfish jerk, he told himself, but he still didn't ask her in. *Coward.*

Her smile, although wooden, widened a bit more. "I could use a little rest, too."

She did look tired. Undoubtedly from dealing with their whole situation.

He helped her get her luggage into her trunk. When she would have just gotten into her car, he pulled her against him, kissing her with all the emotion he couldn't seem to label.

She kissed him back the same way, touching his jaw and stroking his hair.

He chose to see her response as a good sign, a sign he could fix things. "I'll call later to see how you're feeling," he told her.

She nodded, but there was sadness in her eyes. Whether it was because she doubted him, or because she wasn't sure she wanted him to call, he didn't know.

The shrill ring of the telephone woke Ellie as she dozed on the sofa. But by the time she reached the phone, whoever was on the other end had hung up.

She squinted at the clock on the VCR; the glowing numbers read after nine o'clock in the evening. She must have fallen asleep while she was trying to read. Considering she hadn't been able to control her whizzing thoughts long enough to finish a single page, she was surprised she'd been able to fall asleep.

She must have a bug or something. She couldn't remember ever being so tired.

A shower sounded wonderful, she decided, and maybe it would clear her muzzy head. She stopped in her room to undress and pull on her bathrobe, then proceeded to the bathroom.

She'd hoped being away from Mason would help her organize her thoughts, but it hadn't. Too many things had happened that weekend, and she just couldn't seem to sort out her thoughts or her feelings about any of it.

No, that wasn't true. She'd think she had everything sorted out in her mind; then another question would occur to her and her feelings would be jumbled again. Her thoughts were like a string of Christmas lights hopelessly knotted, and when she thought she had one end unraveled, she would realize the other end was still a huge mess.

Only two things had stayed continuously clear throughout all her untangling. Mason, the man she had always considered perfect, had problems. And she loved him—perfect or troubled.

As she waited for the water to get warm, she remembered the shower she'd taken with him at the inn. Even three weeks ago, she couldn't imagine ever being comfortable enough to do such a thing. Her newfound confidence was Mason's doing. He made her feel beautiful and self-assured.

The Natalie thing had shaken her, made her feel like the old insecure Ellie. But she realized she didn't feel upset about the incident now. Maybe she was horribly naïve, but she believed Mason. He had seemed as upset about the whole situation as she'd been.

In fact, he'd seemed flabbergasted when she'd suggested that he didn't want people to know about them because he was ashamed. He had even referred to Ellie as his girlfriend—twice. Granted, it was to a desk clerk whom he'd likely never see again, and to his parents' old friends who hadn't seen Mason's folks in years. But still, it was a start, and she wanted to believe him.

Plus, Mason had told her all about his parents and his marriage. Those were private things. Topics she knew he didn't talk about easily. Yet, he had with her. That meant he trusted her.

She walked to the mirror over the sink. Her image was muted, softened by the beginnings of steam on the glass.

She thought about Mason's compliment in the restaurant. That she was interesting, classic, alive . . . groovy. He didn't have to tell her that. Heaven knew, she was already putty in his hands without flattery.

She rubbed her hand over the mirror, and her reflection stared back at her, now clear and vivid. Could she see the person he'd described? She focused on the woman in the mirror, really trying to see her.

She touched her golden hair, which was thick and shiny, the curls untamed and—unruly. Her hand moved down to her cheek and she smiled. Dimples deepened, making the grin inviting and sort of cute. But it was her eyes that seemed to be the focal point of the face in the mirror. Big, very blue, and pretty, really.

After a moment's hesitation, she let the robe drop to the floor, and she could see bare shoulders and the top of cleavage. The shoulders were rounded, but the skin was smooth and creamy. Nice skin. Her breasts didn't look as heavy as she'd once thought but more full and rounded.

She was that woman in the mirror, and while that woman would never be considered gorgeous, she was nice-looking. She *was* pretty.

Those were only physical characteristics, she realized,

but she doubted her looks more than she doubted any-thing else. She knew she was a good person, a kind person.

Okay, she might have been a bit dull, but she didn't feel that way now. Since Mason had come into her life, she felt alive, interesting, and even a little wild.

She could see the person Mason had described, and it was even more wonderful because the man she loved truly saw her, even before she did.

She left the mirror and stepped into the shower. She closed her eyes and let the hot water run over her, pushing her hair back from her face.

She wanted to be with Mason; it was as simple as that. Was she just a hopeless romantic, clinging to only the good things between them? Probably. But that was who she was, too, a romantic and hopelessly in love.

She had to believe that Mason's opening up to her and flattering her meant that she was important to him. More important than just a simple affair. But she also knew she wasn't going to make things better by pushing him. She had to take whatever Mason could offer. That had been true from the beginning, and she realized nothing had changed.

People in his past had hurt him, made him feel like a failure. Mason had scars that had made him wary and guarded. Today she'd felt him pulling away. But she thought that had more to do with his drinking than her. She hoped. She hoped he'd let her help him. He did need help.

She was amazed at how calmly she was handling this. Old Ellie would have been a mess, but there was one thing that was keeping her composed. Mason had told her he needed her. She believed that.

The steam must be clearing her head. Everything seemed so obvious now. She planned to be with Mason. He might not be in love with her, but he did need her.

* * *

Mason dialed his cell phone again as he drove. Once again, Ellie's telephone just rang until after the seventh ring, he punched the 'end' button.

He'd told himself that he wouldn't go to her. He thought she needed space and time to think, just as he did. Even though he'd been doing nothing all day except wishing he was with her. But he'd also told her he'd call to check on her.

So when she didn't answer after his second attempt, he decided he'd better go to her house and make sure she was okay. What if she was so ill she was unable to answer his call? He had to go check on her.

What if she wasn't answering the phone because she didn't want to talk to him? What if she was thinking their whole relationship was too hard? Too complicated?

Those thoughts caused him to clench the steering wheel tighter and press the accelerator harder to the floorboard.

She wasn't going to end things. She wasn't. He knew he'd seen love, or something very close to it, in her expressive blue eyes. He'd seen it many times. When they made love, at the restaurant, in his bedroom when he'd showed her he'd changed the furniture. But he'd also seen distrust and disillusion after they ran into Natalie. Those emotions hadn't quite disappeared when she'd left today.

He supposed getting intoxicated hadn't improved her faith in him. But he'd been uptight about hurting her, and he'd needed to unwind and think. A few drinks made that easier. Not a big deal.

He should apologize again about Natalie. He had never meant to hurt Ellie. She was the last person he'd want to hurt.

But you are hurting her. By not offering her a real relationship, you are devastating her.

He pulled his car into her driveway behind hers and turned off the ignition. He'd told her about Marla. Surely she understood that he wasn't all that keen on marriage. Marriage was not on his agenda.

But she wasn't asking for marriage. She was just asking for them to be a couple outside of the bedroom. He could offer her that, right? He wanted her, he cared about her. Why was he so damned reluctant to give her more? What was he afraid of?

He got out of the car and walked up to her back door. He knocked, but there was no answer. He knocked again. Nothing. No noise from the other side.

He tried the doorknob; the door was locked. Well, at least she'd gotten more prudent about locking her house. Unfortunately, that made it harder for him.

He looked around for a place where a spare key might be hidden. There was an ornamental frog holding an umbrella sitting in a patch of now-dead daisies near the steps. He picked the decoration up, and sure enough, the little amphibian had a hole in the bottom and an extra key fell out into his palm.

Too easy. Apparently, they still had some work to do on her security system.

He slid the key into the door lock and entered her kitchen. The light over the sink was on, and a lamp in the living room burned. He could hear the faint notes of oldies playing on the stereo, but other than that, the house was quiet.

He walked through the living room and into the hall. At the bottom of the stairs, he listened. He could hear the shower.

Ellie in the shower. Now that was one of his very favorite things. He headed up the stairs, but outside the door, stopped.

What was he doing? He'd essentially broken into

her house, and now he was just planning to barge in
on her while she showered. He really was becoming
a stalker.

He debated leaving, or at least waiting for her in the
bedroom. Or maybe, if he was feeling extra civil, the
living room, but then he changed his mind.

Ellie was his lover. His. And he wanted to see her.
He needed to know she was all right. He needed to
see those expressive blue eyes.

He turned the knob slowly and eased the door
open. She was still in the shower, and from the bil-
lowing steam that filled the room, she'd been in there
for quite a while.

Carefully he pulled the thick bath towel from the
rack near the tub and crept to the toilet, which was situated directly across from the tub. He eased the lid of
the toilet down and sat to wait.

He could get arrested for this sort of behavior.

She began to sing "I Woke Up In Love This Morning," which in Mason's estimations was well worth a
little jail time to hear. Her voice was actually quite nice
and echoed off the tub tiles, making him feel he was
surrounded by her.

She sang to the second chorus; then the shower
stopped. She began to sing again from the beginning.
The shower curtain slid open, and her pleasant
singing turned into a startled squeak.

"Mason!" She gaped at him as she clapped an arm
across her breasts and a hand over her golden curls at
the juncture of her thighs.

A slow grin spread over his lips. She made quite a
picture. Wet, eyes wide, cheeks flushed. "Hi," he said.

She stared at him for a moment longer. Then, to his
utter shock, she moved her hands to her hips, regarding him like he was an errant boy making noise
in the library, and she was, of course, the strict librarian lady.

Although, she was a gloriously naked, wet, and voluptuous librarian. She stole his breath.

"I'm honestly starting to believe you have a penchant for breaking and entering," she said, her voice a bit exasperated, but some of the sternness left her features.

It took several seconds before he could get his overwhelmed mind to make a coherent thought, and even then, he managed only a nod.

She reached around the shower curtain to the towel rack, only to discover it was empty.

Her movement seemed to click something in his brain, and he rose, holding out her towel.

Again, to his surprise, she simply stepped out of the tub and walked into the open terry cloth.

He was torn. He hated to lose the amazing view of her, but he desperately wanted to touch all that warm, damp skin.

"So did you break into my house just to come help me dry off?"

He shook his head, rubbing the towel down one of her arms. "This is a bonus."

She smiled slightly, then held out her other arm for him to dry, all the while staring directly into his eyes.

His heart pounded so hard in his chest he was positive she must be able to hear it. He brushed the towel down her other arm. Then he turned her so he could dry her shoulders and her back. He couldn't help touching his fingers to the twin dimples at either side of her spine, right over her rounded bottom.

He then shifted her back to face him. He looked into her eyes, which were now heavy-lidded with desire. Good, at least he wasn't the only one affected here. Her reaction to his touch gave him hope. Hope that everything between them was okay. That they could just continue on as before.

He patted the towel to her neck, then to her chest, and finally to those full, gorgeous breasts.

She gasped as the towel grazed her nipples.

"Sensitive?" he murmured, mesmerized by the way the rosy buds puckered and pointed. Begging him to touch them.

He wanted to. God, he wanted to. But he had come here with a purpose other than ravishing her on her bathroom floor.

As perfunctorily as possible, he finished toweling her off; then he grabbed her robe from the floor and held it open for her.

She slipped her arms in, but there was a disappointed look on her face as she turned back to him. "I think that is the first time you've actually dressed me."

He smiled regretfully. "Believe me, that isn't my first inclination here, but I think we need to talk."

She hesitated, like she was going to say something. Then she nodded. "I think you're right. Do you want some coffee?"

"That would be good." He followed her downstairs.

She began to move around the kitchen, getting out the coffee and filters, going to the sink to fill the pot.

He leaned against the kitchen door-frame, watching her. The way she moved, the faint sound of her feet padding on the worn linoleum, the way her tiny hands looked graceful doing the simplest things. Somehow, their affair had turned into something more. Something where watching Ellie make coffee was as captivating to him as making love to her.

Okay, maybe not quite as captivating as making love. But as fundamental. As necessary.

It scared the shit out of him. He couldn't have a real relationship. Real relationships just did not work for him.

"Can't things just stay like this?" he said suddenly, whether to himself or her, he wasn't sure.

Ellie paused, a measuring spoon in her hand. "Like what? Me making coffee?"

He nodded. "You making coffee. Us hanging out. Making love. Having fun. Can't we continue on just like this?"

She considered him for a minute; then her dimples deepened enchantingly. "I think we already are."

He returned her smile, but then he added seriously, "Ellie, I don't know if this can ever be anything more. I just don't know. And I can't expect you to settle for this."

She walked over to him and touched her hand to his cheek. "I want to be with you. All I have ever wanted was to be with you."

He didn't know how to respond to the sincerity in her eyes or the gentleness in her touch. He'd told himself that he wanted to see the love in her eyes that he'd seen before. Well, there it was. And now he didn't want to see it. He didn't want her to love him, he didn't deserve it. He should walk away, right now, and let this incredible woman find real love with a real man.

But he didn't. Like the greedy bastard he was, he took the tender kiss she offered him.

She smiled up at him, gently touched his hair, and then returned to her coffee machine. She looked back over to him with an adorable, saucy grin. "Besides, we'd better continue this thing. Or else I'm serving coffee to some strange man who just broke into my house."

Chapter 24

"Prescott, do you know who checked out all the books on substance abuse?" Ellie asked her coworker in a quiet voice.

He looked up from the computer, where he was entering the newly arrived books on tape. "Yes, as it so happens, I do," he said with a slight smile. "Apparently, after Margaret Turnbull's foray into the world of microbrewing as her new hobby, she decided she might have a drinking problem."

Ellie smiled, shaking her head. "Mrs. Turnbull is too much."

"Yep." Prescott turned back to the computer and began logging in data again.

Ellie watched him for a moment, then headed back to her office. Things with Prescott had been okay since she'd told him she didn't think they should date. But there were times, like now, when she thought he was distancing himself from her. She couldn't blame him, given that she'd made him think she was interested in a relationship. But she did miss her work buddy. She missed the easiness they'd always shared.

Of course, she was living in a world of awkward relationships. She and Mason were back to spending every night together and then acting as though nothing was going on in the daytime world. She sometimes felt as though she had imagined the openness, the closeness she'd shared with him in Portland. Now Mason was more detached around her, more circumspect than ever.

So she hadn't brought up his drinking. She decided that if he was already being guarded, he definitely wasn't going to discuss something so difficult with her.

In truth, she had started to doubt he had a problem again. Since Portland, she hadn't seen him drink at all. Maybe she had jumped the gun on her assumption about him. He had been upset that night at the inn, as had she. Maybe that was all there was to it.

And without further proof, she didn't have the energy to bring up the potentially volatile subject. She couldn't seem to shake the flu bug she'd picked up in Portland. She was exhausted all the time. She could easily sleep all day, if that were possible. And occasionally, she had strange bouts of nausea. They didn't seem to last long and never got more significant than a little queasiness, but if the symptoms didn't go away soon, she'd go see a doctor.

Her phone rang. It was Mason.

"Hi, there," he said in his wonderful drawl. "How are you feeling?"

"Still tired, but otherwise fine."

"I need to let you sleep more at night."

Ellie smiled. She might be exhausted, but never too exhausted for his lovemaking. "No, I think my nights are going just fine."

"How about your days?"

His question caught her off guard, puzzling her. "They're fine, too. Not quite as nice as the nights, though."

He was silent for a moment. "Are you going to Chase and Abby's for dinner tonight?"

"Yes, why?"

"Well, Chase just called and asked me to come over for dinner, too."

Ellie was delighted. Nothing sounded nicer than spending the evening with three people she loved.

But then Mason said, "I told him I couldn't make it."

She was disappointed. "Are you working?"

"No, I thought it would be too uncomfortable," he said, and even though the level of his voice didn't change, she felt as if he was moving away, adding distance.

"Oh."

"I just thought it would be more fun for you if you could relax. Not have to pretend, you know?"

She started to agree but suddenly couldn't. The whole situation just seemed ludicrous to her. "So we aren't friends?" she asked. "We can't go and have dinner and act like a couple of people who are friends?"

Silence, then, "Ellie, I know I'm being unfair to you. But it . . . I can't offer you more."

"I'm not asking for more." She did want more, but she did honestly believe Mason was giving her all he could. Whether because of his ex-wife or his family, she knew he resisted commitment. She didn't know if she could handle their situation forever, but she was prepared to give him time. "Mason, I'm willing to accept whatever you can give me. I told you that from the very start. But I don't see why we can't do things together as friends."

Again Mason was quiet for a moment. "I just think it's better if you went alone tonight."

"Okay," she said, crestfallen. "Will I see you after?"

"Maybe. I'll call you."

Ellie listened to the line go dead, but she told herself she could do this. She could give him time. She could wait. She could believe that one day Mason might love her.

* * *

Mason hung up the phone, feeling like a complete ass. He shouldn't have even told Ellie that he had been invited over to Chase and Abby's. But he'd been afraid they might mention it, and she would see his not telling her as another Natalie situation. He wasn't even sure why he didn't want to go.

Could it be that he would have to sit and watch Ellie lie to her sister and brother-in-law? Or was it that he'd have to lie, too?

A lowlife. Isn't that what Chase had called the guy that was possibly seeing Ellie? Well, he was a lowlife, all right. Maybe he should just end things with Ellie. He'd be doing them both a favor. She could date someone nice, someone worthy, and he could . . . he could carry on as he had before.

He didn't know what he should do. All he knew was that things were becoming harder and harder.

A knock sounded at the door of his office. His sentry had left early today; Ginny got her hair done every other Wednesday.

"Come in."

Charlie Grace stepped into the room, and from the look on his face, he wasn't here for a friendly chat. When was the last time the two of them had had a friendly chat?

"What can I do for you?" Mason asked.

Charlie moved to the tweed chair opposite his. He didn't sit but rather rested on the arm of it. "I think you should know Everett Winslow is really putting the pressure on me about this football field."

"So why don't you just tell him that you are going to do the right thing and support the library?"

Charlie nodded. "I could do that. And I would definitely do it if the mayor would do the right thing, too."

Mason pretended to misunderstand him. "I'm already supporting the library."

"Right." Charlie gave him a wry smile. "But I think we both know I'm not talking about that. Mason, you need help."

Mason ground his back teeth, but then he managed to keep his voice even. "When have you seen me take a drink in the past . . . couple months?"

"Better yet," Charlie countered, "why don't you tell me how many times you have taken a drink in the last couple months?"

Mason shook his head, growing frustrated. "Charlie, this is insane. I can apologize only so many times. I made two stupid mistakes. Damn, when did getting drunk twice make a person an alcoholic?"

"We both know you've been drunk more than twice. Hell, I've seen you three sheets to the wind more times than I can count. I should have stepped in sooner, but I thought you'd get it under control. I've known you for years, and I know the type of mayor you were two years ago. And I know the type of mayor you are now."

Rage rose in Mason's chest. "Are you saying that you think Everett Winslow would do a better job?"

"No, not a better job than the old Mason. But I do think that Winslow cares. He may not care for all the best things, but he cares. You've stopped caring. You've given up."

Mason stood. "Fine, back Winslow." He pointed toward the door. "Now please leave. I have a lot of things to *not* take care of."

Charlie headed to the door, but he stopped, looking back at Mason. "People aren't going to turn on you for admitting you have a problem. They'll respect you more. You've been a great mayor. But if you keep going like you have been, the town is going to suffer. As it is, Millbrook is in immediate danger of losing the library. That is going to affect a lot of people."

"Then vote the right way, Charlie," Mason stated.

They stared at each other for a moment; then Charlie left the office.

Mason collapsed back into his chair and dropped his head into his hands. Charlie was acting as though the whole fate of the library was on his shoulders. As though he didn't need the support of the council members.

He sat up, running a hand over his face. He knew the cost of losing the library. He knew people would suffer.

Ellie appeared in his mind. Oh, he knew full well people would suffer.

He glanced at the desk drawer near his right knee. Then he ran a hand over his face again. He needed to figure out a way to convince Charlie he was fine. That he didn't need help, outside of support from the council.

He glanced at the drawer again. Then he slid open the one above it and shuffled through the papers, pens, and staples until he found a small silver key.

He looked at it for a moment, then inserted the key into the lock of the larger drawer. Slowly, he slid it open and stared inside. A half-empty bottle of whiskey lay on its side amongst some papers and folders.

He debated and almost closed the drawer again, but instead he slowly reached in and picked up the bottle.

He didn't have a problem. He didn't.

"Ellie, you look terrible."

Ellie didn't doubt that what Abby said was true, but the statement still stung. "I've been feeling a little under the weather lately."

Abby placed a cup of tea in front of her. "The flu?"

Her sister looked so concerned that Ellie decided she must look absolutely ghastly.

Ellie nodded her head. "I guess I'm going to the doctor's tomorrow." She didn't mention that it was actually her ob/gyn.

"Well, that's good. You are very pale."

Ellie could hear Chase in the kitchen. There was the occasional clatter of a pot or pan. The sound of the refrigerator door opening and closing. The rumble of Chase's deep voice as he talked absently to Chester.

Abby sat down on a chair across the coffee table from her and sipped her coffee.

"Does Chase need any help?" Ellie asked.

Abby rolled her eyes. "Please. He hates having anyone in his kitchen. Plus, you should just relax."

Ellie tried, sinking back against the cushions of the overstuffed sofa. But relaxation seemed far away.

Abby told her about their trip to Boston. It sounded like the newlyweds had had a good time. At least the bits that Ellie had been able to focus on. Abby's story made her think about her trip with Mason. Why couldn't they seem to recapture the happiness of the night at the restaurant or of just lying in bed talking? Why was Mason closing himself off?

"How was your weekend?" Abby asked, startling Ellie out of her reverie. "Did you enjoy the librarians' meeting?"

That had been the excuse Ellie had given Abby as to why she couldn't watch Chester for them.

"It was nice."

"Did you do anything in Portland?"

"Ate out. Went to the Portland Museum of Art."

Abby nodded and reached for her coffee. "Have you seen Mason?"

Abby's question startled Ellie. "No, why?"

Her sister took a sip of her coffee, grimaced, then

said, "To talk about the library. Has anything new happened with that?"

"No." Ellie relaxed. "Nothing, really."

Abby nodded. "Chase invited Mason tonight, but he couldn't come."

"I know." Ellie immediately bit her tongue.

"I thought you said you hadn't seen him."

"I haven't, but—but I forgot, he called. To check in." That was true.

Abby gave her a speculative look but turned her attention back to adding more cream to her coffee.

Ellie heard Chase talking again, but this time either Chester had learned to speak, or someone had joined him. Ellie listened, and the second voice spoke again with a low drawl that curled in her belly and prickled her skin.

At first she thought she must be imagining Mason. She thought about little else; why wouldn't she start hearing him, too?

"Look who decided to join us," Chase said as he walked into the living room, Mason behind him.

"Mason," Abby said, standing. "I'm glad you could make it after all."

"Me, too," he said, looking over to Ellie just briefly, before turning his gray gaze back to Abby. "I figured I'd call it an early night. Millbrook is apparently going to hell in a handbasket. So I might as well have a nice dinner."

Chase frowned, then clapped his friend on the back. "Can't be as bad as that. Let me get you a beer."

"Thought you'd never ask." Mason moved to sit on the sofa next to Ellie, closer than she thought he would. "Hi," he said, his voice low.

Ellie forced a slight smile but didn't speak. She couldn't trust her voice. Why had he come? He'd made it pretty clear earlier that he wasn't comfortable with the idea.

She watched him as he made small talk with Abby. He smiled easily when Chase returned with a beer. There didn't seem to be any of the aloofness in his demeanor that she'd been seeing for the past few days.

"Well, you have great timing," Chase told Mason. "Dinner is almost ready. Does everyone want to move into the dining room?"

The oval table was set for a lovely dinner—for three, so Abby followed Chase into the kitchen to get another service, leaving Ellie and Mason alone.

He immediately approached her, touching her hair. "I missed you," he said softly.

"I missed you, too, but I thought you weren't coming tonight."

"I changed my mind."

Ellie didn't know what to say. She didn't understand what was going on with him. He was acting strangely. His voice wasn't thick like the other times he'd been drinking. But she still got the feeling he had been. Maybe it was the slight vagueness in his gray eyes.

Right that moment, however, his eyes were very focused as he looked into hers and leaned forward as if he was going to kiss her.

"Here we go," Abby said as she entered the room. Her attention was on the plate she carried with silverware and a wine glass balanced on top, and she didn't seem to notice Mason taking a step away from Ellie.

"Okay," Abby said, once the table setting was arranged. "Mason, why don't you sit here. And Ellie, you can sit right there."

Ellie would have laughed at Abby's exactness, but she was too aware of Mason and his eyes on her.

She took the chair Abby indicated, which placed her directly across from him.

He continued to watch her.

She shifted, feeling uncertain. She turned her attention to Abby. "Can I help with anything?"

"You can relax."

Fat chance of that. Ellie sighed. Not with Mason here. Not with Mason, period.

Abby left the room again to get a bottle of wine.

Mason leaned forward. "You don't look very relaxed. Am I making you nervous?"

Nervous, confused, even aroused. Mason had many, many effects on her.

"I'm—"

"Okay." Chase came into the room with large steaming dishes in both hands. Abby followed with the bottle of wine and a corkscrew.

"Here," Mason stood and took the wine from Abby. "Let me help with that."

Chase set down his dishes.

"This looks great," Mason said, retrieving the bottle opener from where Abby had set it on the table. He immediately twisted the curled metal into the wine bottle's cork.

Ellie couldn't help noticing that he filled his own glass before he offered the bottle to the others. "Wine, folks?"

"Please," Abby said, holding out her glass. Chase handed Mason his glass, too.

"Ellie?" Mason asked, lifting the bottle toward her and cocking an eyebrow.

She shook her head. "No, thank you."

"Oh, come on. Just one glass," he urged, his eyes almost challenging. "As a toast to good friends."

He said "good friends" in a quiet voice that was rich with meaning.

Reluctantly she extended her glass and watched as he filled the goblet nearly to the top.

Then he sat and raised his own glass. They all

followed suit. "To good food, good friends, and good drink. Not necessarily in that order."

Ellie couldn't help wondering what order he would put them in.

Everyone chimed in their agreement and their hands met over the center of the table to clink glasses.

Ellie couldn't ignore the brush of Mason's fingers when they touched glasses. She took a quick sip of her drink to hide her blush. Mason took a drink, as well, and he nearly finished his whole glass in one swallow.

Abby started passing around the salad, drawing Ellie's attention away from Mason.

"So," Chase said to Mason, "I never see you anymore. What has you so busy?"

Mason tilted his head and seemed to ponder the question. "I've been . . . uh—well, I've been seeing someone."

Ellie stopped scooping salad onto her plate and stared at him.

"Really?" Chase said, surprised. "Anyone we know?"

Mason nodded. "Yes, actually." He met her wide eyes. "Ellie."

Chapter 25

The table was silent. Then Chase laughed, confusion clear on his face. "Ellie?"

"Yes." Mason's voice held no intonation at all, but also left no room for doubt.

Ellie sat stunned, still clutching the salad tongs as if it was the only bit of reality she had left to hold on to.

What was he doing? Why?

The table was silent again until Abby said in a chirpy voice, "That's—exciting. You know, I swear we had some more salad dressing. Ellie, will you help me for a minute?"

As far as excuses went, it was terrible, but Ellie followed her to the kitchen without argument.

Right now, between her sister and Mason, Abby seemed like the safer choice. Ellie didn't think she could take any more of Mason's little surprises.

"You're dating Mason?" Abby whispered as soon as they were in the kitchen. She grabbed Ellie's arm and pulled her to the far side of the room as if the extra two feet would ensure Mason wouldn't hear them.

"I'm not really sure dating is the right word," Ellie said.

"Well, what are you doing?"

Ellie shrugged and gave her an uncertain look. "Seeing each other, I guess." Seeing all of each other, every night.

Abby frowned. "Well, fine, when did you start *seeing each other?*" She obviously thought Ellie was just being difficult rather than accurate.

"About a month ago."

"And you didn't tell anyone?"

"We decided to keep it private." Until now. Ellie was starting to think maybe she'd rather have kept it private a while longer. She had no idea what had motivated Mason to announce it the way he did, without telling her his plan first. But it did make her think he'd definitely been drinking.

Abby leaned on the counter. "Chase said you were seeing someone."

"Really?" Ellie said, surprised. "He knew?"

"Yes. He came home the day you were late for work and told me he thought you had a boyfriend. I actually didn't believe him because I thought you'd tell me right away." Abby seemed a little hurt.

Ellie patted her arm. "It was a rather—unexpected situation. It still is," she added more to herself than to her sister.

"But you're happy with him, right?"

Ellie thought about it. Right at this moment, not particularly. But there were times when he made her unbelievably happy. And she still felt the happy times were worth all the uncertainty. "Yes."

Abby seemed relieved. "Do you love him?"

Ellie didn't have to consider that question for even a second. "Yes," she said. "Yes, I do."

"So, I'm assuming you're the hickey guy?" Chase asked over a fork of spinach greens.

Mason took a drink of his wine, then said, "Yeah, that's me."

Chase frowned. "Why didn't you say something when I was telling you about that whole incident?"

"We'd kind of agreed to keep things quiet." Or rather he had, and Ellie just went along with his plan.

"Why? And why from us?

"It wasn't you in particular. It was everyone."

"Why?"

Mason couldn't very well tell Chase he'd been right about the whole "love her and leave her" theory that he'd formulated back in the diner. But that had been the plan.

Now Mason had no idea what the plan was. "We just thought it was our business," he said.

Chase finally placed the fork in his mouth and slowly chewed the salad. After he swallowed, he asked, "Is Ellie okay with the relationship?"

"Okay how?"

"She looks exhausted, and I don't know—edgy."

Mason shifted in his seat. He picked up his own fork, then put it down again. He lifted up his glass instead, polishing off the remainder of his wine. He set the glass down with more force than necessary. "What are you saying, Chase?"

"I'm not saying anything," he assured Mason. "I'm asking you, is Ellie okay?"

"Why wouldn't she be?" Mason knew he was getting defensive, but he couldn't seem to stop himself. "What do you think—I'm just dicking her around? Using her or something?" Wasn't he? Wasn't he taking from her and offering nothing in return? That was the definition of using, wasn't it?

"Whoa, whoa, Mason," Chase said, holding up his hands. "That isn't what I was saying. I'm just worried about her. She's like my little sister. I feel a need to look out for her."

"Yeah, well, you don't have to, she's fine. I'm looking out for her now." Mason reached for the wine, disgruntled to discover the bottle was empty.

That's why he'd made this announcement tonight.

He was looking out for Ellie, trying to make their relationship easier for her. He was trying to give her what she wanted.

But when Ellie reentered the dining room, she looked anything but appreciative of his efforts. She regarded him with wary eyes. And Chase was right; she did look exhausted.

"I see you didn't have any luck finding those mislaid salad dressings," Mason said dryly.

Ellie glanced at Abby, and Abby said, "No. No."

Ellie sat down, picked up her fork, and pushed her food around her plate. Abby did much the same thing. Chase glanced back and forth between Mason and Ellie. And Mason wished there was more wine.

Dinner pretty much went downhill from there.

Ellie placed the last dish in the dishwasher. "Okay, I guess I should call it a night."

Abby straightened from trying to find room in the fridge to put all the leftovers. No one had eaten much. "You don't want to stay for dessert? Or a cup of tea?"

Ellie shook her head. "Not tonight. I really am tired but thank you."

"Okay." Abby seemed like she wanted to say something else, but she simply followed Ellie into the living room.

"Good night, Chase," Ellie said. "Dinner was wonderful."

Chase made an almost comical face. "Well, it was something, I'll say that."

Mason rose from the sofa. "I'll walk you home," he said firmly as if he expected her to argue. He crossed over to her and took her hand.

Ellie couldn't help but feel the action was a show of possession, and where that once might have made her feel good, now his behavior annoyed her. What was

Mason trying to prove? She didn't understand what the point of this evening had been at all.

They were silent as they crossed the street to her house. She noticed Mason had parked his car in her driveway, so he must have planned to tell Chase and Abby about them. Although nothing about the announcement had seemed planned. For the umpteenth time, she thought it seemed like the sudden declaration of someone who was drunk.

She noticed as he ascended the stairs to her back door that he was gripping the railing, his balance a little off.

She opened the door, then turned to wait for him to step inside. He did and collapsed into one of the ladder-back kitchen chairs.

Even though Ellie's mind reeled, she calmly moved to the counter and got down the coffee and the filters. She needed to decide how best to approach this, and Mason needed to sober up. She didn't think their conversation was going to be very productive otherwise.

"Chase and Abby didn't take that very well, did they?" Mason said.

Ellie shrugged. "I think they were just a little confused." She could feel Mason's eyes, but she didn't look at him.

"You didn't seem to take it much better."

Apparently there wasn't going to be any thought-out approach or any sobering up.

She leaned against the counter and crossed her arms. "Well, I have to admit I'm a little confused, too. I thought you wanted to continue on the way we have been."

"I thought you wanted me to come to dinner tonight."

"I did, but I was okay with us just appearing together

as friends. I didn't expect you to announce to them that we are seeing each other."

"You don't want people to know?"

"Of course I want people to know. But you've made it very clear that you weren't comfortable with that." She never expected to be arguing with him about making their relationship public.

Mason stretched out his long legs and lounged back in the chair. "I changed my mind."

"Why?"

"I just did."

Ellie hesitated, then realized there was no way to avoid this particular topic any longer. "You changed your mind because you've been drinking. What happens tomorrow when you're sober?"

Mason sat up in the chair, his eyes hard, his mouth an angry line. "Here we go," he said sarcastically. "I knew this was bound to happen eventually. Yes, I did have a few drinks. No, I don't have a drinking problem."

Ellie met his eyes. She wasn't going to shy away from his temper. He needed help. She could see that more clearly with each passing day, in the way he was pulling away from her, in his anger now. "I do think drinking influenced your decision tonight."

He glared at her, and again she didn't look away.

He stood, shoving the chair back so the legs scraped loudly on the linoleum. "You know, I actually thought you would be pleased. I told Chase and Abby for you."

"And I'm supposed to be ecstatic that you had to be drunk to do that." She could feel anger rising in her, too. Did he really believe that she should be satisfied with that? That she deserved that? "If you have to get drunk to tell your best friend and my sister, what are you going to have to do to tell others?"

"What do you know about being drunk?" he said

mockingly. "You don't drink. You don't have a friggin' clue what you're talking about."

Ellie flinched slightly but held her ground. "You're right. I don't know a lot about drinking. But I do know the difference between the Mason who makes me feel beautiful and important, and the Mason who actually thinks I should be satisfied with a drunken admission like the one you made tonight."

He stared at her for a moment, and for that brief moment, Ellie thought maybe she'd reached him, made him see how he was acting. But then it passed. His eyes hardened again. "You know, you're right. It's becoming very apparent to me that I really can't make you happy. In fact, I'm starting to think you are better suited to Charlie Grace. You two actually have a lot in common."

He turned and headed for the door.

Ellie rushed across the room, cutting him off. "Mason, you can't drive."

He looked down at her, fury clear on his face. "I can drive just fine." He started reach around her for the doorknob, but she pressed herself to the door.

"Please, Mason, don't." The anger she'd felt drained away, replaced by concern.

He moved very close to her, trying to intimidate her with his size, with his strength. But she wasn't. Mason wouldn't hurt her, of that she was certain. At least not physically; emotionally was another matter.

"Mason," she said softly. "Please, just stay and have some coffee. Let's talk about this reasonably. If you want to go after that, you can."

His eyes were still cold as he stared down at her, but he nodded, just a slight dip of his chin. He stepped away from the door, and after a second Ellie moved away from it, too.

She kept an eye on him as she went back to the

counter and started preparing the coffee again. He stood several feet from the door, observing her, too.

She scooped a spoonful of the ground beans into the filter before she realized she didn't have enough to make a full pot. She shot a quick glance at Mason. He still stood in the middle of the kitchen.

She crouched down to open the cupboard door. The shelves were filled with canned goods, and it took her a few seconds to locate the new can of coffee. She closed the cupboard door and stood.

When she looked over to where Mason had been, the room was empty, and the back door stood ajar.

She ran over to see if she could catch him, but he was already backing out of the driveway. She watched his taillights until they disappeared around the corner of her street.

The next day Ellie wasn't surprised when, by that afternoon, she hadn't heard anything from Mason. She'd followed him home last night to make sure he got there all right, and then she'd just returned home herself. She'd spent the night tossing and turning, trying to figure out how she could help him. But ultimately, she didn't think there was much she could do if he wasn't ready to admit he had a problem.

She picked up the phone in her office and dialed the number to Mason's office.

It rang three times and then a recording of Ginny's voice answered. "You have reached Mayor Sweet's office. He is either in a meeting or away from his desk. Please leave a message, and he will return your call as soon as possible. Thank you."

Beep.

Ellie hung up. She'd tried to call him earlier today and had actually spoken with a live Ginny. His secretary had told her that Mason was in a meeting, but she'd let him know Ellie had called. That was at eleven this morning.

Ellie definitely wasn't going to be able to help him if he refused to talk to her.

She glanced at the clock on her computer—nearly 3:15 P.M. Her appointment with Dr. Kelley was at 3:30 P.M., but after last night, birth control seemed rather unnecessary now. Then she decided she might as well go, if for no other reason than to question the doctor about this lingering malady that she just couldn't shake.

She arrived at the doctor's office at exactly 3:30 and was shocked when she got right into the examination room.

"Ellie, how are you today?" Dr. Kelley, an easygoing woman with blond curls, much like Ellie's, and a warm smile, asked as she entered the room.

Ellie cast a withering look at the paper johnny she wore, then smiled. "As well as can be expected."

"Yeah, that is a loaded question when it comes to visiting your gynecologist. Not many people are thrilled to see me."

Ellie smiled sympathetically.

Dr. Kelley sat on a black vinyl stool on wheels and took a pen out of her coat pocket. She opened the file that the nurse had left on the counter when she had shown Ellie into the room.

"Okay, let's see. It looks like you had your last annual in May. So I assume you must be here for something else."

Again Ellie felt a bit stupid. It looked like her sex life had probably come to a screeching halt. But she said, "I'm here to get birth control."

Dr. Kelley nodded. She made a notation in the file.

"Okay, have you thought about which birth control you're interested in?"

The request didn't appear to be stupid to Dr. Kelley, which for some reason made Ellie feel better. "The pill."

"Okay, when was your last period?"

Ellie tried to recall. "I guess, the end of August."

The answer didn't seem strange to Ellie, but Dr. Kelley frowned. She considered Ellie's file. "I do have a note here that you've never had regular periods, but have you been having intercourse during this time?"

Ellie nodded, feeling a little embarrassed. "Protected, though." *All but the first night.*

Dr. Kelley nodded. "Well, I would feel better if you took a pregnancy test for us. Just to be safe." She opened a drawer under the counter she'd been using and took out a plastic cup covered in clear cellophane. "Go right down to the bathroom at the end of the hall and pee in the cup. You can just leave it on the nurse's station when you are done."

Ellie stared at the innocuous little cup for a second before taking it. She headed to the bathroom feeling like she was in a dream. Could she really be pregnant? *No.*

She did as Dr. Kelley instructed, and when she brought the cup to the nurse's station, the nurse, a young, perky brunette, told her to go back into the same exam room. "Dr. Kelley will be back with you in a few minutes."

Ellie settled on the crinkly paper that covered the examination table and waited. Her heart raced, but she told herself she was being ridiculous. She wasn't pregnant. She wasn't.

Time seemed to creep by until finally she heard the rattle of the doorknob. Dr. Kelley entered the room, and Ellie's breathing stopped. She didn't even need the doctor to say the words; the other woman's expression said it all.

"Ellie, you are pregnant."

The rest of the exam was a blur. Dr. Kelley estimated her due date, which was the end of June. She did the pelvic exam and took blood samples. She gave her prenatal vitamins and pamphlets on what to expect during pregnancy. But it was as if everything was happening to someone else.

Ellie was just an observer. It wasn't happening to her.

"Ellie, I can tell you are shocked," Dr. Kelley said at the end of the exam. "Is there any chance that you aren't going to want to keep this baby?"

Her question was the first thing that really seemed to pierce the numb shell that surrounded Ellie. Keep the baby? Of course. She would never give up this baby. Even if she and Mason were over, she wanted this baby. Their baby.

"No," she stated, "I'm keeping it."

Dr. Kelley patted her arm. "Congratulations," she said with the deepest sincerity. "See you in a month."

Ellie thanked her and watched as the doctor left the room. She automatically started to dress, again feeling distanced from everything. She'd never considered pregnancy, although now it seemed so obvious. The tiredness. The nausea. How could she have missed it?

Because she and Mason had had unprotected sex only that first night. Who got pregnant the first time she had sex? Only every teenage girl in those afterschool specials she'd watched on TV growing up. But she wasn't a teenage girl.

She paused in buttoning her shirt. Thankfully she wasn't a teenage girl. She could do this. She could raise a child alone. She didn't know how Mason would react, but if he didn't want anything to do with the child, she could do it alone.

She finished dressing and headed to the front desk in the waiting room to make her appointment. It wasn't until she'd told the receptionist that she needed a prenatal appointment for November that she realized that Ginny, the town gossip and the secretary of the father of her baby, was sitting in one of the uncomfortable tweed and wood chairs.

When Ginny saw Ellie glance at her, she raised the magazine she was holding in front of her face and pretended to be reading.

Great, all of Millbrook was about to learn that Ellie Stepp was knocked up.

Chapter 26

Two days had passed since Ellie had discovered she was pregnant, and as of yet, nobody else in town seemed to know. Apparently Ginny *could* keep a secret.

She decided that maybe Ginny wasn't talking because she didn't know who the father was. If Ginny did know, Ellie was sure the temptation would have been just too much. It was definitely good gossip.

Of course, the father didn't know either. She had tried to call Mason twice. Not to tell him about his impending fatherhood, but simply to see where they stood. But given that she couldn't locate him, she had to believe they didn't have any standing outside of over. She was devastated at the idea, but she didn't know how to fix things. She didn't think she could.

Even if their relationship was finished, she didn't plan to keep the pregnancy a secret from him. It would be impossible in a town this small, but more importantly, she would never deny Mason his child.

She had thought about going to his office since she'd probably be able to find him there, but she'd chickened out. Somehow the phone just seemed less upsetting than seeing him face to face. Considering that he didn't want her anymore.

"Ellie?" Abby leaned forward so her face was directly in Ellie's line of sight. "You keep zoning out on me. You're starting to give me a complex."

Ellie smiled weakly. "Sorry, I have a lot on my mind."

"Anything you want to talk about?"

Ellie shook her head and began to scoop out the slimy innards of the huge lopsided pumpkin she was carving. A cool autumn breeze stirred the leaves on Abby's lawn and ruffled Ellie's curls.

They sat on the painted floorboards of Abby's front porch, carving jack-o-lanterns to take to the Halloween Festival that evening. When Abby had called Ellie to see if she would go tonight, Ellie's first inclination had been to say no. To stay home and feel awful. But then she decided she might as well go. It was doing her no good to stay home and alternate between sleeping and eating, occasionally sitting in a depressed daze just to add a little variety.

She knew Abby was worried about her. And she knew Abby was dying to ask what was going on with Mason. But to her sister's credit, she'd remained quiet but was trying to be around if Ellie needed her.

"I think I'm going to make mine scary," Abby decided, using a black marker to draw the face on her perfectly round pumpkin.

Ellie smiled absently, then picked up a marker to draw the face on hers.

They worked in silence. Ellie pictured what it would be like to be doing this kind of thing with her child. A child. Sometimes the pregnancy didn't seem real. And other times, it was so real she could barely breathe under the shock of it.

The sun was starting to set when Chase drove into the driveway in the beat-up old pickup truck that he loved. He came around the front of the house to see them.

"Hey, what are my favorite ladies up to?" he asked

as he climbed up onto the porch and sank into a deck chair near Abby.

"Getting ready for tonight's festivities." Abby held up her nearly finished pumpkin. "Isn't he scary?"

Chase shivered dramatically. "Very. Is yours scary, too?" he asked Ellie.

Ellie shook her head. "No, mine is just smiling." And then for no reason in particular, she burst into tears. Or maybe there were just too many reasons to pick only one.

Abby slid over and hugged her tightly. Ellie was glad when she still didn't ask any questions.

Halloween was a big holiday in Millbrook. Maybe because the area easily lent itself to a spooky atmosphere in the fall. Trees were gray and bare; piles of dried, dead leaves rustled eerily in the breeze; and the nights were clear and crisp.

Mason had to admit, it did seem like a town right out of *The Legend of Sleepy Hollow* or, probably more accurately, any of Stephen King's novels.

Mason hadn't wanted to attend the festival, but as mayor, he was sort of expected to make an appearance. The event was held in a field on the outskirts of town, which, as fate would have it, was owned by his dear old dad—another reason people assumed he would attend.

The field was lined with makeshift lanes of food and game booths. There was a haunted hayride and a haunted woods walk where teens dressed as Jason and Michael Myers and other horror flick favorites jumped out at brave festival goers with fake knives and real chainsaws—minus the actual chains, of course. For the less daring, there were best costume contests and jack-o-lantern carving contests.

Mason stood at the last one, looking at the wide

array of lighted, toothy grins. He took a sip of his beer and stared at a pumpkin that looked remarkably like Ed Asner.

He was pondering how different *The Mary Tyler Moore* show would have been if Lou Grant had been played by a large orange gourd when a familiar figure in the crowd caught his attention.

He stepped back, using the milling partygoers to hide himself as he watched Ellie. She walked around the jack-o-lanterns, stopping to admire many of them. She looked wonderful, and he couldn't tear his eyes away from her.

He'd been avoiding her. Ginny had told him several times that Ellie had called his office, but he hadn't called back. He knew he was behaving like a coward, but he didn't know what to say about his actions at Chase and Abby's house. Ellie had been right to be angry. Just announcing they were a couple while he was a little tipsy. The whole episode had been insulting.

He supposed he could simply go up to her and tell her he was sorry. He knew she would probably forgive him, but then there was her concern about his drinking. Somehow he didn't think she would let that subject drop as easily. And he was tired of defending a problem that wasn't a problem.

Ellie was wearing her jeans, the ones he loved, and another of her long sweatercoats. This one was blue, just a shade or two lighter than her eyes. She was talking to a woman with a baby, and the smile on Ellie's lips was bittersweet.

He frowned, wondering about that look. Was she upset about him? Would she want to talk to him? Could she forgive his behavior the other night?

"Hey." Chase appeared at his side, following Mason's gaze.

"Hey." Mason felt uncomfortable and tried to act

like he'd been looking at a gigantic pumpkin with the White House carved in its side.

"You need to talk to her," Chase said. "She's miserable."

Mason didn't pretend not to know who "she" was. "I think we have some real problems. I'm not sure they can be fixed." That was as candid as he'd been with anyone about this relationship. In a way, the admission felt good.

"Ellie is one of the most forgiving people I know. I'm sure she'll give you another chance."

Mason glanced at his friend out of the corner of his eye. "You're sure I'm the one to blame, huh?"

Chase grunted. "No doubt in my mind."

Mason looked back over at Ellie. Damn, he did want to talk to her. Seeing her made him ache.

Gathering his courage, he started to weave through the crowd toward her when Chase's hand on his arm stopped him.

"Maybe you should give me the beer," his friend said.

Great, not another one. But Mason handed over his cup.

Chase nodded in Ellie's direction. "Good luck."

Mason knew he needed it.

When he got close to her, she was actually talking to, of all the people in Millbrook, Prescott. He hung back and watched the two interact. She smiled up at Prescott and nodded at something her coworker said.

Mason felt like he was reliving the fair. Only this time he wasn't going to slink off to wait for her to come home and find him there. He wanted to be with Ellie, and he wanted everyone to know it. Especially pesky Prescott Jones.

"Hello, Ellie," he said as he approached the couple.

Ellie twisted around and stared at Mason like she was seeing a ghost. Somewhat appropriate, given that she was at a Halloween festival and he had just seemed to materialize out of thin air after vanishing for days.

"Mason," she said, trying to keep the surprise out of her voice.

"I was hoping I could talk with you," he said, looking only at her and ignoring Prescott.

Ellie didn't, however. "Prescott, do you mind if I catch up with you later?"

Prescott gave Mason a distrustful look and then smiled at Ellie. "Sure, I'll be somewhere around the costume contest. My nephew's entered. He'll be one of the half dozen Harry Potters."

After Prescott left, she turned back to Mason. Her smile faded.

"How are you?" he asked.

Pregnant, was her first thought. Missing him desperately, was her second thought, but she said neither. "I'm okay. How about you?"

He looked tired, almost haggard. "I'm . . ." He caught her wrist in his large warm hand and tugged her away from the crowd.

He stopped under an ancient oak some distance from the festivities. "I need to talk to you. Really talk, without people milling around us, stilting our conversation."

She waited for him to continue. In truth, she was too amazed he was here and looking so contrite. She'd been positive things were over, that he'd ended things for good.

"I'm sorry I haven't been in touch for the past couple days," he said, still holding her arm. He rubbed the pad of his thumb back and forth over the sensitive inside of her wrist. The simple touch sent tingles dancing through her.

"I was being a complete coward and avoiding you," he told her. "You were absolutely right to react the way you did the other night. I shouldn't have announced that we are a couple to Chase and Abby like that. I should have talked to you, and then we should have told them together."

"Are a couple," Ellie repeated, focusing on the only part of his explanation that was in the present tense. "Are we a couple?"

Even in the shadowy night, Ellie could see the sincerity in his eyes. "God, I hope so. I want us to be." His thumb continued to caress her wrist while he brushed the fingers of his other hand down her cheek. "Ellie, I've missed you. I haven't thought about anything but how to make this mess up to you. About how to convince you to forgive me."

Her heart pounded against her breastbone. His fingers felt like fleeting touches of heaven.

"Please tell me we can work things out," he said in his low, persuasive drawl. "Please tell me you can forgive me for all the crap I've put you through for the past few weeks. And please, please let me tell all the folks of Millbrook that I am dating the most wonderful woman in the world."

Ellie couldn't believe he was saying all this. It was like he was articulating every hope, every dream she'd had since their affair began. For just a moment, giddiness surged through her. Unfortunately the emotion was short-lived.

"I want that, Mason. But we fought about more than just your decision to tell Abby and Chase about us."

He was nodding even before she had finished her sentence. "I know. I know. And I will definitely admit that I drank too much that night. But there *were* mitigating circumstances for my drinking. I had another run-in with Charlie Grace that day, and I just got upset. It was dumb."

Ellie studied him. He looked so earnest that she

wanted to believe him. "But why would you do the very thing that Charlie is accusing you of?"

"I don't know. It was stupid." He played with a lock of her hair. His thumb swirled over the pulse in her wrist.

It took all her concentration not to simply lose herself in his touch.

She wanted to believe him. To believe everything was going to be all right. Of course, making their relationship official was a far cry from becoming parents together. She couldn't begin to know how he was going to react to that information. But they had no chance of working through that situation if they weren't together at all.

"I want to be with you, too." She barely had the words out before Mason was kissing her senseless.

She clung to him, savoring him. He felt so right, and she had to have conviction that everything would work out.

They broke the kiss, but they remained close, their foreheads touching, their eyes locked.

"I'll make everything up to you," he whispered.

She smiled. "This is a wonderful start."

He kissed her again.

She cupped a hand to his face, tracing his jaw, then sank her fingers into his hair. She pressed against the hard, lean length of his body.

He groaned. "I do want to show you off, but right now, I really want you in my bed where I can spend hours making love to you."

"Mmm, that does sound awfully nice."

He smiled, obviously pleased with her response. He linked his fingers with hers and started to lead her toward the part of the field sectioned off as a makeshift parking lot.

They were nearly there before she yanked him to a

stop. "Wait, I really should tell Abby and Chase where I'm going. I came with them."

"Okay," he agreed. "Chase was over at the pumpkins."

Still hand in hand, they walked back to the crowds. Ellie could tell Mason was eager to find her brother-in-law, but she knew it was for the same reason she was impatient. Hours of lovemaking did sound very, very nice.

She spotted Chase over by a booth that was selling fresh-roasted pumpkin seeds and hot apple cider. She started in that direction. Mason, who had practically been dragging her, suddenly lagged behind.

She frowned back at him. She pointed toward the booth. "I see Chase right over there."

He nodded, looking in the same direction, but she realized that he was actually staring at the couple talking with Chase.

"Those are your parents, aren't they?" she asked.

"Yes," he said flatly.

Ellie stopped. "You don't want to see them?"

He hesitated, then offered her a stiff smile. "I just didn't expect them to be here. This isn't really my dad's scene."

He started walking toward them. As he got closer, his grip on her hand grew tighter.

"Here comes your son now," Ellie heard Chase say as they reached the threesome.

"Mason." His mother, a petite, slender woman with short hair the color of polished silver and sparkly blue eyes, hugged her son.

Mason returned the hug with one arm because he was maintaining his hold on Ellie's hand. "Hi, Mom."

His mother stepped back, glanced at Mason and Ellie's linked fingers, and her finely arched brow rose curiously. "And who is this lovely young lady?"

"You know Ellie Stepp," Mason said, pulling Ellie

against his side, leaving no doubt they were a couple. "Millbrook's librarian extraordinaire."

Ellie saw recognition in the older woman's eyes as she smiled warmly. "Of course. I'm showing how *un*-well-read I am by not recognizing you right away. Nice to see you, Ellie."

Ellie tried to release Mason's hand to shake his mother's, but he held her fast. Ellie held out her other hand, the handshake awkward, but the attempt made both women laugh genuinely.

"I'm glad to see my son is getting a bit more cultured, however. He hated to read when he was little. And please call me Liz."

Ellie agreed, immediately feeling an affinity with the elegant, gracious woman. The tall man at Liz's side, however, was a different story. Mason's father didn't have any of the warmth that Liz emanated. But there was no denying where Mason got his looks. Mason was a younger version of his father.

Mason's father didn't look at her; he was glowering at his son.

"Hello, Dad," Mason said with a definite lack of enthusiasm.

"I stopped by your office twice this week," his father said, ignoring Mason's greeting, "and you weren't there either time. Didn't you get the messages I left you?"

Mason nodded. "Ginny gave them to me."

"I don't know how you normally conduct your business, but I can't imagine that ignoring messages ingratiates you with your voters."

"No, but I don't imagine you planned to vote for me anyway," Mason said dryly.

"Boys," Liz said in a warning tone, "can you play nice for a change?" She rolled her eyes and said to Ellie, "They are just alike, which for some bizarre reason makes it impossible for them to get along."

Ellie smiled sympathetically. But outside of their looks, she couldn't see any similarities in the two men. Mason could be cool and aloof, but even at his coldest, he was downright toasty when compared to his dad.

"I was just telling your folks that the costume contest is about to be judged," Chase added, obviously trying to help keep the peace. "Abby's already there. Why don't we all head over?" He gestured in that direction, a steaming Styrofoam cup in each hand.

"Actually, we—" Mason started.

"Oh, no, you don't," Liz cut her son off. "It took me hours to convince your father to come here tonight. And you're not taking off so soon." She reached forward and linked an arm through Ellie's. "Plus I want to get to know your new girl."

Mason looked at Ellie, and she shrugged. It didn't seem as if they were going to get away anytime soon.

The group began walking toward a ring where the participants circled past, parading their costumes before the judges and the audience.

Abby greeted them and pointed out Willie, the little boy she and Chase sometimes watched for the child's mother, Summer-Ann.

Willie was dressed up as Buzz Lightyear. The little boy waved excitedly at them.

"So how long have you and Mason been dating?" Liz asked, still holding Ellie's arm.

"Don't grill the poor girl," Mason warned his mother good-naturedly. "You'll scare her off."

"About a month," Ellie answered the older woman, despite Mason's admonition.

Liz made a face at her son, and Ellie could tell that Liz and Mason were close.

Mason's father didn't join in, but Ellie noticed that he wasn't as remote as he had initially appeared. He watched his wife and son, flashes of melancholy in his familiar gray eyes.

He just didn't know how to relate to his son, Ellie realized. And she got the feeling Mason didn't know how to relate to his dad, either. The situation was sad.

"I talked to Charles Grace—during one of my visits to Town Hall." His father said the last part pointedly.

"Did you?" Mason sounded far more nonchalant than he was. Ellie could feel the tension in his body as he held her close.

"He was saying that Everett Winslow is really putting the pressure on him."

"Yes," Mason said, "he's told me that, too."

"Well, Charles has always been one of your biggest supporters. What the hell are you doing that he's even considering backing Winslow?"

"Jim," Liz cautioned, "we're here to have fun."

"That's right," Mason said with a forced smile. "Ellie, are you thirsty? That cider smells wonderful."

Abby nodded, holding up her cup. "It is."

"Want some?" Mason asked Ellie.

"Okay."

"Mom? Dad? Can I get you some?"

Both of his parents agreed.

"Do you want me to come with you?" Ellie asked.

He shook his head. "Nah, I've got it. You stay and root for Willie, or rather Buzz." He leaned down and gave Ellie a sweet, gentle kiss.

When they parted, Ellie beamed up at him, happy to be with him and proud he was handling his father's criticism so well.

He gave her another quick kiss and then headed toward the cider booth.

Ellie smiled to herself, feeling like things just might work out. They could.

Then across the ring, she caught sight of Prescott. He watched her, a disappointed expression on his face. Some of her happiness fled.

Chapter 27

Mason gritted his teeth, irritation coursing through him. Of course his father would assume Mason was the one doing something wrong with Charlie. That he was failing as a mayor.

He waited for the teenage boy behind the counter to get the ciders. He didn't need more of his father's disapproval. He'd had enough to last a lifetime.

He just wanted to spend the night making up with Ellie—not listening to his father interrogate and criticize him.

He stared at the board on the end of the counter that listed the booth's wares, not really seeing the words written in thick white chalk. Until one of the items caught his attention.

Hard cider $2.50

"Excuse me," he called to the teenager. "Can I change one of those regular ciders to a hard cider?"

"Sure."

"You know what? Make that two."

He didn't have a drinking problem, he said to himself as he took the first drink of the tart, acidic liquor. He had problems that required a drink or two. Simple as that.

* * *

At first Ellie didn't notice the difference in Mason. She'd been too busy watching the festivities, talking with Liz and Abby and eating delicious goodies to detect the subtle changes in his demeanor. But she had noticed that Mason kept disappearing for a few moments every now and then, and by the close of the evening, it was clear to her that Mason had been drinking.

He had become vague, not following the conversation. But when he did join the discussion, his comments were very cynical and even disrespectful. Especially the ones directed at his father.

Several times Ellie also saw him stumble. Once he used her to steady himself.

"Mason," she whispered when the others were busy talking with Ned Philbrick, who had grown this year's largest pumpkin, "have you been drinking?"

He gave her an offended look. "No."

She watched as he wandered over to the others. He swayed slightly.

Ellie had no doubt. He was drunk.

But only once they had wished everyone a good night and just the two of them were at his car did she bring up the subject again.

"Mason, you're drunk."

"I'm not drunk." He attempted for the third time to get the key into the door's lock.

She snatched the car key away from him. "Let me drive."

"I can drive," he insisted, holding out his open palm.

She didn't budge, standing between him and the vehicle, his key clutched tightly in her hand.

Finally he submitted, throwing up his arms. "Fine, you drive."

Mason was quiet for the remainder of the trip. Ellie glanced from the road over to him. He leaned back in the seat, his eyes closed, and she thought he might have passed out. But when she pulled into her driveway, he sat up, peering around.

"Why did we come here?"

"It was closer," she told him. In truth, she had decided to come to her house because she had serious doubts he'd stick around after she told him what she was thinking about his drinking.

He accepted her reasoning, very happily, in fact. "Good idea. I never thought I was going to get you alone tonight." A slow, sexy grin turned up the corners of his lips and, despite her concern, her body reacted.

They entered the house, and Ellie didn't even get the kitchen light on before she was pulled tightly against Mason's solid body. He kissed her hungrily, and her own need raced through her body. She clung to him.

She couldn't taste the tang of liquor on him as she had the other times. He tasted like apples and cinnamon. It would have been quite easy to pretend there was no problem, but she couldn't.

After a few moments, she managed to gain some control and pull away. She wasn't just looking out for herself now. Soon there was going to be a little person who needed Mason, too.

She crossed the room to flip on the light. When she turned back to him, he was regarding her with another sexy grin. "Should we break in your kitchen table?"

He moved over to her, pulling her back into his arms. It took all her willpower to pull away again. "Mason, you have been drinking."

For a split second his expression hardened, but then he offered her an almost repentant smile. "Yeah, I did have a couple hard ciders."

That explained why she couldn't taste anything other than the tartness of apples.

"I really needed a couple," he explained, moving closer to her, trying to win her over with his nearness. "Just to calm me." He touched her hair. "You saw how my dad hassles me. He just picks and picks." He gazed in her eyes, his head coming closer to hers. "Like the Charlie Grace thing."

Ellie tried to focus on his words rather than the hypnotic movement of his wonderful lips.

His father . . . his father was a difficult man. "I know your dad is hard on you," she said sympathetically, looking into Mason's gray eyes rather than at the mouth she wanted to kiss. "But I don't think drinking helps the situation."

Mason laughed humorlessly, straightening up. "You'd be surprised."

Ellie took a deep breath, able to concentrate now.

She didn't want to have this conversation. Not when they had just gotten back together, but she knew things weren't going to get better if she ignored them. If she fell into bed with him. A wonderful method of postponement, but still only that. A delay.

"Mason," she said slowly. "I think—I think Charlie Grace was right. I think you have a drinking problem, too."

A muscle twitched in his cheek, and all sleepy amorousness vanished from his eyes.

"I'm really starting to feel like everyone around me is a broken, goddamned record." His voice was low and angry. "You know, I avoided you for the past couple days for this exact reason. And here we are, not even back together for, what? Six hours? And here we go again."

"I could say the same thing," Ellie said. "Six hours, and you're drunk again."

"Ellie, I told you, I just needed a few to relax."

"Isn't that practically the definition of alcoholism? That you think you need to drink?"

Mason's eyes grew darker, grayer, like a storm about to rage. "This is complete bullshit," he growled. "I wanted us to be together, but I won't deal with another person who isn't happy with who I am."

"But this isn't you. I tried to tell you that before. When you drink, you're not the real Mason," Ellie told him.

He snorted. "How do you know?"

"Because I've spent lots of time with the real Mason."

"Maybe this is the real me now," he said derisively; then he threw his hands out to his sides. "Maybe this is as good as it gets."

Ellie shook her head, feeling pain for him. Pain for this amazing man who didn't know how wonderful he was. "No, this Mason is running and hiding."

He turned away from her, crossing to the kitchen table. He braced his hands on the tabletop and hung his head for a moment.

Ellie was staggered that a man with such broad shoulders and a strong back could appear so broken. She went to him, placing a gentle hand on his back, rubbing the taut muscles between his shoulder blades.

He allowed the touch for a moment, then shrugged away. "Do you remember the night of Chase and Abby's wedding?"

She nodded. "Of course."

"Do you remember our dance?"

"Yes."

"Do you remember telling me that if I was yours, you wouldn't change a thing about me?"

The hurt in his voice nearly shattered her. Tears tightened her throat, and heaviness contracted her chest. "I don't want to change you," she said. "I want you to want to change yourself."

The pain left his voice, replaced by fury. "There isn't any difference."

He started toward the door, but she caught the sleeve of his jacket. He paused, glowering back at her.

"There is a difference," she pleaded. "There is."

He faced her, his expression no longer furious, just empty. She wanted the anger back.

"I'm not going to be a coward this time," he told her dully. "I'm just going to deal with this relationship now. We're over. Done."

She didn't argue, didn't beg, even though every cell in her body told her to. She knew it wouldn't do any good. It wouldn't change anything. The emptiness in his expression said it all. He didn't want or need her help.

But still she couldn't help asking, "What if I told you I love you, that I've loved you for as long as I can remember? Would you get help? For yourself? For us?"

He laughed humorlessly, the sound as cold as frostbite. "Yeah, maybe, if I actually loved you, too."

For once, Mason wished he'd blacked out last night. But every word, every single syllable of his fight with Ellie was still in his mind. Loud and clear.

He sat behind his desk, staring blankly at a stack of papers that he needed to review and then sign.

How had he turned into such a bastard? Ellie's wounded blue eyes appeared in his mind. No, she'd been more than wounded. He had devastated her. She had actually recoiled at his final words to her as if he'd physically hit her. Those vicious, cruel words that had likely hurt her more than an actual blow.

She'd offered him her heart, and he'd thrown her

love back in her face. He hadn't been thinking about anything but defending himself, protecting himself.

She refused to believe he wasn't a drunk. She said she loved him, but she didn't believe him. Her disbelief was painful, much more painful than anyone else's doubt in him.

He'd been spiteful to her, nasty. Their relationship coming to an end was painful enough without his adding to that pain.

There was nothing he could do about it now. He didn't intend to talk to her again. Not on a personal level. Any conversation now would just drag out the hurt. It was better to just cut all ties. Eventually they'd both move on.

She'd find someone to truly love her.

That idea made his chest tighten, his stomach clench. But that would pass, too. It had to.

He took a deep breath and focused on the papers in front of him, one of which was a surveying proposal of the property that housed the town garage. This was something that Charlie would know more about, given his work with real estate.

He looked at the clock on his desk. It was just after five o'clock; maybe Charlie was still here.

Even though he wasn't in the mood for a lecture, Mason decided to take the document down to Charlie and get his opinion.

When he stepped out of his office, Ginny was concentrating on her typing; she didn't even look up at him.

"Hey, Ginny, working late, I see?" He made a big show of looking at his watch. "It's after five; shouldn't you be long gone?"

Normally Ginny would have made some smart-ass response to him. But she only nodded. Not even an impertinent, "Yes, boss."

He found her reaction strange but didn't give it too

much thought. He had enough on his mind without dissecting his secretary's behavior.

When he reached Charlie's office, Mason heard that the councilman was with someone. He could ask Charlie about this later.

He started to turn to leave when the visitor's voice stopped Mason in his tracks.

"As you can see," Everett Winslow said in his overly amiable way, "it's time to jump ship. If you stay with Sweet, you are going to go down, too."

There was a pause. "You're sure about this?" Charlie sounded absolutely dumbfounded.

"Heard it directly from the lips of his secretary myself. And we all know Ginny knows of every speck of dirt in this town. She's quite invaluable, really. I hope she will agree to keep working for me after the election."

Mason frowned. He knew that Winslow thought he had a good chance of winning this election, but the man sounded like he knew the win was already in the bag.

"I just find it hard to believe." Charlie still sounded dazed.

"Well, believe it, friend. It's time to change sides. Mason Sweet is going to be lucky to get any votes after the folks of Millbrook discover he has impregnated the nice librarian lady."

Mason staggered down the hall, his breathing shallow, his head spinning. Was it true? Ellie, pregnant? Why hadn't she told him? Because he'd dumped her before she could.

He reached his office, still trying to grasp what he'd heard, when he saw Ginny still at her desk. She was gathering her coat and purse to leave, but she froze when she saw him.

"Is it true?"

Ginny didn't even pretend that she didn't understand what he was asking. She nodded. "I saw her at Dr. Kelley's office. She was making an appointment for a prenatal checkup."

"When? What day?"

"Three days ago."

So Ellie had known at the Halloween Festival.

"Why did you tell Winslow? Are you unhappy working for me?"

She shook her head adamantly. "No. I didn't tell him. He overheard me at the diner talking with Summer-Ann Bouffard. I would never tell him." She gave him a pleading look. "I was only going to tell Summer. She wouldn't have told anyone. I am very happy working with you. I would never purposely hurt your reputation."

Mason believed her. Maybe it was the guilt in her dark eyes.

"How did you know I was the father?" he asked.

Ginny gave him an apologetic look. "I know everything that goes on here."

When Mason arrived at Ellie's house, he was relieved to see she was already home from work. She answered the door on the second knock.

"Mason," she said, obviously surprised to see him, but then the surprise left as she saw the look on his face.

"Did you think you could get away with not telling me?" He slid past her into the kitchen before she could ask him to leave or simply shut the door.

She paused for a moment before closing the door and turning to face him. Just like Ginny, she didn't bother to act like she didn't know what he was talking about. "I was going to tell you. Eventually."

He nodded, his emotions warring between anger and hurt. "How long have you known you're going to have my baby?"

"Three days."

"So Ginny really is in the know," he said sarcastically. "She's known as long as you have."

"Technically, I've known a little longer," she said. Her matter-of-factness strengthened his anger.

"How long did you intend to make me wait? A week? A month? Three months?"

She bristled. "I would have told you last night, but I didn't think it was the best timing. You know, given the fact you were drunk and breaking up with me."

Mason had never heard that kind of angry sarcasm in her voice before. It startled him. He tried to calm his own bitterness. "Things wouldn't have ended last night if I'd known the truth."

Her eyes widened with mock gratitude. "Really? What, we would have made it another few days before it ended? Great. Now if you don't mind, I was in the middle of making dinner." She moved back to the door as if to show him where to go.

Sarcasm did not suit her.

"Ellie," he said, keeping his voice low and gentle. "This changes everything. We need to talk."

She stared at him, her eyes flat, devoid of any emotion. "Yes, it does change everything. We're going to be parents. You, a dad. Me, a mom. But it doesn't change anything between us. We're over."

"No, we're not," he stated. "You are going to marry me."

She laughed, the sound brittle. "Really? I don't think so."

Mason stalked toward her as if by sheer physical intimidation he was going to change her mind. "Yes, you are."

She held her ground, staring up at him with those

empty eyes. "No, I'm not. I refuse to marry you just because we're having a baby. That's no reason to marry."

"It seems like the best one to me."

"You of all people should know a marriage based on a charade just doesn't work."

"What?" He didn't understand her reasoning. "Why would it be a charade?"

For just a moment the old Ellie appeared in her eyes. "If we married, it would be a total farce. Pretending we're happy. Pretending we care about each other. You coming home every night and acting like I'm the woman you want. How long before you don't come home? Before you find someone that you can really love?"

"It wouldn't be like that. We could have a good marriage. I care about you. I want you."

She shook her head, her eyes lifeless again. "No. I won't keep you out of your child's life, but I won't marry you."

"What about your reputation?" he asked, desperation filling him. "You'll be a single mom." He was reaching for straws.

"Yes, but I'm pretty tough. You see, I grew up with people talking about me. So I suppose I can survive it again."

"Please, Ellie—"

"No," she said, her eyes as cold as chilled blue crystals. "Now please leave."

He hesitated, looking at her. The old Ellie was gone. Replaced by a woman who was detached and cold.

He didn't know what to say, how to reach her. There was a wall around her, and he'd laid the foundation for her to build it.

Chapter 28

Ellie continued making her dinner. She worked around the kitchen as if she were on autopilot, all the while telling herself she wouldn't feel anything. No hurt. No sorrow. Nothing.

Last night she'd cried. After Mason had told her he didn't love her, she'd cried, her heart broken. But she wasn't going to cry anymore. There was no point.

It wasn't like any of this could honestly be a shock to her. After all, she'd known from the moment she accepted Mason's proposal that they'd eventually end things. She'd also known she'd never have his heart.

But somewhere over their time together, she'd lost sight of those facts. She'd dared to imagine a different outcome. She'd believed that Mason Sweet might love her.

She'd never, never be that stupid again.

A knock sounded at the door, and she paused in stirring the tomato sauce she'd been heating. She took a breath, then went to open it.

Abby waited on the other side, concern clear on her face.

"Are you okay? I know your relationship with Mason isn't any of my business, but I was outside and saw him tear out of your driveway."

Ellie nodded. "We don't have a relationship anymore," she told her sister, coolly.

Abby tilted her head, giving Ellie a sympathetic look. "How—how are you?"

"Pregnant," she said, her eyes dry, her heart frozen. Maybe life would be easier now that she couldn't seem to feel anything.

By Ellie's estimations, all of Millbrook knew about her baby by that Friday. So she was quite shocked when the town's head gossip showed up at the library that same day.

Ginny came in looking as if she expected lightning to strike her dead at any moment. But to her credit, she did also look very contrite as she asked to speak to Ellie in private.

Once in Ellie's office, Ginny immediately broke into an apology. "I'm not here to try to convince you that I'm not to blame. I am. But I'm not the one who told the whole town. That was Everett Winslow."

"Everett Winslow? How did he find out?"

Again she looked ashamed. "Well, he overheard me at the diner telling Summer-Ann Bouffard. But I never intended to hurt you or Mason."

"How did you know that Mason was the father?"

Ginny sighed as if suddenly her amazing scandal-mongering abilities were too much to bear. "I know everything that goes on in Town Hall. I knew all along that you two were seeing each other."

Ellie was impressed, both that she knew and that she hadn't shared that bit of news with anyone. Either that or no one had cared about that part of the story.

"I did come to apologize." She fidgeted with the strap of her purse before finally adding, "But I also came to see if you would talk to Mason. I'm really worried about him."

Ellie's heart lurched. What was wrong with Mason? But she quickly smothered her worry. Why should she

care? He wasn't her concern. Still, she couldn't re-
frain from asking, "Why?"

"He hasn't come in to work for the past three days.
I've called him, and he just mutters he's sick and
hangs up on me. We both know he's sick, but it's not
the flu." Ginny gave Ellie a significant look.

Ellie's first thought was to play stupid, but she
couldn't. "Yes, I know he has a problem."

"Will you help?"

Ellie sighed. "Let me think about it."

Ellie had decided that she had to help Mason if she
could. After all, he was the father of her baby, and she
couldn't, in good conscience, allow something to happen that might eventually hurt her child. But she also
knew she couldn't deal with him personally.

So later that night as she sat in Chase and Abby's living room drinking herbal tea, she asked Chase, "Will
you check on Mason? Ginny came to me today, concerned, saying he hasn't been to work in a few days."

"Ginny came to you?" Abby asked, appalled. "After
all the damage she's done?"

"She claims she wasn't the one to spread the rumor.
She says it was Everett Winslow who has told practically the whole town," Ellie told them.

Abby grunted. "Well, if she hadn't told anyone in
the first place, then Everett Winslow wouldn't have
overheard it to repeat."

Ellie shrugged indifferently. "It doesn't much matter. The truth would have come out soon enough, and
the end result would be exactly the same."

Abby looked like she wanted to argue that, but she
just took a sip of her coffee.

"So, Chase, will you go check on him?"

At first Chase didn't answer.

"Please," Ellie cajoled.

Abby made a disgruntled noise as she took another sip of her coffee. "Who cares if he's okay or not?" she said after a moment. "Butthead."

Ellie smiled at her sister's protectiveness. "Well, he is the baby's father. I feel like I should make sure he's okay. But I can't go there."

"No, you can't" Chase agreed. He sighed. "All right. I'll go."

"Thank you," Ellie said with relief.

Mason groaned and rolled over. His body ached, and he was shivering. He opened his eyes, then closed them again. The bright light was too much, too blinding. He lay there for a moment.

Damn, he was probably missing work again. When was the last time he'd been to work? What day was it?

He didn't really care. He started to doze again, but he woke because he felt like he was sleeping on a granite slab. A freezing granite slab.

He opened his eyes and tried to focus, but he couldn't comprehend what he was staring at. It was too bright and a little blurry. But after several blinks, he realized he was on the kitchen floor, staring up at his opened refrigerator. Why the hell would he be doing that?

Struggling to sit up, his hands slipped on something and he fell back heavily. His head whacked loudly on hardwood.

"Damn," he groaned, his voice sounding strange to him, like someone else's, all raspy and slurred.

He remained on the floor, trying to get his bearings. Why was he here? Why did he feel so awful?

Ellie. He'd been drinking because of Ellie. Because she was pregnant with his baby. Because she didn't want to marry him. Because . . . because he didn't deserve to marry her.

He levered himself up to a sitting position, using the butcher block to haul himself to his feet. The room was spinning. That must be why all the cupboard doors were wide open. And why dishes and glasses were smashed all over the floor.

No, wait. He frowned around himself. He had done this because . . . he was angry. Angry at Ellie. No . . . angry at himself? He'd been angry.

He staggered around the island, and he felt a piece of glass slice his foot, but he couldn't feel any pain. Why could he still feel the pain of Ellie's rejection? He drank and drank, yet he couldn't seem to kill that pain.

He stumbled over a container of rolled oats and nearly fell, but he caught himself on the kitchen doorframe. Why the hell did he have rolled oats? He hated rolled oats. He needed more booze.

He picked his way through the dining room, which was destroyed, too. He didn't remember doing that. He'd forgotten turning over a heavy oak table, busting a couple chairs, but Ellie's cold face was still clear in his mind. Empty blue eyes like a doll's eyes.

Where the hell was the booze?

He tripped again, this time over a lampshade. He cursed. The word came out more like a combination of "puck" and "tuck" rather than the actual expletive he was going for.

How the hell was he supposed to go find more booze with the room spinning and things all over the floor tripping him?

He finally got to the library. He'd have something to drink there. He searched the bar, but it was empty. Had he really gone through everything?

He leaned against the bar, a wave of vertigo hitting him hard. He had to go buy more. He had to forget. And liquor did that.

A violent wave of nausea overcame him, followed by the vertigo. He needed to get to the bathroom.

He swayed from the library and started up the stairs, clutching the banister. Another rush of nausea hit him, and he stopped and closed his eyes. Sweat broke out on his brow, but he was still freezing.

The feeling passed, and he made his way to the bathroom before the next one hit him. This time he couldn't suppress the sickness, and he vomited into the toilet, the sound loud and wretched in the empty, silent house. He finished and collapsed limply against the cold tile floor.

How could Ellie want this . . . him? She had every right to send him away. She had every right to hate him. He was a selfish bastard. And a failure.

She's right. I'm nothing but a lousy, pathetic drunk. She deserves so much more.

Those were his last thoughts before he slipped back into blackness.

"Mason?" Chase's voice sounded far, far away. "Oh God, Mason?"

Mason tried to answer, but he couldn't seem to crawl out of the darkness enveloping him.

"Shit!" Chase sounded more panicked; then Mason felt himself being shaken. "Come on, Mason. Wake up."

"Chase," he said, his throat raw and painful. He managed to open his eyes.

Chase stood over him, fuzzy and concerned.

"Mason, we need to get you to a hospital."

Mason struggled upright with help from Chase. But even sitting was too much, and he slumped against the icy porcelain of the toilet and closed his eyes.

"Mason, what happened? Your house is in shambles. Your feet are bleeding," Chase told him.

Mason didn't bother to open his eyes to look. He didn't care.

"I love Ellie," he told Chase.

Chase didn't answer for a moment, and Mason almost forgot he was there until he said, "Then we need to get you to the hospital."

Mason shook his head, the action slow. He swallowed before he said, "No, I'm not sick like that." He opened his eyes, centering on Chase's face. "I've got a problem."

"I know," Chase said softly.

"Chase, I need help." He closed his eyes again. "I need help," he whispered.

Mason had no idea how Chase got him up and to a clinic that night. He had no memory of it. But he did remember coming home to the house he had destroyed. All that damage had become a symbol to him of his drinking problem. When he'd been trashing his home, he had thought he was making himself feel better. When in fact, he'd simply created a huge mess, where he had to pick up the pieces and try to fix things. His drinking had done the same thing—except on a much larger scale.

He walked down the steps of Town Hall, enjoying the biting cold of the early April wind on his face. He breathed in deeply, feeling the same sting in his lungs. It was nice to be able to feel again. Even if it was painful.

Over the past few months, things had been pretty painful. But it still felt—better—wasn't the right word. It felt real, as if he was living again. No longer numb.

He stopped at the bottom of the granite steps and looked toward the library. A thin layer of snow still covered the roof, but in a few more weeks, all the snow would be gone, replaced with mud and eventually green grass and spring flowers.

It would be only a few weeks until his child arrived, as well.

He checked his watch. It was a little after six o'-clock. Ellie would be gone now. He rarely saw her. Just the occasional glimpse of her entering the library, or walking down the sidewalk to the diner.

But he grasped those brief moments, trying to absorb every change in her, every subtle difference. Did her belly appear larger under her winter coat? Did she look healthy? Did she look happy?

He started down the sidewalk in the direction of the library. He hoped she was doing well.

She refused to talk to him. He could understand that. He'd caused her a lot of pain. And she didn't trust him. Why should she?

Twice he'd called her, but she had simply told him that she was busy and she couldn't talk. She hadn't sounded angry or hurt. She sounded inaccessible.

So he didn't call her again. But he did get reports from Chase and Abby. Even though they were concerned about Ellie, they seemed to be equally worried about him. He didn't deserve their worry, but he accepted it. Their friendship was his only link to Ellie. He had to hold on to that.

He knew that her pregnancy was progressing well. All her tests so far had been fine. She didn't plan to find out the baby's sex. She had cravings for cheeseburgers and chocolate malts, and she was sure if the baby was a girl, she should probably name her Gidget. Moondoggy wasn't on the list for boys' names, however.

Mason sighed, feeling an odd mingling of amusement and sorrow. He wanted to be with her. Not just because of the baby, although he did want desperately to be a part of that, too. He wanted to be with

her because he loved her. He loved Ellie so much
he ached with it.

But he knew he was too late. He'd lost his chance
with her the moment he'd outright rejected her love.
Of course, he now realized she'd been offering him
her heart over and over throughout their relationship. When she'd believed his lies. When she'd
defended his career. And when she couldn't fathom
why his ex-wife wouldn't want him over anything else.
But most of all, when she had told him he had a
drinking problem and that he needed help. She'd
done everything out of love.

But when he'd refused her love that last night,
throwing her feelings back at her and actually saying
he didn't love her, that had been the end. Even
someone as generous and bighearted as Ellie could
take only so much rejection before she had to walk
away.

He pushed open the door of the library. The warmth
felt as good on his skin as the cold had. He pulled off
his gloves and headed toward the periodicals.

His meeting wasn't until seven, but he always came
right from work and waited, reading in one of the
worn chairs at the back of the stacks. In part, because
it made no sense for him to drive all the way home
and then all the way back again. But mostly because,
here, he felt close to Ellie. Sometimes, he could swear
he even smelled her scent in the air.

Like now. He lifted his head, catching the delicate
aroma of lavender.

Then he heard her soft, melodic laugh. He spun
around, sure he was losing his mind. But there she
was, walking up to the front of the library, Prescott beside her.

She looked at her coworker, a smile on her lips, her
adorable dimples framing her pretty mouth.

"I think Hercules might be a bit more classic than

I was thinking. I was thinking something more like David or Michael."

She turned and glanced in Mason's direction. Her eyes locked with his. She stumbled.

Mason started forward to catch her, but Prescott steadied her first, grabbing her elbow.

She continued to stare at Mason for just a moment before offering Prescott an appreciative smile.

Mason shifted, not sure what he should do. Maybe he should just turn away and pretend to peruse the magazines. Maybe he should leave and come back when the meeting started. But he couldn't. There was no way he could walk away.

"Hello, Ellie," he said, his voice as unsure as the rest of him.

She hesitated, then nodded. "Mason."

He didn't speak again for a moment, just eating up the sight of her. She looked beautiful. Her hair was knotted on top of her head in those chopstick things he loved. Curls brushed her neck and her cheeks. She wore a red corduroy jumper, and for the first time, he could truly see she was showing, her stomach a perfectly round sphere under her clothing.

He longed to place his hand there. "How are you?" he asked instead.

"Fine," she answered coolly, and Mason watched as a cold, indifferent mask seemed to drop over her features. Her eyes lost all emotion. They were as expressionless as her voice had been on the phone.

"Are you feeling okay?" He knew he had essentially already asked that, but he couldn't think of anything else to say.

"Yes."

For the first time, he noticed she had her coat draped over her arm. She was on her way out. Leaving. He wasn't ready to let her go. Not when he hadn't had her this close in weeks—months.

"Were—were you discussing baby names?" he asked, keeping his voice polite. Like good manners would make any difference.

She hesitated; then her chin came up, just a fraction of an inch. "Yes, actually."

"I think I have to side with you, then. I'm not a big fan of Hercules."

She nodded, but her face stated that she couldn't care less what his opinion was on the subject.

She turned her attention back to Prescott. "Okay, so we've got everything done for the spring literacy fair?"

Prescott nodded. "I think so."

Ellie shook out her coat and pulled it on, hiding her belly under gray wool. "Good night, then."

She tottered to the exit, not glancing in Mason's direction again.

After the doors closed, Mason realized Prescott was watching him, sympathy in his eyes.

Instead of giving the man attitude as he would have a few months ago, Mason simply asked, "Is she really okay?"

"Yes," Prescott said, although his eyes weren't as positive. "She's okay. Not great, but okay. She's happy about the baby, and she focuses on that."

Mason nodded, fiddling with the edge of the magazine he didn't even realize he was still holding until that moment.

"I've gone to a couple of her appointments with her. Just for company, when Abby can't go," Prescott said.

Mason fought the swell of resentment that surged through his chest. Prescott wasn't telling him this to offend him; he was just reassuring Mason that she was being cared for. He could see that in Prescott's guileless expression.

The same expression Ellie once exhibited so easily, so readily. Before Mason showed her that exposing her emotions would only get her hurt and leave her bitter.

Mason sighed. "I'm glad you're here for her. She deserves a guy like you. Someone who won't let her down. Someone she can trust." He forced a smile, then lifted the magazine. "I guess I'll go read while I wait for my meeting."

"Hold on," Ellie muttered at the door as she heard the phone ringing on the other side. She managed to get her key in the lock on the first try and rushed across the kitchen to grab the receiver.

"Hello," she said, a little breathless.

"Hi, Ellie. It's Prescott."

"Prescott?" Why would he be calling? She just left him. "Is everything okay?"

"Actually, no. I think you need to come back down here."

Ellie frowned. "Why? What's happening?"

There was a pause. "I just need you to come down here." Prescott sounded troubled.

"What's wrong?"

"It's a . . . a—I just think you need to come down here," Prescott insisted.

Ellie hesitated, then decided she'd better return. Prescott had never called her to come back to the library after she'd left for the day, so if he needed her there, she supposed he really did. Even if he couldn't seem to tell her why.

"Okay. I'll be there in a few minutes."

"Good," Prescott said with obvious relief.

Ellie hung up the phone and headed back to the door, which was still ajar. What could possibly be wrong at the library? Why couldn't Prescott tell her?

She didn't want to go back there, not tonight. Seeing Mason up close, talking to him, had been too difficult. Too agonizing. She didn't want to risk the chance of seeing him again. Of letting him make a chink in the wall she'd managed to keep erected around herself. She really thought he might be able to, with his sad eyes and his tentative smiles. That scared her.

But she did get in her car and head toward the library. She checked the digital clock on her dashboard. It was nearly seven. By the time she got there, Mason would be in the A.A. meeting, and she wouldn't have to see him.

She knew that he was attending the A.A. meetings regularly and that he had been for almost six months. Not only the meetings in Millbrook, but a couple in Bar Harbor, too, Abby had just recently informed her.

In fact, both Abby and Chase felt the need to keep her informed of his actions. He was very dedicated to his recovery and was doing well. Even though Ellie didn't show any interest in their reports, her indifference didn't seem to stop either of them from updating her regularly.

Ellie was glad that Mason was getting the help he needed. She just didn't want to be a part of it. She couldn't be a part of it. She had to protect herself, her heart.

He had looked good tonight, though. Better than she'd seen him look in a long time. He wasn't as pale or as worn-down as he had been in the fall.

Okay, if she were being honest, he'd looked downright gorgeous. His hair mussed from the wind. His cheeks slightly reddened from the cold air. His eyes, while heartbreaking, were clearer, grayer. She had wanted to touch him, to press her mouth to his full lips.

But she knew she couldn't think that way. Not if she wanted to remain safe and unhurt. She wasn't about to make herself an open target again. Not when she knew that Mason, while he still might want her or care about her, didn't love her.

She pulled into her parking place and hoisted herself out of the car. Her belly was getting almost comically round, and she knew she was beginning to waddle when she walked. She didn't mind. She loved the tangible evidence of the little person growing inside her.

As fast as she could, she tottered her way up to the library entrance. When she entered, Prescott waited at the front of the library. He stopped pacing when he saw her, his expression a combination of relief and uneasiness.

"What's wrong?" she asked, immediately anxious herself.

"Julie," he called to the teenage girl who helped around the library a couple evenings a week, "could you watch the front desk?"

Julie appeared from the stacks. "Sure."

Prescott linked his arm through Ellie's and led her back to her office.

Once inside, Ellie asked again, "What's wrong, Prescott?"

"Will you please sit?" he asked, pulling out her desk chair.

"You're scaring me." But she did sit as he'd asked.

He came around the front of the desk, then took a calming breath before he said, "I think there is something you need to hear."

Ellie frowned as she watched him reach for the intercom and flip on the switch labeled *Bay Front Meeting Room*. The speaker came to life, a voice she didn't recognize saying, "It took me nearly twenty years to admit I had a problem."

Ellie immediately snapped the switch off. The speaker was silent. "What are you doing?"

"I think you might hear something you really need to hear."

"What?" Had Prescott lost his mind? He demanded she come back here to eavesdrop on an Alcoholics Anonymous meeting? "We can't listen to those people. It's private."

"You need to. You need to listen to one of those people in particular." He flipped the switch again.

She immediately slapped the knob back down. "Prescott, why are you doing this?"

"Ellie, you know I'm not fond of Mason."

"Well, that makes two of us." She laughed humorlessly.

Prescott shook his head. "Both you and I know that isn't true. You may want it to be true, but it's not. And from what I saw of Mason tonight, I know he loves you, too."

Ellie started to stand. She didn't want to talk about any of this. She was working hard to move on, to stop caring. This wasn't helping. Why would Prescott think this would help her?

"Please, Ellie, listen to me."

She hesitated, but the pleading in Prescott's pale blue eyes stopped her. She sat back down.

"You know how I feel about you," Prescott said. "Heck, part of me wants to just let you go on giving Mason the cold shoulder. Then maybe"—he offered her a weak smile—"maybe there is a chance you might turn to me."

Ellie started to speak, but Prescott cut her off. "But that wouldn't be the right thing for you. You love Mason Sweet, and you need to give him another chance. So please listen."

Prescott turned the knob again.

Ellie stared at the small silver box as voices started to fill her office. The woman from earlier was finishing her story of alcoholism. The group applauded.

This wasn't right, Ellie thought. It was wrong to listen to other people's private conversations. She started to reach for the switch when the words of another anonymous voice said, "Mason, this is your six-month anniversary. Would you be willing to share your story?"

There was a rustle of people shifting in their seats. A cough. Then Mason's voice saying clearly, willingly, "Sure."

Ellie knew she should shut off the intercom. She had no right to hear this, but her hand wouldn't move. Couldn't move.

"I've been an alcoholic for about two years. I started drinking when my wife and I split. She wanted a life that I didn't. And I guess I started to drink because I thought it made me feel better. Feel like less of a failure.

"I felt like I'd failed my wife, my father. The alcohol seemed to make those feelings disappear. But they didn't disappear. I just got numb, indifferent. The alcohol didn't solve any of my problems or fix any of my insecurities. It just created more problems. And then suddenly I was more concerned with drinking than I was with anything else. Anything. And that was when I really did become a failure. I failed at my job, my friendships. But most importantly I failed a person who truly loved me and wanted to help me."

Ellie's heart began to beat fast in her chest. She didn't want to hear any more, but she couldn't stop.

"She asked me if I would get help. If I loved her enough to get help." Mason said, his voice low and filled with pain. "Such a simple question, with such a simple answer. But I didn't answer, not with the truth. I told her I didn't love her. Because I wanted to hurt her for daring to say that I had a problem.

"And even after I knew that I had hurt her so badly, I still justified my actions to myself. I blamed my inability to tell her I loved her on my ex-wife. I blamed it on my parents. Hell, I even blamed it on this woman herself. But it wasn't any of them. The blame was all mine. And the fact that I am an alcoholic.

"I couldn't tell the most wonderful and amazing woman who'd ever walked into my life that I love her because I was too concerned with protecting my addiction. I put my drinking above the best thing that ever happened to me."

There was a pause, and Ellie stared at the speaker, wishing she could see Mason's face. Wishing she could touch him.

"I'm not sure I can ever fix this part of my past," Mason said, the anguish in his voice clear. "But I will stay sober not only for myself but for her, too. She once asked me if I would get help, not just for her but for both of us. Out of love. And I do love her. I will always love her."

Ellie felt the tears running down her cheeks before she actually realized she was crying.

Prescott flipped off the intercom and then tugged a tissue from the box on the corner of her desk. He held it to her with an encouraging smile. "Don't you think he's worth a second chance?"

She accepted the tissue, unable to respond. It was like a dam had been broken, and she couldn't seem to stop crying. All the tears that she'd held back over the past months wanted out. But the tears weren't painful but rather—freeing. The wall of ice she'd insulated herself with was melting. Her heart was thawing.

By the time Prescott handed her a fifth tissue, her tears were finally starting to abate and a light, almost blissful feeling filled the place in her chest that had felt so heavy for so long.

Mason loved her. He'd loved her then. He loved

her now. And he said he'd love her forever. It was incredible, so very incredible.

She took a deep breath and offered Prescott a tremulous smile. "I think I'm ready to offer him that second chance."

Prescott returned her smile with a pleased one of his own and opened the door.

After the meeting let out, Mason stayed behind to talk with his mentor, Frank, and he and Frank were the last to exit the assembly room. At first Mason didn't see Ellie sitting in the same chair that he had been sitting in earlier. Then she stood.

He stopped, surprised to see her again and then concerned because she had obviously been crying.

"Ellie." He strode to her and, without thinking, took her hands. "What's wrong? Are you okay?"

"I heard you."

Mason frowned. "You did?" He had no idea what she was talking about.

"I heard what you said in the meeting. I listened over the intercom." She glanced around him to Frank. "I know that was wrong, probably illegal, in fact."

Frank shrugged. "I never heard any of this," he said with an enigmatic smile and disappeared into the stacks, leaving the two of them alone.

"What did you hear?" Mason asked, still a bit dazed that Ellie was here, that he was holding her delicate fingers, touching her smooth skin. And more astoundingly, that she gazed up at him with those wide, trusting, absolutely breathtaking eyes he'd missed.

"I heard you say you love me," she said.

"I do," he stated. "I love you more than anything in the world."

"And that you plan to love me forever."

He nodded. "Yes, I don't have a choice in the matter."

"Why is that?"

"Because you have my heart."

She smiled up at him, all her emotions clear on her adorable face. "Well, that works out well, you see, because you have mine, as well." And she rose up on her tiptoes and kissed him.

Epilogue

Mason stood at the podium in the center of the high school gymnasium. The people of Millbrook cheered and applauded.

Ellie was struck by how incredibly beautiful he was—that golden aura surrounding him again.

He grinned at the crowd looking like he'd just won the presidency of the United States rather than a mayoral election in a small town in Maine. But Ellie knew this position was more important to him than any old presidency.

Not only had he won, but he'd won fair and square, despite all of Everett Winslow's machinations. It seemed that the folks of Millbrook admired a man who could stand up and admit his mistakes. Thank God.

He lifted his hands to quiet the crowd, and they gradually settled down. "Don't worry," he said reassuringly. "I will keep this short and sweet. I know everyone wants to get out to that barbeque set up on the football field. I just want to thank all the folks here. I will make sure to keep Millbrook the best place in Maine to live."

The crowd applauded uproariously.

Ellie smiled as Emily, their three-month-old daughter, started at the sudden commotion; then she

burrowed closer against Ellie's chest and drifted back
to sleep.

"I want to thank my supportive council members,"
Mason continued, nodding at Charlie, who Ellie saw
gave him a thumbs-up sign. "And all the other folks
who have helped me in the past with my position as
mayor. And most of all, I want to thank my wonderful wife, Ellie." His eyes met hers, his gaze filled with
love and happiness.

She grinned back at him proudly.

"Thank you. Thank you, everyone, for your support," he said and stepped down from the stage,
heading directly toward his wife and their daughter.

Mason had pushed for them to marry a week after
that night in the library, which, in his opinion, wasn't
a day too soon. Ellie still suspected he'd been worried
that she might change her mind about him.

She hadn't wanted to wait, either. They'd spent too
much time apart. Too much time alone.

They'd moved into Mason's house, which Chase
had helped them fix up. She and Mason had picked
out furniture together. They had worked on the nurs-
ery. And now she couldn't believe she'd ever felt like
the place had belonged to anyone other than them.

"Hi, Mister Mayor," Ellie greeted him with a proud
grin. He leaned forward and kissed her.

He straightened and pulled back the blanket to
look at their beautiful baby girl with her father's
sullen chin and her mother's dimples and wild blond
curls. She slept away, oblivious to the celebration
around her.

"Emily doesn't seem terribly impressed with her
dear old dad."

Ellie laughed. "She will be. But not quite as impressed as your wife."

He smiled. "Why are you impressed? I'm the one
married to the most remarkable woman in the world."

"Mmm," she gave him another kiss. "You know flattery is going to get you everywhere, don't you?"

"Mmm-hmm," he agreed with a slow grin. He started to lean forward to kiss her again when a hand on his shoulder stopped him.

He turned around, the easy smile on his face slipping as he saw who was behind him.

"Dad" he said.

Mason's father stood with Liz, although Liz quickly came over to hold the baby. Abby and Chase appeared, too, everyone fussing over oblivious Emily.

"You won by a landslide, I hear," his father said his in no-nonsense way.

Mason nodded. "That's what I hear, too."

"That's good. You look good." His father shifted his weight from one foot to another.

"Thanks." Mason shifted, too.

"I also hear the town voted to keep the old football field."

"Yes."

Ellie knew that particular vote had been just as important to Mason as his own votes.

His father nodded, a look of approval on his face. "Well, I guess folks must have realized if it had been good enough for Mason Sweet to play on, it was good enough for their kids."

The compliment was given in such a matter-of-fact way that it took a moment before Mason comprehended that it was a compliment. "Maybe," he finally responded.

"Now let's see this little angel," his father said, walking over to Mason's mother.

Mason's father took Emily from Liz, cooing down at the sleeping infant. Looking proud.

Ellie came back to Mason's side, watching their family.

"Your parents are thrilled with their granddaughter," she said happily. She hugged his arm, pressing her cheek to his shoulder. "And with their son."

Mason took a deep breath, and Ellie had the feeling that he was overwhelmed. Today was a very good day.

Finally, he murmured, his voice a little shaky, "I'm thrilled with you."

She smiled up at him, feeling almost giddy with love. "Good, 'cause I'm here to stay."

He pulled her into his arms and kissed her, his touch sweet and gentle. "No, I think it's the other way around, angel," he said as he gazed down at her, his gray eyes sparkling with love. "You're the one who's stuck with me."